PROTOCOL

MM HOLT

Copyright © 2018
All rights reserved by the author.
No part of this book may be reproduced in any form without permission in writing from the author. Reviewers may quote brief passages in reviews.

ISBN 9781795379335

Table Of Contents

Prologue
Part 1: Shore Duty ………………. 6
Part 2: The Mission (1) ………….. 97
Part 3: The Mission (2) …………. 218
Part 4: Excidium ………………… 296
Aftermath …………………………358

Dedicated to the continuing struggle against the Accord Of Nations.

Prologue

I LOWERED THE barrel of the heavy, alien rifle, easing it gently down until my left hand rested on the dripping edge of the building's roof, eighty floors above the rain-soaked streets below.

Seeking the target.

I scanned along the rooftop of a skyscraper fifteen hundred yards away, one of many giants in a cluster of skyscrapers along the edge of Hong Kong Harbor. The crosshairs moved over the clutter of air conditioner intakes, stairway entrance hutches, exhaust outlets, all of them veiled by heavy, tropical rain.

Then, I found what I was looking for: the dark S of Octavia's lustrous ponytail, glistening with raindrops, holding its own against the deluge in a way no human hair ever could.

Because Octavia was no human.

I ranged the rifle scope down the length of Octavia's blue uniform. The patches on her chest came into view. On one side, a badge indicated her high rank; on the other, the insignia of her alien nation. Further down, the crosshairs traveled along the glory of her figure, the narrowness of her waist, the swell of her hips, and the extraordinary length of her legs. Octavia was a male fantasy, the kind that had been forbidden on earth for centuries.

Keep your focus, Burns, I told myself. Keep your focus.

I moved the heavy sights gently up again. Now Octavia's face came into view. It was another miracle of beauty: womanly yet girlish; vulnerable yet strong; soft yet determined. She wore makeup, which itself was bizarre because no Earth female had worn makeup in living memory, not since the establishment of the Accord of Nations hundreds of years ago. The same with her hair. Most women of the Accord wore their hair short or even shaved.

But Octavia was not most women.

She appeared to be my age, no more than thirty, but it was impossible to determine how old she actually was in alien years. She might have been just a few years old; she might have been hundreds of years old, or thousands, or hundreds of thousands. Her age, like her appearance, like her spacecraft, and the nature of her planet, were unknown to everyone on earth, as mysterious as the night sky.

I breathed out slowly, keeping the sights steady— and I watched her, waiting until she was still. Fifteen hundred yards is far. I had to be sure I would hit my target, because if I missed, Octavia would not give me a second chance.

She moved slowly about the roof, sniffing the rainy air with rabbity twitches of her nose. The nape of her neck came into view. It looked so vulnerable, so easily snapped, or crushed, or blown away by a blast from the rifle. But one shot would not be enough—not even one from a weapon made by her own kind.

Perhaps no weapon would be enough.

I breathed out slowly and counted my heartbeats, keeping Octavia in the crosshairs of the virtual sights.

And then Octavia turned to sniff the air in my

direction.

The shot was on, but a question nagged at me. Could I really shoot a woman—even an alien one? It was unthinkable, but it was necessary. I had to keep telling myself that. It was necessary—for everyone, for earth.

And I had done it once already.

Octavia frowned. Had she sensed I was nearby? It certainly looked like it. Now, the situation was about to become far more dangerous, as if it wasn't dangerous enough already.

I was Octavia's obsession. Yes, me, Alex Burns, a twenty-six-year-old lieutenant in the Accord of Nations Navy. A week ago, I was a nobody, languishing on shore leave, with few achievements and fewer prospects. My only distinction was that I had trained myself in military arts of marksmanship and hand-to-hand combat, because the Navy no longer valued the skills of war.

Oh, and apparently, I looked like a film actor, the one who always played the villain from the pre-Accord years: tall, well over six feet, fair-haired, blue-eyed. I was what Navy called 'too oppressively male in appearance.'

Now I was infamous: a traitor, a deserter, a murderer, and a thief, with a list of Navy Spirit code violations as long as your arm. I was wanted by the military. I was wanted by the Harmony Police—and, of course, I was wanted by Octavia and her invasion force.

Despite it all, I was also one of only three people to have actually been on board the alien vessel, the only one to have somehow drawn the infatuation of its leader, the only one, as far as I knew, to know about her plans of invasion.

So, if I were ever going to pull the trigger, it should be now.

The rifle's small light blinked, signaling its readiness.

Now or never, Burns, I told myself. Now or never.

I breathed out slowly and centered the crosshairs on Octavia's ear.

I had made my decision.

Before I squeezed the trigger, I whispered some final words into the rain, just in case I didn't survive the day.

'I'm sorry,' I said. 'I say sorry to everyone I've disappointed. Sorry to you, Kresta, my mother. Sorry for wasting my life. Sorry for causing the loss of yours. Sorry to you, Dad. I never took the time to know you. And sorry to you, Katherine Le Seaux and Andrew Chen. I wish we'd had more time before the mission went so wrong.'

I paused and drew a breath. I wasn't finished.

'But I'm not sorry for what I did to all you admirals, captains and commissioners. Not sorry at all. In fact, I curse you. Curse you all. You are the ones who made us believe your lies—the lies that kept us down for hundreds of years. The lies that deceived us and prevented us from seeing the truth.'

I know, because I was the most deceived of all.

After such a tirade it was difficult to slow my breathing and steady my heartbeat. I wasted even more seconds clearing my mind.

Finally, I was ready.

I breathed in. Breathed out. Repeated.

Then, I caressed the weapon.

And fired.

Part 1: Shore Duty

'There shall be no borders between nations. The Accord Commission shall govern all.'

Accord Of Nations Constitution

1

Three Days Earlier

The night before the aliens arrived, I had a dream.

I was standing on the quarterdeck of a large sailing ship, the really old kind we saw in paintings in the Accord museums.

I stood in the cool breeze, shifting my weight from one foot to the other as the deck pitched and yawed. It was night and the surrounding sea was dark except for the tops of the white caps rolling towards ship's port side.

Above me, gray and white sails rose high into the darkness, spread out along the nine yards of three towering masts.

Before me, the deck stretched away towards the ship's plunging bow, and along the gunwales, cannons were ranged, held fast at their ports by thick rope tackles.

The ship's timber groaned and creaked with each pitch and roll. The ropes either side of me answered with groans and creaks of their own.

I sensed a presence to my left. I turned to face it slowly.

Then I saw him.

He was dressed in a blue naval coat, an impressive garment, with great brass buttons, white lapels, and two braided epaulettes. No stripes, so I couldn't tell his rank. But by the look of the coat, the rank was high. It might have been the kind of ceremonial coat worn by the navy officers in the evil pre-Accord era when Western powers oppressed the world.

The strange man looked familiar. He was my height, with the same hair and face as me, but more weathered. His skin was not that of a twenty-six year old. It had taken some serious sun and wind, like an older version of myself.

He leaned on the taffrail, one elbow on the glistening timber as if waiting for me to notice him.

'Who are you?' I said, in my dream voice.

I heard him reply in a strange accent.

'You know,' he said. I barely heard it over all the creaking and yowling. The way he said it sounded like, 'Ye noo.'

'You know,' he said again. 'Don't you?'

'No,' I said. 'I don't.'

He looked at me, one eyebrow raised.

'Then, you're not ready,' he said. 'You look strong enough. You look like you can fight. Maybe you can command. But you're soft. It's obvious. You don't have the stomach, not for what's coming, not for what they'll do to you. You don't have the belief.'

'What's coming?'

'It's too late now,' he said. 'She's already here.'

'Who?' I said. 'Who's already here?'

He shook his head.

And then, I heard the sound of wind chimes. They were playing nearby, somewhere behind me, totally out of place among the creaking ropes and cracking timber. The man in the huge navy coat raised his eyebrow even further.

'Time's moving on, Lieutenant Burns.'

2

The ship faded away. The captain in the blue navy coat disappeared. The wind chimes rang on. I reached out from under the covers, found my handheld, and switched the chimes off. Then, I rolled out of the bunk, rolled up the blinds and began my morning exercises while the cold light streamed into the small cabin.

It was 6:00 a.m. on December 29, 249 AONE, the Accord Of Nations Era, and it was going to be a big day.

I followed my usual exercise routine, the one for mornings when I wasn't going to either the base gym or to the base combat simulator, or to one of the Navy Spirit training courses, or to the special martial arts courses I took off the base with a civilian named Diaz.

Fifty pushups on my knuckles. Fifty stomach crunches with twists to left and right. Twenty pull-ups hanging from the metal bar that ran across the cabin ceiling, which wasn't strictly allowed by Navy Spirit.

No, it wasn't a real work out, but it was enough to get my heart pumping and my muscles throbbing—not that I needed any more excitement. Today, as I said, was going to be a big day.

Then, I grabbed my towel, soap and razor, and hit the showers. I had to be nice and clean for when I met Captain Paine.

I toweled off, came back to the cabin and dressed in my blue NWU, the Navy Working Uniform. Name patch for Burns on my right side, lieutenants stripes on the collar, the letters of AONN and AONT USA over my left pocket. The Accord of Nations Navy. Accord Of Nations Territory, USA.

The only letters not on the uniform were AONS Harmony, which meant Accord Of Nations Ship Harmony, the base where I'd been on shore duty for two long years.

I checked my watch. I was still early. The meeting with Captain Paine wasn't till 8:00. In the meantime, I had to attend the morning pledge and anthem recital, just like every other sailor and officer on the base.

So, I switched on the radio. It was tuned to the local station. The female newsreader said police had caught the vandals who defaced the Accord rainbow sculpture in the nearby town of Dworkin. Meanwhile, preparations were well underway for Accord Establishment Day Celebrations. This year, the announcer said, it was the turn of AONT China to host the ceremony in the southern coastal sub-territory of Hong Kong. Today's weather here in AON sub-territory California, cold and clear, as usual.

I stood up, paced around the room. I hadn't been this on edge since the same time last year. Back then, I'd gone to Captain Paine's office hoping for but not really expecting anything good to come out of it. And I had been right. I had saluted and left that office and gone straight back to the training courses, all three hundred and sixty-five days of them.

But this year felt different. Something was in the air. Call it intuition, a feeling that something was going to happen. There were other signs too. The dream, for instance. The one about the sailing ship and the Captain in the PAE Navy great-coat.

I checked my watch. I was still early, but decided I'd get out of the cabin anyway. I checked myself in the small mirror beside the bunk. My uniform was new and pressed, my face shaved and clean. Hair combed and neat. All Navy patches correctly placed and even.

Lieutenant Alexander Burns was ready.

Almost.

There was one last thing to fix. I dropped the small grin. If there was one thing Captain Paine hated, it was male personnel who smiled. A male smile signaled male entitlement, which was one of the worst things in the Navy. It was one of the worst things in the Accord too. A male smile was a direct link to the pre-Accord days centuries ago when the patriarchal system tyrannized the world. Every male in the Accord bore the shame. It was every male's duty to eradicate it like they eradicate pests.

So, I forced the smile away and replaced it with the slack face of the dedicated male sailor: humorless, non-threatening, resigned to whatever the Navy ordered.

But behind it, I was still hoping.

Today might be the day I'd finally be ordered to my first mission at sea.

3

Just as the radio predicted, it was a typical morning for AONT USA, sub-territory California: cold, clear and still. I looked at the sky as I walked. It was an unblemished light blue, as always.

I walked past the Accord Of Nations flagpole. At its top, a hundred feet above, the oversized flag was held in position by a rod, so that it that flew proudly, breeze or no breeze. It was a Navy requirement that the full face of the flag should be visible at all times from all parts of the base. So, the symbols of a dove perched on a rainbow on a brown background always stood proudly.

I reached the parade ground with a couple of minutes to spare. Ten thousand sailors, all dressed in blue Navy NWU were gathered, chattering in loose rows, waiting for the ceremony to begin. I saw Lieutenant Strick near the back and went and stood beside him.

'T.E.D., Strick.'

'T.E.D., Burns,' Strick said, as I fell in beside him.

T.E.D. was the standard Accord greeting.

'So, who was the enemy this morning?' Strick said, smiling. 'Rogue nations, meat eaters or patriarchal states that reject the Accord values?'

I'd known Strick (preferred pronoun 'He') since I'd been assigned to AONS Harmony two years ago. We'd done several Navy Spirit courses together. Strick was always a joker, even after two high profile missions and two promotions.

Strick's first mission was aboard AONS Gender Spectrum on a tour of AONT Asia. The second was on AONS Jenner to AONT Russia. There were patches on his NWU representing distinguished service on each of the missions. Rumor was he had been recommended for the Navy Cross for a speech he gave in AONT China about the oppressive nature of capitalism.

But for the moment, Strick was on shore duty too.

'I was scheduled to fight climate change deniers,' I said, 'but I canceled because of a meeting with Captain Paine.'

'Climate change deniers,' Strick said. 'Are there any left? I guess it's possible there might be climate change deniers somewhere—AONT Australia, maybe. Were they violent?'

Strick was referring to my usual morning routine of weapons combat training in the base simulator.

'Depends on what level of danger you choose,' I said. 'If you want they can be harmless rioters in an open space, or you can crank it up and fight them with weapons in a city at night.'

Strick shook his head. 'You still think all that stuff will do you any good, Burns? I mean, what's the actual likelihood of any action these days?'

Throughout his career, Strick had done no training

involving fighting at all. It certainly hadn't done his career any harm. He'd been promoted as fast as the Navy Spirit Code permitted. But I had my own ideas about what skills a Navy person should have. In my view, you had to be both competent and dangerous, even if you never used your skills. Not using them gave you character; knowing that you could use them gave you power.

But I never dared to say this to anyone.

'If you want my advice,' said Strick, 'stop trying to be an old Navy guy and start being a new Navy guy. Combat training and battle training are from the days when the dinosaurs roamed the Earth. These days we win the war of minds, Burns, not territory. Take it from me. You'll never get anywhere if you if train for actual sea battles, old pal, unless you're planning on fighting a war of your own.'

'I know,' I said. 'I know. But there are still worthwhile skills to learn.'

'Like what?'

'Like seamanship, like Naval history. It's the Navy, after all, not a civilian department.'

'You wanna get on a mission, don't you?' Strick said.

At the front of the massed group of sailors was a raised platform with a podium and a microphone. An AON flag flew beside it. No loudspeakers were necessary because we would all listen to the speaker and the anthem through our handheld headphones.

Behind the platform were the docks at which three battleships were tied up: AONS Tolerance, AONS Equality, and AONS Diversity. They languished at their moorings, like old giants. None of them had been to sea for decades, not even on goodwill missions. Peace had reigned across the world for two hundred years, thanks to the Accord, so there was no need for the Navy to be an actual fighting force.

And now, the old battleships were deemed too aggressive to be seen by civilians. So, they'd been ordered to shore duty too, and their guns had been sealed against the weather with rainbow-colored tampions.

'Heads up,' said Strick.

At the front of the crowd, a tall woman in NWUs walked purposefully to the podium, and yelled out, 'Atten-shun!' Everyone snapped their feet together and placed their hands over their hearts. The mass of sailors was now organized into tight rows.

Then the music came up and the anthem began.

Equality of outcome
  Accord Values for all
  Nations without borders
  The patriarchy must fall

Diversity is our strength
  Tolerance for all
  Gender is a spectrum
  The old ways must fall

From Greenland to New Zealand
  From Nigeria to Nepal
  The great Accord of Nations
  Its Values protect us all

And on it went until the music ceased and everyone shouted the words, TOLERANCE, EQUALITY,

DIVERSITY and then cheered. Strick and I cheered too, as you had to do, but it was at this point that I always wondered how strange it was that the names of the three old battleships were also Tolerance, Diversity, and Equality, and by cheering it was like we were mocking them for being tied up and going nowhere.

But I didn't have long to think this thought, because the Navy Spirit captain was on the microphone again and yelling, 'And now for our dishonorable discharge.'

The ten thousand sailors booed and jeered as the individual concerned was lead onto the platform in handcuffs, wearing a light-blue Navy prison jumpsuit. He stood, head down, a Master at Arms either side.

'Ensign Ernest Lorna,' boomed the officer at the microphone. 'You have been found guilty of sexual misconduct against a lower-ranking Navy personnel member who identifies as female. You have violated Navy Spirit's most important codes. You have offended the feelings of a promising sailor. You have brought the Accord of Nations Navy into disrepute and you have shamefully ignored the values of the Accord. You are to serve a prison sentence, then you are to be discharged.'

The crowd jeered as he hobbled away and down the steps.

'What did he do?' I shouted over the noise.

'The usual,' said Strick. 'Drinking. Morning after. She reported him.'

'Was there a hearing?' I asked.

'What does that matter?' said Strick. 'If she said he did it, he did it, right? What's the matter with you, Burns?'

The Navy Spirit captain dismissed the sailors. They wandered away, some to the mess for the late breakfast shift, others to their duties around the base, or to the Navy Spirit courses, but not every one. Beside us, three female cadets lingered. The three of them were around eighteen years old. Each had their hair clipped short, as usual.

Strick nudged me.

'It's happening again, Burns.'

'What is?' I said.

'It's not me who they're smiling at.'

I looked across at the cadets. 'I better get going,' I said.

'Good morning, Lieutenants,' said one of the cadets.

'Good morning,' said Strick. 'Don't I know you from AONS Restitution?'

'I don't think so, sir.' And then she added. 'It is sir, right?'

'Absolutely it's sir,' said Strick. 'Just as it was on the cruise down the coast of AONT India, remember?'

'No, sir. Never been aboard.'

'Well, we'll have to see about getting you some sea legs,' said Strick.

'How about your fellow lieutenant?' said the second cadet. 'We've saluted him after the last three pledges and the lieutenant didn't notice us once.' She looked at me coyly. 'Don't you like our salutes, Lieutenant?'

As I said, I was tall, over six feet, with yellow hair and blue eyes. The movie villain from the oppressive, pre-Accord West. This resemblance should have caused me to be a figure of hate, and yet, almost every day on the base I would catch winks, smiles, nods, sly catcalls and even direct propositions, often from superior officers, and from right across the whole sexual spectrum, which as everyone knew was limitless.

'What's the matter, Lieutenant? Don't you like us?'

Some might say I was in an enviable position having so much attention. But the risks were too great. One report of sexual misconduct and my career would be over. Just like that. Just like Ensign Lorna's career.

Of course, that didn't mean other personnel couldn't enjoy themselves. Strick for example. Strick was everything the Navy wanted and promoted: a female who had transitioned to a male. He could do and say what he liked, which was exactly what he did.

'I've got to run,' I said.

'You sure?' Strick said. 'I've got release forms if you're worried.' He patted his pocket. 'Can't get safer than that.' He turned to the three cadets. 'You don't mind, do you, cadets?'

'Don't get your hopes up Lieutenant,' laughed one.

'It's not that, Strick,' I said. 'I've got a meeting with Captain Paine. I can't be late for it.'

'Captain Paine?' said Strick. 'Captain Paine?' he said again.

'Is there any other?' I said.

'What's it about this time?'

'I'm about to find out,' I said. I didn't want to mention that it was about a mission. I didn't want to get everyone else's curiosity up. I had enough trouble keeping my own hopes under control.

I returned the salutes of the three cadets.

'T.E.D.,' they all said.

'T.E.D.,' said Strick.

'T.E.D.,' I replied.

And then I walked toward the stretch of the base known as Navy Way.

4

Navy Way was the administrative heart of AONS Harmony. It stretched along the length of the docks, running north to south. It contained all the departments necessary to running a modern Accord Naval base.

Each department had its own building with its name on a large sign outside each one. I walked by Plenty (the quartermasters), Togetherness (staff recreation), Sustenance (the main mess), and the largest building of all, the Navy Spirit building for Navy's personnel department.

Finally, I got to the building called Leadership, the one where Captain Paine's office was located. I saluted the two guards at the entrance and then walked through the doors beneath a large metal crest of the Accord dove and rainbow.

I got to Leadership and Captain Paine's office at 7:55, five minutes early. Lieutenant Commal was waiting at the desk outside in his blue NWU, looking intently at a computer screen.

'T.E.D., Commal,' I said. 'I'm here for the eight

hundred.'

'T.E.D., Burns,' Commal replied without looking up. 'You'll have to wait. The Captain's busy.'

'OK,' I said. 'How long?'

'I'm not psychic, Burns. You know where the seats are, don't you?'

'Sure,' I said and walked over to the three seats placed in a row opposite Commal's desk.

Commal had been friendly once. We'd completed several courses together as part of officer training. He was good company back then, but these, days Commal was hostile to everyone but senior officers, who wouldn't put up with the slightest hint of insolence.

The rumor was that Commal had a change of heart after gender reassignment surgery. Commal wanted to identify as a male again, but Navy Spirit had refused permission on the grounds that to return to being a male would bolster the patriarchy, and bolstering the patriarchy was against the spirit of the Accord.

The Accord knew best, as ever.

Meanwhile, Commal's resentment grew. He'd started working out and bulking up, and not taking his hormone pills. He'd even cut his hair short. Males who had transitioned to females wore their hair long whereas females who were female wore their hair short like men. It was just one of those things. Commal now looked like a bulldog with breasts.

'What's going on in there?' I asked nodding at Captain Paine's door.

'Captain Paine's meeting with Captain Odilli from Navy Spirit about a new initiative from Admiral Zhou,' Commal said.

'What kind of new initiative?'

'What's it to you?'

'It might affect me,' I said. 'What's it about?'

'I don't know, Burns. Some new equity initiative for the Accord. They haven't announced it yet.'

'I'm just wondering if it'll affect my chances of a mission.'

'Listen, Burns,' said Commal. 'Don't think your cisgendered white maleness entitles you to any privileges around here. You'll soon find out what it's about.'

'OK,' I said. 'I'm just asking. You're lucky enough to have been on a mission, Commal. This might be my first. I don't want anything to go wrong.'

Commal looked up from his screen. 'That was eighteen months ago, after my reassignment surgery.'

Then he looked back at his screen.

At eight ten, Commal looked up from the screen. 'In you go, Burns.'

'T.E.D.,' I said walking towards the door. 'Wish me luck.'

'No, you wish me luck,' said Commal.

5

Inside, I saluted Captain Paine, then rotated to the second person in the room, Captain Odilli from Navy Spirit.

'Tolerance, equality, diversity,' I said, then I stood at attention in front of Captain Paine's desk, keeping my face expressionless, hiding any hope I had for good news.

Neither of the two officers appeared to notice me. They were having an argument. It was the kind where they pretended to be polite but actually wanted to shout at each other.

'It's all very clear in the Rainbow 17 initiative document,' said Captain Paine. 'I've got to increase the quota of T.W.O.C. in the missions immediately—and that takes priority over everything else.'

From the other side of the room, Captain Odilli spoke. 'It's equally clear that I'm to have more T.W.O.C. in my training courses,' said Captain Odilli. 'And if the T.W.O.C. don't do the courses, especially the I.F. unit, they won't be allowed to go on any mission. I'll forbid it.'

The two officers glared at each other in silence.

T.W.O.C. stood for transgendered women of color. I.F. stood for intersectional feminism. Understanding these two oppressed groups was a key part of Navy mission training.

'Then we'll just have to take it up with Admiral Zhou,' said Captain Paine.

'Fine by me,' said Captain Odilli. 'Admiral Zhou understands the importance of Accord values, Captain.'

'Admiral Zhou also sets the quotas for the missions, Captain.'

'Are you saying Accord values aren't important? Because that's what I'm hearing.'

They glared at each other again. At the mention of Accord values, they appeared to reach a stalemate. No one wanted to be accused of disrespecting Accord values. When an argument reached the stage of Accord values, and whether or not someone disrespected them, the argument was usually over.

I saw Captain Paine look down at her desk, blinking furiously. In my peripheral vision, I saw Captain Odilli looking at the floor, shaking her head as if she were carrying on the argument in her thoughts. Then, Captain Paine looked up at me and frowned deeply.

'What do you want?' zee snapped. Captain Paine was in her early thirties, slim, and wore her brownish hair in the cropped style of all female officers. Zee had earned her Captain's rank after two years as a lieutenant aboard AONS Cohesion on a global goodwill mission. Ever since the mission ended, zee had been on shore duty, spending zer time working zer way up the Navy list, aiming for the exalted position of

Admiral. Zee was thin-lipped, lined and constantly irritable.

'Sirra,' I said, making sure to use Captain Paine's current preferred pronoun. 'Lieutenant Alexander Burns. I'm scheduled to meet with you regarding my upcoming mission.'

At the mention of the word 'mission,' Captain Odilli began to snigger. 'The Mission is part of the E.O.O. program,' I said. E.O.O. stood for the Equality Of Outcome program, which required each member of Navy personnel to be given the same opportunities as every other sailor and to receive the same score afterward.

Captain Odilli sniggered even more.

'Kayla,' said Captain Paine to Captain Odilli. 'We can continue talking later. There's no need for you to stay here for this. I'll ask Commal to come in. Commal can be the third person.'

Zee was referring to the Navy requirement for three people to be present whenever a cisgendered male met with anyone who identified as female.

'No way,' said Captain Odilli. 'Watching you deal with this lieutenant is going to make my day. Just hold on while I get my cis male tears mug.'

I was still standing to attention, still looking over Captain Paine's cropped hair at the photos on the wall. Zee had placed the usual pictures there: the Accord flag, the list of Accord values, a painting of the Accord Establishment Day ceremony, and a large photograph of the Accord Commissioners themselves outside the Accord Headquarters in AON sub-territory Los Angeles, all of them dressed in uni-sex Accord smocks.

'At ease, Burns,' Captain Paine said at last, as zee

tapped at her computer. I put my feet apart and stood with my hands behind my back. Then Captain Paine looked up and said, 'Do you believe in the values of Accord, Burns?'

'Yes, sirra.'

'You're committed to the ideas of diversity, tolerance, and the necessity to rid the Accord of privilege, sexism, and the patriarchy?'

'Yes, sirra,' I said.

I was usually asked these kinds of questions whenever I was in a meeting. It was because of my appearance, again. I looked exactly like a privileged guy over whom the struggle had to be won, a living relic of the pre-Accord era.

'You've been here two years.'

'Yes, sirra.'

'And you haven't been promoted, and you haven't been on a mission.'

'Sirra, this year will be my first,' I said. 'That is…if there is a mission, sirra.'

Captain Odilli was snuffling back laughter.

Then, Captain Paine sat back in her seat. I sensed bad news was coming.

'Look, Burns,' said Captain Paine. 'Things have changed. The Equality Of Outcome program is out of date. It's been replaced by Rainbow 17, which was issued last week. According to your profile, I'm afraid you don't fit the new requirements.'

'Don't fit, sirra?' I said.

'Rainbow 17 is quite clear. It's just the rules, Burns.'

'Yes, sirra.'

Captain Odilli said, 'Ask him why he thinks he deserves a mission.'

Captain Paine steepled her fingers across her shirt front. 'OK, Burns. Tell us why you deserve a mission.'

I cleared my throat. 'Well, sirra. I believe I have completed all the training required to be eligible for a mission. Many courses were completed with distinction. I was top of class in the courses for Diversity, Purging Toxic Masculinity and Destroying The Patriarchy. I was second in the class for courses for Anti Sexism and the Intersectional Feminism course that Captain Odilli just mentioned.'

Captain Paine said, 'High scores are examples of patriarchal meritocracy and oppression, Burns. They are no guarantee of advancement. In fact, they reduce the likelihood of promotion. You ought to know that.'

'Yes, sirra.'

Zee began been tapping at her screen, frowning at something. 'Says here you took extra courses as well.'

'Yes, sirra.'

'Extra courses in what?'

'In marksmanship, sirra, as well as hand-to-hand combat and Naval strategy. I also obtained a pilot's license specializing in Navy Slingshot aircraft, and J-Pack deployment. I also volunteered to help at a civilian LGBTQ shelter, and I requested to study pre-Accord era naval battles, but permission was denied by Navy Spirit.'

'Naval strategy and hand-to-hand combat?' said Captain Paine, head slowly shaking. 'What on earth made you think they would help your career in the Navy?'

'The Navy is still a fighting force in some ways,' I said. 'There might be an emergency that requires fighting capabilities at some point in the future. I was training for such an emergency.'

Here, both Captain Paine and Captain Odilli both laughed together. Suddenly, they were great pals. The both of them leaned forward, their mouths open wide, laughing, almost as if they were going to slap each other's knees.

When they had calmed down, Captain Paine said, 'Burns, it ain't going to happen. Your application is problematic, as I said. You're ordered to shore duty until further notice. We'll let you know about any missions coming up. In the meantime, you're dismissed.'

'Permission to speak, sirra,' I said, standing my ground.

'Make it fast, Burns.'

'May I ask why specifically I am not eligible for a mission and why I am problematic? I have completed all the requirements. I have waited for two years. My name is at the top of the roster. I have no Navy Spirit code violations. The Navy Spirit charter states that equality of outcome must be the first consideration, it...'

Captain Odilli climbed to her feet.

'Are you trying to tell me about the Navy Spirit charter, Lieutenant? Because if you are, you won't just be on shore duty, you'll be doing all those courses all over again.'

'No, per,' I said, making sure to use Captain Odilli's preferred pronoun, which was even more critical than getting Captain Paine's pronouns because per pronouns changed so often.

Captain Odilli walked over to me. Per wasn't as tall as me. Per head reached only as far as my shoulder, but per anger made per seem a foot taller.

'You really think you deserve this mission, don't you, Burns?'

'I believe I have a case, per.'

'You think you deserve it because of your privilege, don't you, as a cisgendered male—and a white male at that?'

'No, per,' I said.

'You probably think you deserve a promotion too, don't you?'

'No, per.'

'How about we give you a battleship to command as well?'

I didn't answer, but I was thinking that battleships had not been effective in naval warfare since the development of aircraft carriers in the pre-Accord era.

'You think I have time to worry about your disappointments, Burns? A privileged male like you? You heard Captain Paine. You're dismissed. Now get out before we call the MAs.'

'Hold on, now Kayla,' said Captain Paine. 'Burns might deserve a little more explanation as to why he's not going on the mission. He's been waiting for two years.'

Captain Odilli, shook per head and sat back in per chair. 'Explanations are not required where privilege exists.'

Captain Paine tapped at the computer. 'It's simple, Burns. Others on this base have moved higher on the Oppression Hierarchy.' Zee read from a list. 'Lieutenants Cestor, Neves and Lennox have all changed their sexual identities over the last six months. Lieutenants Tieffer, Ndougoo and Redondo have actually had gender reassignment surgery. Lieutenant Pereira has changed racial identity. And, Lieutenant Knab now identifies as non able-bodied. So they all get missions first. It's only proper, Burns and it's only fair.'

'Yes, sirra.'

'If you want to get on a mission, Burns, you've got to place higher on the Oppression Hierarchy.'

'My apologies, sirra,' I said. 'I identify as a male—a straight male, and I'm able-bodied.'

'Well, then there's nothing we can do for you.'

'Yes, sirra.'

'Right then,' zee said. 'Burns, you are to report to Navy Spirit immediately to await new orders. Until then, you are on shore duty till further notice. Your mission is over.'

'Permission to speak, sirra.'

'No, Burns. You're dismissed.' Zee smiled at Captain Odilli and in a mock army sergeant's voice said, 'Dismissed!'

They both smiled. Their previous hostility to each other was now behind them. They had found common ground, something they could agree on.

Suddenly, a ping sounded in Captain Odilli's pocket, followed by a ping in Captain Paine's pocket, and two more pings from outside the office door.

Within seconds, someone knocked. The door opened before Captain Paine could speak. Commal stood there, eyes wide.

'Beg your pardon, sirra,' he said to Captain Paine. 'Beg pardon, per.'

'What is it, Commal?' said Captain Paine.

'AON Navy headquarters is calling. Admiral Zhou's office. They say it's urgent.'

'How urgent?' said Captain Paine.

'Very urgent, sirra. Code Unicorn,' said Commal.

Captain Odilli looked at Captain Paine. 'Code Unicorn?'

'What could it be?' said Captain Paine.

'It's probably about the Accord Establishment Day ceremony,' said Captain Odilli. 'AON sub-territory Hong Kong is having trouble with the location. They think holding it by the harbor, as the Commission requested, will trigger unconscious ancestral memories of colonization by the pre-Accord powers arriving by sea.'

'I think this is something more important than the Establishment Day Ceremony, per and sirra,' said Commal.

Captain Paine's expression turned dark. 'Nothing can be more important than celebrating the establishment of the Accord,' zee said. Then, zee noticed me still in the room. 'Burns, I said you're dismissed.'

'Yes, sirra. T.E.D.'

As I walked away, I heard all three handhelds ping again, and again.

And again.

6

I trudged out of Leadership, past the two guards at the entrance. I almost forgot to salute them. Then, I turned left and drifted toward the Navy Spirit building.

It wasn't yet 8:30 a.m.

Outside, the sun was still shining on AONS Harmony. Blue sky, green lawn, sailors in their blue NWUs. It was a beautiful scene, more like a university campus than a Naval base. Only the three old battleships brooding at their moorings tainted the mood—them and my bitter disappointment.

I was frustrated. Two years of shore duty, two years of extra courses and disciplining my mind to purge my toxic maleness, and here I was facing two more years of the same.

And the only way out of it was to change my gender or to identify as someone non-able-bodied or someone with ancestors from a nation oppressed by the pre-Accord Western powers.

I shook my head, wondering.

What would it take to make the Navy change its ways? Would it require a war? An actual war?

Something to shake up the whole Accord? Would that mean the Navy would be forced to choose the most battle-ready personnel as crew, not just the most oppressed?

Would it mean they would choose me, Alexander Burns?

It was a wonderful thought. To be at sea serving the Accord in an active role! It was all I had ever wished for. But thinking that way would get me exactly nowhere. The whole Accord was at peace. There hadn't been a war since the overthrow of the pre-Accord powers centuries ago. The peace grew stronger every day.

And, if I were being honest, really honest, I'd concede that there wasn't a need for a military at all. There were no nation states, so no conflict. Which is how the Navy had gotten to its present state where the only way to serve it was to not serve it, and the only way to be your best was to be your worst, denying your own abilities and skills.

It was hard to understand, just like a lot of things about the Accord.

I shook my head. Bad thoughts, Burns. Bad thoughts. Must be due to the old shame. That's what we'd been taught since first grade. I was a descendant of the pre-Accord West, a male descendant too, which meant I bore responsibility for the crimes committed by my ancestors, the crimes of colonization, capitalism, and oppression.

The Accord never let me forget.

Bad thoughts, Burns.

I was so absorbed with thinking, I hardly noticed that I'd almost walked as far as the three battleships.

The Navy Spirit building was now behind me.

I stopped in the building's long shadow, turned around and looked up at the Accord flag flying at its entrance. The rainbow and the dove represented diversity and peace. They were also meant to express the concepts of inclusion and harmony among all people, but when I looked at the flag, I saw it differently. I saw it as a symbol of a new kind of oppression that replaced the old kinds from the pre-Accord era.

I shook my head. Captain Odilli was right. I needed to take the courses again.

So, I turned around and walked back toward Navy Spirit. Better get started on the courses, Burns. You've got a lot of work to do.

And that's when someone slammed into my shoulder.

7

Whoever it was had been running hard. They hit me from behind with a whomp that spun me half around and almost knocked me over. The collision didn't really hurt me, but it hurt the slammer. He or she or they hit the deck hard. They fell onto the lawn face first, sending their handheld clattering along the sidewalk.

'Are you all right, sailor?'

The sailor was a young female, dressed in blue NWU and a cap with the same short haircut as Captain Paine's, except her hair was fair, not brown. She was on her knees clutching her chest, her mouth open. I took a step forward to help her. I bent down and reached out my hand.

Just in time I came to my senses.

Touching a female was dangerous—for any reason, even if you were trying to help a female in trouble. You could find yourself in a sexual harassment case in an instant, especially if you were her superior officer. At the very least, helping a female was seen as an example of oppression by a cisgendered male. Females never needed male help. That was the first lesson in Navy training 101.

So, I withdrew my hand, and stepped back a good yard, out of her reach. Already I was worried at how this scene appeared to anyone watching. A female lay on the ground, clutching her chest, and a tall, male officer stood over her. I looked over my shoulder, watching for the first person to begin shouting the denouncements.

But the female really did look hurt.

'Can I call someone to help you?' I said, bringing out my handheld. As I did, I pushed the video record button. Can't be too careful. 'Can I call someone for you? Are you hurt?'

'No,' she gasped. 'No.'

She scrambled to stand up but slumped down again. Dammit, I thought. I stepped forward again and crouched on my knees in front of her. 'Is it all right for me to help you up, cadet? Just say no if you're feeling oppressed.'

In a flash, she had grabbed my arm and yanked on it, almost pulling me down on top of her. 'Woh! Careful, now,' I said, but then I realized what was happening. This was a trap to claim sexual assault after all. And I had fallen into it head first.

I waited for her to start screaming ASSAULT, RAPE, HARASSMENT, and so on. Then witnesses would arrive. Then the MAs would arrive. Then charges would be made. The girl would be believed without question by Navy Spirit. There would be a hearing, but I would have no right to explain my side, and no right to question her. The handheld recording would not be allowed as evidence.

But the girl did not scream. Instead, she yanked herself to her feet, her face in a convincing expression of panic. Then, she pushed past me and ran unsteadily along the path towards the doors of the Navy Spirit building. No doubt she was going to make her accusations directly to the base S.H.O., the Sexual Harassment Officer.

I watched her disappear inside. I saw the door close behind her. But I didn't move. Didn't walk away. Didn't even take a step. To leave the scene would implicate me further. So I stayed where I was. I knew the MAs would come streaming out of the building in about forty seconds. I might as well enjoy the sunshine and freedom while I could.

But the MAs did not come running through the doors. Nobody did. It was strange. In fact, now that I was looking around, there was something unusual about the base in general. Something I hadn't noticed in my disappointment after the meeting with Captain Paine. The lawns and sidewalks were empty. The Navy personnel was scattered. Sailors in all the different uniforms were running across the parade ground, panic on their faces.

This wasn't a drill.

So, what on Earth was going on?

I noticed a column of smoke rising from the northeast, over near the town of Dworkin. Nothing ever happened in Dworkin, except maybe on Accord Establishment Day. It was probably one of the quietest towns in AON sub-territory California.

Now, something was definitely going on.

Then, my handheld pinged. Once, twice, three times, like someone ringing a warning bell. I took it out and read the message.

RETURN TO BARRACKS. STAY CALM.
AWAIT ORDERS.

What was going on?

I looked up from the handheld. This time, I saw something. A large, dark aircraft hovering over the three docked ships, AONS Tolerance, AONS Diversity, and AONS Equality. The aircraft was shaped like nothing I'd seen before, neither civilian nor military. It was shaped like a giant black teardrop turned on its side. It made no sound, fired no weapons. It just hovered—as if it had been placed there by an invisible force.

Was it an AON Air Force craft? It didn't look like it. There was no livery on its sides, not even the rainbow and dove flag. It was just a dark object that reflected no light, like a teardrop made of whatever black holes in space were made from.

The sight of it made me uneasy. Was this 'the something big' I had sensed earlier in the morning?

Then, the strange object began to rotate—slowly and malevolently.

8

The nearest barracks were on the far side of the parade ground. The strange object was on its western side. To reach the barracks, I would have to walk a hundred or so meters in the object's gaze. Or I could follow the cadet and go into the Navy Spirit building. It was closer.

I chose the barracks.

The object remained indifferent as I walked. It looked as if it were resting, or scanning, or stalled. How did it stay suspended in the air? I couldn't see or hear any jets or propellers. It didn't look like a balloon, either, because it was unmoved by the breeze coming from the ocean. And what had it done to make the female cadet so scared?

I kept my eye on it all the way across the parade ground.

At the barracks, sailors were crowded around the lobby area. No-one was panicking. Some were actually smiling. Maybe they thought the object was something to do with the Accord Establishment Day celebrations.

'Who is in charge here?' I said to an ensign at the

edge of one of the groups. He'd been smiling at something one of the group had said, then he looked around, saw me, and snapped to a salute.

'T.E.D., sir.'

'Who's in charge?'

'No-one, sir. We're waiting for orders.'

As he said this, there was a clatter of pings as every handheld in the area sounded an incoming message, followed by silence, as everyone reached into their jacket pockets.

'At ease,' I said to the ensign. 'Check your messages.'

He reached into his jacket, brought out his handheld and looked at it.

'Well?' I said. 'What's it say?'

'There's going to be an official announcement from the Accord about the object, sir?'

'Where?'

'On the TV, sir. The news.'

As he said this, people began moving away to the barracks TV room.

'OK. Thanks, ensign. Dismissed.'

He saluted and then ran to catch up to the rest of his group. I stayed watching the object through the entrance. It was still turning slowly above the three ships at the dock as if it were making up its mind what to do next.

'Why so serious, Lieutenant?' said a cheerful voice beside me. 'The Accord says to stay calm, so there's nothing to worry about.'

Standing there, smiling, was one of the three cadets I'd met earlier with Strick.

'That's not how it looks,' I said.

'The Accord's got this,' said the cadet, smiling. 'It's

probably a prop they're using for Establishment Day.'

'Let's hear the official announcement first,' I said.

'What else could it be?' she said.

I looked at her name patch. The name was Fowler.

She followed my eyes. 'It's Frank,' she said.

'OK, cadet,' I said.

I walked with the cadet through the corridor to the TV room. Sailors stood watching the big TV screen or looked down at their handhelds. Others were yelling 'Shhhhh,' as the TV news anchor from Unity appeared beside an image of the object. Unity was the official Accord news station.

'...dubbed the Friend Ships in Accord English, the objects are believed to be carrying intergalactic visitors. Officials from ASA, the Accord Space Administration say the visitors have not yet made contact but were expected any moment to make an announcement. Accord Commission representative, Commissioner Alain De Forrest stated that the Commission valued diversity and so welcomed the opportunity to extend the Accord's hand of friendship to visitors from other worlds. The appearance of the Friend Ships was met with excitement around the Accord. Children from every territory hosted welcoming parties for the visitors...'

The screen then cut to shots of children smiling, holding up welcome signs and drawings of the object itself. But just as they were showing an image from AONT China featuring children holding hands to form a heart shape, several loud booms sounded outside, shaking the room.

The announcer on the screen repeated the words, 'We're sure our visitors will appreciate the very same values that have made the Accord of Nations and its people so happy and equal, valuing our diversity, just as we will…' when there was an even louder boom which shook the room even more. People fell against each other. The TV itself fell from the wall, hit the floor and fell face first onto its screen.

'Get out!' someone yelled.

I shoved through the crowd, past several people looking at their handhelds. Like all well-drilled people of the Accord, they trusted the official news more than their own eyes.

When I got to the building exit, I stepped through the crowd and onto the edge of the parade ground. Black smoke was billowing furiously from the docks.

'What did it do?' I said.

One of the sailors wide-eyed with fright, said, 'It was just up there, and then it did something to the ships.'

'Like what?'

'Like a…I don't know. I didn't see the shot or whatever.'

Beneath the thick smoke, the three ships at the dock, the AONS Tolerance, AONS Equality, and AONS Diversity, could be glimpsed. They were reduced to twisted and tortured metal.

Frank came up beside me, then stopped and stared at the scene.

'Are we being attacked?' she said. 'The Accord says the objects are friendly.'

'It's a strange way of showing friendship,' I said.

'Maybe it's their culture,' said Frank. 'We have to be tolerant.'

The rest of the group were silent, stunned by the sight of the destroyed ships and fires. None of us had seen action before. No-one in the entire military had ever experienced actual fighting. The only battles waged were the Accord's battles against sexism, racism, the patriarchy, homophobia, and inequality.

But this was real.

And no-one was in charge, mobilizing the base defenses.

'What's it doing?' someone said. 'Is it coming over here?'

'Maybe they're going to land then come out,' someone else said.

Up in the sky, the object moved away from the smoke, hovering sixty feet high above the docks. Then it moved silently over the parade ground, drawing a tear-shaped shadow behind it. When it reached the parade ground's center, it halted. Then it lowered itself until it was about twenty yards high.

Then, like a collective cymbal clash, all our handhelds pinged again. This time, it was the special ping noise used only by the AONT USA Navy Head Quarters in sub-territory San Francisco. I pulled my handheld from my chest pocket and read.

NO DANGER FROM VISITORS IN FRIEND SHIPS SO LONG AS WE ALL UPHOLD ACCORD VALUES. ALL PERSONNEL RETURN TO STATIONS.

So what did that mean? Hadn't they heard what just happened? And then I realized, the Navy command hadn't ever seen any action either. To them, a military response, actually deploying the Navy's weapons, would be to evoke the bad old days of the pre-Accord. Instead, they deployed the Accord values, as if the values would stop a laser beam.

My handheld pinged a second time, a single ding after the cacophony seconds before, but I didn't check it. I was too busy watching the parade ground. Now the object wasn't alone. Someone was walking towards it from the parade ground's southern edge.

By the short cropped hair, it looked to be another female cadet. She was wearing the blue NWU, and no cap on her shaved head. She walked slowly but steadily as if mesmerized. She held out her arms in what looked like a gesture of welcome. When she reached the object, she stood in its shadow and reached out to it.

'Shhhhh,' someone yelled. 'What's she saying?'

'Hey! Don't presume to know this person's pronouns. They might not like she.'

'Shhhhh.'

The mob quietened down and listened. We could just hear her words over the roar of the fire on the docks.

She shouted, 'Tolerance, equality, diversity. You are welcome, visitors.'

The dark object remained still and silent, hovering above her. 'You are welcome!' the cadet yelled again. 'You are welcome in the name of tolerance and diversity.'

Then, a hatch opened in the object's side. A thick blue beam shot down. It hit the female's head first and then covered her entire body down to her boots. She didn't exactly explode; it was more like she melted. Then the beam ceased and the port hatch closed. The female—what remained of her—was a smoking pile on the ground, about the size of a stack of dinner plates.

'Why isn't someone doing anything?' called someone to my right. 'Why isn't anyone doing anything? They're going to attack us.'

'Shut up!' yelled someone else. 'You're othering the visitors. It's offensive. Think of our values. Think of the Accord.'

'I just feel someone should do something. Isn't anyone doing anything? Where are the officers in charge? Who is the responsible?'

Nothing happened. No Navy jets came rocketing across the sky, firing missiles. No guns blazed from around the base. No armed personnel came running around the corner. Nothing. It seemed the Accord Of Nations Ship Harmony, the largest base on the west coast of AONT USA, had given itself up without a fight.

'Everyone, stay where you are!' yelled a commander who had walked up the corridor from the TV room. 'You've got your orders. Stay inside and wait. The Accord's got this.'

'What's she talking about?' some yelled.

'She?' the voice said. 'It's zee.'

'Commander, are we going to mount a response to this attack?' I said.

Zee looked at me with pure hostility. 'What's your name?' zee said, even though my name patch was right there.

'Lieutenant Burns.'

'Well, Lieutenant, didn't you hear? We're not under attack, so there's no need to defend the base.'

Zee walked away.

My handheld was busy again. This time, it wasn't pinging. It was ringing. I looked at it. No caller ID, which meant it was probably someone calling from inside the base.

I pressed the green answer button.

'Lieutenant Burns speaking,' I said.

'Burns, why haven't you been reading your messages?' It was Commal. He sounded angry, his masculine voice was even deeper than before.

'There's been a lot going on,' I said.

'Captain Paine is going nuts. Zee's been trying to reach you for the last half hour.'

'My apologies to the Captain,' I said. 'I was following the orders to stay inside.'

'Well, now you've got new orders. You're to report to the Captain's office right now.'

'Right now? Didn't you see what happened?'

'Yes, Burns. We've all seen what happened, including what happened to the cadet who ran onto the parade ground.'

I looked back outside at the blue pile beneath the dark object.

'What does the Captain want?'

'I don't know. You'll find out when you get here.'

I looked back at the parade ground. There was no exit from the barracks except ones that lead directly onto it. If I was ordered to Captain Paine's office, I would have to pass the object, drawing its gaze. Is that what they were expecting me to do?

'Did you hear me, Burns?' said Commal.

'Yeah, I heard.'

'Are you moving yet, because I don't hear any footsteps.'

'I'm coming, Commal. Calm down.'

'If it's the object you're worried about, just stay away

from it.'

Easier said than done.

I hung up. I could have argued with Commal. No, I should have argued with Commal. What Captain Paine had ordered was potentially suicidal.

But strangely and for reasons, I didn't comprehend, I wanted to go. I wanted to pass the object and to run the gauntlet of its lasers.

'Lieutenant Burns.' It was the commander, back again. 'Go to the TV room and order everyone to their seats. There's going to be a special broadcast about tolerance from HQ.'

'Sorry, Prasana,' I said, reading the name patch. 'Orders from Captain Paine.'

'What orders?'

'To report to the Captain's office immediately.'

'In Leadership?'

'Does she have any other office?' I said, then corrected myself. 'Yes, the office in Leadership.'

Prasana looked outside at the object, hovering over the steaming blue pile that was once a cadet.

'You're not going out there, are you?'

I shrugged. 'Well, I can't tunnel my way there.'

I stepped toward the exit. Frank tugged at my sleeve. 'It's crazy. You saw what happened.'

I said nothing and then I pushed open the heavy glass door and stepped outside.

9

I stepped further into the open. Navy Way and Captain Paine's office lay on the far side of the parade ground. The object hovered in between, motionless and indifferent to the black smoke and twisted wreckage behind it. It stayed that way while I edged along the parade ground's perimeter.

Ten yards out, I looked back to the barracks entrance and saw the faces of the Frank, the Commander, and the rest. Frank was waving for me to come back. I turned away and kept on going.

Twenty yards along the wall with eighty or so to go and I was feeling more confident. The black object hadn't moved. It hovered there, dignified and serene, the way some insects appear when their prey is in front of them—waiting for the moment to strike. I kept my eyes on it and walked steadily on.

Forty yards to go. Should I run? I could have made it to the buildings on the ground's eastern edge in seconds if I did. Forty sprinted steps and I could be there out of sight, out of danger.

Twenty yards now. Almost there. No need to run.

Just keep things steady. The black object hovered in the sun, strangely outlined against the blue sky, like the objects in the combat simulator's world, hyper-real, ten percent different to reality, reflecting no light.

Tens yards to go and all was well. The object wasn't interested in me. It would stay where it was while I got to Navy Way and to Captain Paine.

And then, without knowing why, I took a step away from the perimeter and onto the parade ground's open space. I just turned right and walked out there. I took five steps. Nothing. Ten steps. Still nothing. So I kept on walking until I was thirty steps away from the perimeter, exposed and in full view of the object.

This isn't like me, I thought. I'm not this reckless, not this foolish. And yet, there I was out in the open, challenging the object's dominance of the territory. Risking the same fate as the female cadet.

Then, my handheld sounded.

I froze. It had only been one ping, and yet the effect was as if a large bell had tolled and was now echoing around the parade ground.

I looked at the black object, prepared to run if it moved. But it stayed motionless in the air. Then again, maybe it had moved after all. Its shadow had been over the pile of blue sludge. Now the shadow was in front of it.

The object had moved closer to me.

I reached down to my pocket, cursing myself for not switching off the handheld before I left the barracks. On the screen was a message from my mother, asking me to call her. I switched the handheld to silent and slid it back into my side pocket.

Then, I looked across at Navy Way, and then behind

me at the barracks.

Is it better to go on, I wondered, or to go back?

But the object was already moving.

The shadow was now at least twenty yards from the pile of blue sludge. Without me realizing, the object had drifted away, like a boat on the tide.

But each time, I looked at it, the object appeared to be at a standstill.

Seconds passed as I debated what to do. Walk or run? Forward to Captain Paine's building or back to the perimeter and the barracks?

I chose to walk the shortest route, directly across to Captain Paine's building. I took the first few steps, moving confidently as if nothing was wrong. I'm just another Earth creature keeping out of the way, like the others back there in the barracks.

Then, I heard the blast.

I ducked instinctively, hands over my head, chin into my chest. I stayed that way for twenty-seconds. Then I looked up. The object was still there, black and malevolent, but the barracks were destroyed. They'd been turned into rubble and dust, bricks and roofing falling around it onto the parade ground.

I could hardly believe it. There had been hundreds of personnel in there, including Frank and the other commander.

I looked back at the object, expecting it to be rubbing its wings in satisfaction, but it was as impassive as ever, as if the blast had been fired from somewhere else.

Time for me to get out of there.

This time, I didn't run or creep. I strode back towards the barracks. There might still be people alive in the rubble.

I hadn't moved more than ten paces when I felt the shadow pass over me and grow larger.

The object was not only moving; it was also descending, and it was going to block my way. Silently, it lowered itself in front of me, dropping down until it was six feet above the ground and we were virtually nose to nose, like a scuba diver meeting a killer whale. I stopped and stared straight into the black hull.

Fear told me to bolt, to turn and run for my life. Maybe, I'd escape before it fired its beams. Maybe, I could zig zag and escape the first blast. But I didn't move. I stood my ground. If this was the end, I was not going to die running away with a shot in the back.

Instead, I looked closer at the object's hull. It was looming and silent, and strangely cold. I could feel a chill radiating from it.

A disturbing thought insinuated itself in my mind. If I reached out, I could touch this bizarre object. It was just three feet away and I could touch it.

I raised my right arm and held up my hand and reached forward across the gap. The hull glistened as my hand moved closer. Now it was darkly translucent. I could almost see shapes behind it, rounded shapes, mechanical shapes, moving shapes, like organs squirming beneath skin.

Then, I saw something loom up into the translucence.

It can't be possible, I thought. It can't be.

No sooner had I thought this when the object was gone, rising silently upward at an impossible velocity, up into the flawless blue sky until it became a dot and then nothing.

10

Within seconds of the object's disappearance, I heard the fire and rescue units screaming towards the barracks and the docks. In my pocket, my handheld vibrated over and over. I took it out. No caller ID.

'I'm almost there, Commal,' I said.

'You better be. Captain Paine's been on the intercom every two minutes.'

'You heard the blast, right?'

'We're monitoring everything, Burns. The rescue units should be there already.'

'They are, but they're going to need help. Tell Captain Paine to wait. I'll get back when things calm down.'

'Negative, Burns. Your priority is Captain Paine. Personnel are on the way to the barracks already. They'll take care of it. Your only orders are to get here right now.'

'What's the urgency, Commal? Thirty minutes ago, Captain Paine didn't want anything to do with me. Now she can't do without me. Surely she can wait.

There are people inside the barracks.'

'Just get here, Burns.' And he hung up.

I left the parade ground and hurried along Navy Way to the Leadership building. The guards at the building entrance were gone, the crest of the rainbow and the dove was askew. Inside, the lobby was empty. The reception desk was un-personed. The elevators didn't respond when I pressed the buttons.

So I took the stairs instead.

As I climbed, I couldn't help but wonder what Captain Paine wanted. I guessed it was something to do with the arrival of the object, though I couldn't say what exactly. Otherwise, it might have been a harassment claim lodged by the female cadet outside Navy Spirit.

But there was one other possibility, a very small one. Maybe Captain Paine had changed her mind and was ordering me on a mission.

When I got to the Commal's desk, he was sitting there wearing a helmet.

'T.E.D., Commal,' I said.

'Finally!' he replied, his voice still deep.

'It wasn't easy to get here,' I said. 'I had a close encounter with the object back there.'

But Commal wasn't listening. 'Straighten your uniform, Burns,' Commal said. 'Some very senior people are here. And straighten your hair. You know how yellow hair makes Captain Odilli angry.'

'Are you listening?' I said I was out there when the object attacked, just after the blast at the barracks. I saw something inside it.'

'It wasn't an attack, Burns,' Commal snapped. 'You're othering the visitors, and that's totally against Accord values. We don't know the visitors' culture, so we're not in a position to judge them. As a transgender woman who is transitioning back to being a man, I know all about being other-ed, and it sucks.'

'Is Captain Paine ordering some kind of response?'

'Save your war plans for the combat simulator, Burns. The Captain is waiting. No, not in there. She's waiting in the Affinity Room.'

'The what room?'

Commal came out from behind his desk and began walking down the corridor. 'This way,' he said.

'What's the Affinity Room?' I said following behind.

'It's a conference room used for special situations.'

'Special situations like an attack on the base by aliens?'

'You're othering them again, Burns. Luckily for you, we're old friends, or I'd report you.'

'Well, how do you describe what just happened out there? Three ships sunk, a barracks destroyed, who knows how many personnel killed, maybe more attacks in other parts of the Accord. That doesn't sound like a friendly visit.'

'Keep your voice down,' said Commal, pushing the elevator buttons.

'The elevators are out,' I said.

'Not this one,' said Commal. 'Separate power supply.'

We stepped inside. Commal scanned a card over a sensor. The door closed and the elevator descended.

'Why does Captain Paine want to see me?' I said. 'There are more important things to do.'

'Such as?'

'Such as everything I've said so far. Then there's

liaising with the Army, and the Air Force…'

'Calm down, Burns. You'll have to wait and see what the Captain wants.'

'Don't you know?'

'I only know that I've got about two hundred AWOLs to track down and that Captain Paine and Navy Spirit won't let me be who I really am. That's as much as I can deal with at the moment. You'll soon find out what zee and per want any minute now Burns.'

We reached ground level but the elevator kept on descending.

'But why me? Why now?'

'Who knows?' Commal said. 'Maybe they're going to give you a mission after all. Someone has to get what they want.'

Commal's change of tone from hostile to complaining was interesting. The crisis had brought out a different side to him.

The elevator halted far below ground level. The doors opened. Cool, stale air rushed in. A dark corridor painted Navy blue stretched away from us and ended at a large set of double doors. Two MAs stood before them, wearing sidearms.

One of the MAs took out a scanner and ran it over both Commal and me.

'What's going on?' I asked.

'No questions, Lieutenant.'

Then, the MA stood back and opened the door.

I took a step inside, then turned back to Commal. He hadn't moved.

'What about you?'

'Not me,' said Commal. 'You're on your own.'

11

Inside, was a conference room. There was a large horseshoe-shaped table with a bank of TV screens at one end. No windows. The walls were bare and concrete, except for a large painting of the Accord Commissioners wearing unisex smocks, and on the opposite wall, a plaque displaying the list of Accord values.

The TV screens showed footage of AON military bases. All of them seemed to have been attacked. There were burning buildings, aircraft hangers in ruins, and ships sunk at their moorings. And not just in AONT USA either. There were bases on fire from AONT Delhi to AONT Moscow. The attack had been global.

Three people were at the table. On one side was Captain Paine. Zer face was strained, her lips looked thinner than usual. On the other was Captain Odilli, per arms crossed, a frown on per large face. The third person had their back to me, but I knew who it was from the short dark hair and the thick Admiral's epaulettes resting on thin shoulders. Without a doubt, it was Admiral Zhou.

This, I thought, is an actual war room, or crisis room, despite being called the Affinity Room. This was a room where decisions were made about the deployment of defenses, of ships, aircraft, sailors, soldiers. It was the kind of room I'd only heard about as being used in the very first days of the Accord when real wars had been fought against the pre-Accord powers.

And now I had been ordered down here to help. Probably they needed my opinion of the aliens. I had just seen one after all. Or maybe, they had me in mind for some special task. I tried to keep my enthusiasm hidden, but I couldn't help but think all my extra courses, all my waiting might now pay off.

'Tolerance, equality, diversity,' I said, saluting.

'At ease, Burns,' said Captain Paine.

I put my feet apart and my hands behind my back, and stood at the end of the table.

Captain Paine said, 'This is Lieutenant Burns, Admiral.'

The thin shoulders turned. The Admiral rotated on the seat until she faced me. Her hostile, dark eyes looked me up and down, from my face, to my belt, to my boots, then back to my hair, frowning all the way, as if she'd never seen a male before. Maybe, like everyone else, she saw my likeness to the movie actor who played the pre-Accord bad guys. It was not a good first impression.

'Not diverse enough,' said the Admiral. 'Not diverse enough. What can they be thinking?'

'They were very specific,' said Captain Paine. 'They named Lieutenant Alexander Burns.'

'Then, they have lost their minds,' said the Admiral.

'We have policies to prevent this sort of thing from happening.'

Here, Captain Odilli spoke. 'Exactly, Admiral. Just look at his appearance. What's the matter with you, Burns? Is that any way to appear before senior officers?'

'Per?'

'Your uniform and hair—they're a disgrace.'

'My apologies, per. I was outside when the aliens… the visitors…' I paused and chose my words carefully, not wishing to blow my chances with a slip of the tongue. 'When the visitors demonstrated their culture,' I said. 'Captain, I actually managed to get a close up look at the…'

'Get someone else,' said the Admiral.

'I don't think we have time,' said Captain Paine, looking at the screen. 'The Commission is about to start the conference, and we don't yet have the full list of Commissioners' preferred pronouns.'

At the mention of pronouns, the three of them stiffened, as if they had suddenly had a weapon pushed into each of their backs.

'Commissioner coming up,' said a voice to my left. I turned and saw someone standing by the wall. They were about my own age, dressed in an Accord smock. Probably some government liaison person. Gender unknown.

'Which commissioner?' said Admiral Zhou.

'Commissioner Jimenez,' said the government liaison person. 'Commissioner for The Accord Space Agency.'

'Preferred pronouns?'

'Xe, Xem and Xyrs.'

'How do we address xem?'

'Use xer,' said the government liaison. 'Very important that you use xer.'

They all turned to the screen, and sat up straighter in their seats, as the screen changed to an image of a woman with short dark hair, dark complexion, and no eyebrows.

'T.E.D.' xe said.

'T.E.D.' Replied Admiral Zhou, Captain Paine and Captain Odilli.

'I'll get straight to the latest and how it concerns the military,' said Commission Jimenez, blinking over and over with some kind of nervous tic. I didn't know much about this Commissioner. Xe was almost never in the news. The Accord Space Agency conducted no missions since the Commission ruled space exploration to be patriarchal and colonialist.

'As you know,' xe continued, 'the visitors in the friend ships have ceased demonstrating their blue beam culture. Now, they have now made contact. They sent a message in which they identified themselves as coming from the planet we call Rome.'

'Rome?' said Admiral Zhou. 'Never knew there was a planet called Rome.'

On the screen beside the Commissioner, a view of the galaxy appeared with its stars arranged in a spiral pattern. At one edge, a circle highlighted the location of Earth; on the opposite edge, another circle highlighted planet Rome.

'Why is it called Rome, xer?' said Captain Paine. 'I thought we named planets by numbers.'

'Good question,' said the ASA Commissioner. 'The planet was discovered in the PAE by an amateur astronomer who had an interest in ancient Rome. Rome was a city-state empire that existed from 2600BAON to 1500BAON. Very imperialist. Very oppressive to minorities. I can't even imagine how they treated ancient LBGTQ people.'

'Truly shocking,' said Captain Odilli.

Everyone shook their heads. They all knew about pre-Accord conquest and oppression.

'The pre-Accord male who discovered the planet,' said Commissioner Jimenez, 'had naming rights at that time, so he used his rights to call it Rome. The ASA plans to rename the planet, but we haven't yet decided on a final choice.'

'Why not, xer?' said Captain Paine.

'Some groups want it named after a heroic feminist; others want it named after a leader of an oppressed minority. We haven't decided.'

'I suggest we name it after all of them,' said Captain Odilli.

'Thank you for the suggestion, Captain,' said Commissioner Jimenez. 'I'll take it to the committee responsible. However, for the moment, the name is Rome. The visitors themselves know we call it Rome.'

'The visitors know that we call it Rome?' said Admiral Zhou. 'Surely they must know how oppressive Rome was.'

'Yes, Admiral,' said Commissioner Jimenez on the screen. 'They know quite a lot about ancient Rome.'

'How do you know that, xer?' said Admiral Zhou. 'How do they know anything at all about an oppressive pre-Accord power from so long ago?'

'Well, for one thing, Admiral,' said Commissioner Jimenez, blinking, 'they communicated to us in Latin.'

12

The room was silent for a full twenty seconds as this last piece of information sunk in. I could imagine what the three of them were thinking. Why not use one of the Accord languages to contact us?

Eventually, Admiral Zhou replied.

'In Latin, Commissioner?'

'Yes, in Latin, the language of the ancient Romans. They even refer to Earth as Hyacinth, the Latin word for blue.'

'And what does the message say?' asked Admiral Zhou.

'After we translated it,' Commissioner Jimenez said, 'we found it said that the Romans want to meet a delegation of four people from Hyacinth. Nothing more. They didn't ask for anything, nor offer anything, nor mention what was to be discussed. They just wanted to meet four people, whom they were polite enough to name. The message was sent by the officer in charge of their friendship flotilla of ships, which is presently located beyond our moon.'

An image appeared on the screen beside

Commissioner Jimenez. 'This photo was taken by a telescope in AONT Spain, sub-territory Canary Islands.'

The sight of the image caused all three people at the table to gasp in astonishment. The friendship flotilla looked enormous beside the moon, like a giant beehive or an impossibly large bunch of extended dark blue grapes.

Eventually, Admiral Zhou returned everything to the business at hand. 'And who is the officer in charge of this ship, this flotilla?'

'The visitor's name is Admiral Octavia Caesar,' replied the Accord Space Agency commissioner.

'That's a woman's name, right?' said Captain Paine. 'Octavia is a woman's name.'

'At this stage,' said the Commissioner Jimenez sternly, 'I don't think we can take any step as dangerous as presuming the Admiral's gender.'

'No,' said Captain Paine. 'Of course not. I…'

'Who are the four people they want to meet, xer?' said Admiral Zhou, cutting in. 'Surely they will want to meet our Accord Commissioners, or perhaps the three heads of the Army, Air Force, and Navy.'

'No, Admiral,' said the Commissioner. 'That's the strange part. The people they want to meet are a mixture of civilians and low ranking military personnel.'

'Civilians? Why not senior leaders?'

'They didn't say.'

'Civilians? It doesn't make sense,' said the Admiral. 'Why civilians?'

Commissioner Jimenez ignored her.

'We have tracked down who we believe to be the

people they've requested. I have their identities here.'

An image came up on the screen of a middle-aged man wearing a traditional African robe.

'The first is Kenneth Okwanko, from AONT Africa sub-territory Nigeria,' said the Commissioner. Then, an image of a pale, fair-haired woman came up. She wore an AON Army battle dress uniform. 'The second is Captain Katherine Le Seaux from AONT Eurabia sub-territory France.'

Next, an image of an Asian male came on screen. 'The third,' said the Commissioner, 'is Andrew Chen Wai Hing, a civilian from AONT China, sub-territory Hong Kong.'

The pictures were set beside each other on the screen in a straight row.

Everyone looked at the three people who would form the delegation.

'Insufficiently diverse,' I heard Captain Odilli say. 'Insufficiently diverse. Way too insufficiently diverse. There are no partially-abled people, no obviously LGBTQ people, and no women of color.'

'Yes, we know,' said Commissioner Jimenez. 'We're as concerned as you are, but let's finish the list first before we move on to adjusting it. The fourth person the visitors requested is from AONT USA. In this case, we didn't have to search the census to find out who this person might be. Strange as it seems, the Romans provided a photograph of their own.'

The photograph came up on the screen. It showed my face in close up, frowning, my features contorted. In the background was AONS Harmony. I realized with a shock that this must have been taken from onboard the black object not thirty minutes ago.

'This is Lieutenant Burns, currently serving at your base,' said the Commissioner.

Captain Paine looked at Captain Odilli. They both looked at the Admiral. Captain Odilli then turned back to the screen.

'He is a cis-gendered male,' said Captain Odilli. 'A cis-gendered male,' she said a second time. 'And he has never even been on a mission. How can we send him?'

'We're as unhappy about it as you are, Captain,' said Commissioner Jimenez. 'However, they asked for Burns specifically. You saw the photograph.'

'We've got to propose other candidates,' said Captain Odilli. 'No, we must *insist* on other candidates. We can tell the visitors that they don't have sufficient training for space travel.'

'No-one in the Accord has any training for space travel,' said Commissioner Jimenez.

'Then we have to stall them,' said Captain Odilli, 'until we find a better solution. This is the Accord of Nations. We can't just send anyone.'

'I see how inappropriate it looks,' said Commissioner Jimenez, 'but we must respect and tolerate the visitor's culture and the wishes of this Admiral Octavia. Tolerance is a cornerstone of our values…along with diversity, of course…and equality.'

'Well,' said Admiral Zhou, 'if we must send up this insufficiently diverse group, the next question is how do we send them? Or do the visitors want to meet here in the Accord? We could invite them to the Accord Establishment Day celebrations.'

'It's already been taken care of,' said Commissioner Jimenez. 'The visitors will send a shuttle tomorrow morning to take the four emissaries up to their ship.

They named a location in the AON China Sea.'

'That's it?' said Captain Paine. 'Just like that.'

'Not entirely,' said Commissioner Jimenez. 'The Commission has decided that we will insist on conveying our Accord values to the visitors. It's the proper protocol.'

'Well,' said Admiral Zhou. 'It looks like our delegation to meet the very first visitors from the galaxy will be an insufficiently diverse group of Okwanko, Le Seaux, Chen and Burns.'

They all turned to look in my direction.

'Of all the people in all of the Accord,' said Captain Paine.

I kept my face blank. I didn't care what Captain Paine thought. I didn't care what any of them thought. I was going on a mission. It wasn't the kind of mission that I had ever imagined, but it was still a mission.

And there was nothing anyone could do to stop me.

Or so I thought.

13

That night, I packed for the transfer to AONS Accord Values, the ship that would be waiting at the designated coordinates in the AONO China Sea.

Not much was required: my NWU, which I would wear for the transfer up to the Roman ship, and then a blue Service Dress uniform to wear in case of formal meetings or ceremonies. No-one knew exactly what would happen, but Admiral Zhou wanted me to take the uniforms just in case.

I finished packing at eight p.m. The transport would be leaving at two a.m. the following morning. Not much time to be prepared, but there were some things that I thought shouldn't be left out. I picked up my handheld, found the page I wanted in the address book and pressed the green command button.

'Hello,' said the voice on the other end of the line.

'Hi, mom. It's me,' I said.

'Don't call me that,' said my mother's voice. 'Why do I have to tell you that every time?'

'It's the truth,' I said. 'Why not?'

'You know very well why not, Alex,' said my mother.

'I have to tell you every time,' she said again.

It was Accord policy that children should refer to their parents by their first names, not the pre-Accord patriarchal names of mom and dad. The family unit was one of the first things the Accord changed when it saved the world. Moms and dads were out. The Accord was your parents, your partner, your employer, your benefactor. Everything.

'OK, Kresta,' I said.

'I don't know where you get it from, Alex.'

'Sorry, I'm only kidding.'

'It's not natural. No one I know says their children call them mom or dad.'

'OK, Kresta.'

'I didn't work all those hours to raise you so you could disrespect me every time you call.'

Kresta worked a few days a week at the AON sub-territory Los Angeles Department of Diversity. She had done since she was twenty-two.

'OK, Kresta. Forget it.'

'With all the news about the friend ships, it's not appropriate to joke around.'

'OK,' I said. 'No more mom stuff, Kresta. Just forget about it.'

'You must get it from Cal.' She meant my father. 'It doesn't come from me.'

We let the conversation drop for a moment.

'Are you still a lieutenant?' said Kresta.

'Yes, mom. Still a lieutenant.'

'Don't take it to heart, Alex. You know why, don't you?'

'Yeah, I know,' I said. I could have added that they never let me forget.

'It's just the way the Accord is about people like us. It's not our fault.'

'But it is our fault, Kresta. That's what it's about. Even if it doesn't feel like our fault, it's still our fault. We bear the shame, no matter how many centuries ago.'

'Don't take it to heart.'

'I won't.'

We went silent for a moment.

Then, I said, 'Did you see the friend ships?'

'Everyone saw them. They've been on the news all day. It's a great moment for the Accord,' she said. 'Everyone's talking about them and what it will mean. Great days are coming, Alex. Perhaps the greatest days since the Accord was established.'

'Yes,' I said. 'Nothing like this has happened before, not even in the PAE.'

'A great day for diversity,' she repeated. 'And tolerance.'

'What else did you hear?' I asked. 'About the friend ships?'

'The same as everyone else. That they'd visited several of the cities in the Accord, hovering in the sky and then leaving. Why? What have you heard? Do you know something we don't?'

'No, Kresta.'

'They're not against Accord values, are they? Not dangerous?'

'We get the same TV as you, Kresta,' I said, but I was thinking of the destroyed barracks and the pile of blue sludge on the parade ground.

'A great day for the Accord,' she said again.

'Listen,' I said. 'Do you know how to reach Cal?'

'Cal? Why do you want to talk to him?'

'It's just been a while. I just want to, you know, keep in touch with him.'

'He doesn't call me,' she said. 'I haven't heard from him for a year now, which is fine by me, after what he did.'

'But you don't know where he is.'

'I think they move him around,' she said. 'Last I heard from him, he was in a re-education facility somewhere up north. Maybe in AONT Canada.'

'OK, Kresta,' I said. 'It's no big deal.'

In the background, I heard a door close and someone speaking.

'Listen, Alex. Regina's just come home.' She put a hand over the mouthpiece. 'Hi, hon!' she yelled to the background. Then I head what sounded like a kiss. Then she said, 'I better go.'

'OK, Kresta,' I said.

'Are you all right?' she asked.

'I'm fine,' I said. 'Talk again, soon.'

She hung up. Her photo disappeared from the screen of my handheld.

I flicked through the address book until I found a different picture, the one of Cal. It had been taken before he'd been sent away. I pressed the green call button, but I knew it wouldn't do it any good. The Accord would have taken his phone.

Cal always encouraged me to call him 'Dad.' It was just one of the many reasons why the Accord wanted him out of the way, and why he had to be re-educated.

I put the handheld under my pillow and lay down. Then I thought about the mission. There wasn't much time until the transport would arrive. I thought I should at least try to get some rest—even though I was too worked up to sleep. If I was being honest, I was also apprehensive. In all the talk about extending the Accord's values to the galactic visitors, no-one had mentioned that the mission might be dangerous. No-one mentioned how strange it would be for us to meet people from another world. Everyone believed the Accord's values would protect us like armor.

And no-one had wondered how these visitors might look. They hadn't even mentioned it, not even in passing. The reason was plain, of course. It was intolerant to even wonder about their appearances. So, the subject passed by untouched, and, as it happened so often, I felt like the only person in the world to have such bad thoughts.

I closed my eyes, trying to keep my imagination from throwing up images of aliens from outer space— monsters with scales, giants with hideous faces. Luckily, I was so tired that it wasn't long until I drifted far away and woke up into a dark and surreal dream.

14

I was back on the quarterdeck of the old sailing ship at night.

The ship was under more strain than before. It was close hauled against the wind and the ropes and timber complained loudly. The ship itself leaned to starboard and pitched forward and back over waves unseen in the dark.

Down below on the deck, out of sight, a bell tolled.

'Four bells,' the voice said beside me. I turned to my left. There stood the same figure as before: the man of my height and my face wearing an enormous blue naval coat with huge brass buttons. 'That's six o'clock in the morning on land,' he said. 'But of course, you should know that, Lieutenant Burns.'

He was wrong. Bells and bell time had been abandoned by the AON Navy centuries ago. It wasn't for technological reasons. It was to distance the Accord Navy from the practices of the military in the PAE.

'Who are you?' I asked again.

'You still don't know?' he said in his strange accent. 'Why don't you tell me?'

He cocked his head. 'You know, I could have you punished for addressing a captain in that way, Lieutenant. We're in different Navies, but it's still the custom to respect rank, is it not—even in your world?'

I knew this was all a dream, so I didn't argue. Instead, I changed my tone.

'Sir, would you mind telling me who you are?'

'I think the question to ask,' he said, 'is who are you, Lieutenant Burns?'

I kept quiet.

'But since you ask, let me introduce myself. I'm the captain of this ship,' he said. 'His Majesty's Ship Vengeance, a one-hundred gun, triple-decker ship of the line.'

'Ship of the line, sir?'

'The line of battle,' he said, 'with a crew of seven hundred and twelve men.'

I looked about the ship, saw the old pre-Accord cannons and the mass of sails.

'Very impressive,' I said. 'But I still don't know who you are…sir.'

'My name,' he said, 'is Captain Alexander Burns of the Royal Navy.'

'The Royal Navy, sir?'

'The Navy of King George the third.'

We looked at each other, Burns to Burns.

'Why are you in my dreams, sir?' I said.

'Why are you here in my reality?' he replied. 'You're the one who appears on my quarterdeck like a ghost, scattering my crew with your bizarre clothes and hat.'

I looked down at the deck of the ship. Saw no one. Then, I looked back at Captain Burns. His face was in shadow, but I could see the smallest of smiles.

'Sir, I think you already know who I am.'

'Yes, I know who you are, Lieutenant Burns,' he said. 'I think you know who I am too. The clue is in the name, laddy.'

We stood silently as the ship pitched and rolled, and the ropes complained. When HMS Vengeance re-settled itself, I said, 'What year is this? Sir?'

'The year thirteen. Eighteen hundred and thirteen.'

We stood in silence while I calculated the generations and the years. If this guy was some kind of ancestor, he would be my great grandfather twenty-eight times over.

And this would be the pre-Accord era, the evil pre-Accord era that everyone in the Accord had been warned about. I looked at my ancestor with caution.

'The person you mentioned, sir, the last time we were here…I know who you mean now. You were trying to warn me about her, right?'

'And?'

'I know who she is. Her name is Admiral Octavia?'

'Is that what how describes herself—as an admiral?'

'Yes, sir. Admiral Octavia Caesar.'

'Admiral Octavia Caesar,' he said. 'An admiral's rank and a famous Roman name. Very fancy for a most dangerous individual.'

'She's here, sir, with a great ship moored behind the moon. I'm to be deployed there tomorrow.'

'So soon?'

'Yes, sir. Admiral Octavia and the ship just arrived. She asked for me by name.'

'How big is this ship?'

'They say it's very large, sir. About the size of a town.'

He shook his head. 'About the size of a town. And how many crew are aboard this great ship?'

'We're not sure, sir. The Admiral didn't mention crew.'

He said nothing, just kept slowly shaking his head.

'Sir, it's strange.'

'What is?'

'That you aren't surprised about Octavia's ship.'

'That is just the beginning of the strangeness,' he replied, at which point he turned to look out into the dark, as if sensing something out there on the unseen waves.

'Sir, I am deploying in a few hours,' I said. 'Last time, you said you would give me some advice.'

He turned back from looking out to sea. 'All the advice in the world won't help you against her, Lieutenant—even if we had time for me to advise you, which we don't. You're not the only one on a mission. This ship, the Vengeance is ordered to find an enemy vessel, the French ship Indomitable, which I expect to engage at dawn.'

I looked into the dark and thought I could see a fringe of gold in the distance. Then, I said. 'Sir, any advice would help.'

He was about to reply when there was a call from high above us in the rigging.

'On deck there!' yelled a voice. 'On deck there!'

'Yes, Evans,' replied a second voice, down on the deck.

'Sail ho, sir.'

'Where away?'

'Larboard bow, sir. Hull down.'

How had he seen anything in the dark? Unless, of

course, from high in the rigging, he could see the dawn and perhaps the sunlight on a white sail.

Within seconds of the exchange between deck and lookout, there were footsteps on the ladder leading to the quarterdeck. Then, a figure emerged, also dressed in a blue naval coat and with the same long hat as the captain. He was about my own age and looked very warily at me. He didn't come more than a foot onto the deck.

'Yes, Mr. Collins, I heard the call,' said Captain Burns. 'Evans's eyes are as sharp as always, even in this light.'

'Yes, sir,' the young man said. He too had a strange accent, though different to Captain Burns's accent. 'Should we beat to quarters, sir? We aren't certain it's the Indomitable.'

'Yes, Mr. Collins. We shall beat to quarters.'

'Aye, sir,' said Mr. Collins and clattered down the stairs.

'Mr. Pound!' he called once he had reached the deck. 'We shall beat to quarters.'

Instantly, there was shouting on the deck below, then whistles, drums, and hundreds of feet moving on the timber.

'It's nearly time, Lieutenant,' said my ancestor. 'You wanted help, so let me give you a few pieces of advice.'

'Yes, sir.'

'And if it won't help you, it might at least open your eyes.'

No one had ever spoken to me this way—with this mixture of respect and concern.

'Stand up for yourself. Don't believe all you're told. Think your own thoughts. Don't look at me like that,

Lieutenant. You know what I mean. All the lies they tell you about the world and about women and men and power. It's shameful. It's wrong. And the way you let them push you around—it's worse than shameful. It's time to be who you really are, and who you are capable of being. You are a Burns, a descendant of a great Naval family, the inheritor of a great fighting spirit.'

I looked at him not sure what to say.

'Well, Lieutenant. Don't stand their with your mouth open like a fish. You heard me.'

'Sir, I…'

'Yes, I know. You've been waiting to hear this all your life. Is that what you want to say?'

'Sir, I…'

Mr. Collins appeared at the top of the stairs again, still wary of me.

'Yes, Mr. Collins,' said Captain Burns.

'A change of course to intercept her, sir? To cross her wake and gain the weather gage?'

'Not yet, Mr. Collins. Not until we're sure it's her.'

'Aye, sir,' said Mr. Collins and disappeared again. More shouts below. Men appeared on the rigging, climbing aloft.

The Captain turned back to me.

'You've never seen action at sea, have you?' he said. 'Never tested yourself, never known victory; never known defeat. Never come close to dying. Never lived. You've just followed orders and been pushed around. Well, Lieutenant, you better prepare yourself to either fight on your feet, or to die on your knees.'

I wanted to ask him more. I wanted to ask about everything. What did he know about the Accord?

About life? About the sea? About women and men and power? About the pre-Accord era? About my family? About everything?

'It's time,' he said.

'What else should I know?' I said.

He drew himself up to his full height, stepped closer to me and said, 'A-riamh deiseil.'

'What? What's that mean?'

But before he answered, the sea, the sails, the rolling ship, the coming dawn, and my ancestor's scornful face all vanished, and I was gone from the fighting ship, HMS Vengeance.

15

Next morning, I raced across the metallic blue of the AON China Sea in a Navy helicopter.

On board were the two pilots and Captain Dravid from Navy Spirit. Captain Dravid had met me after I landed that very morning at AONS Equality of Outcome on the AONT sub-territory Luzon. He said he would escort me in the chopper the rest of the way.

Now we were barely an hour away from AONS Accord Values, one of the AONN's larger aircraft carriers. It had been ordered by Admiral Zhou to halt its goodwill voyage to AONT Vietnam, and steam northeast to the exact location designated by the galactic visitors at 18°49'23.7"N 116°34'14.2"E in the AON China Sea between AONT Philippines and AONT China, sub-territory Hong Kong.

'Forty minutes,' said one of the pilots through my headset.

Captain Paine and Admiral Zhou had gone on ahead to meet onboard AONS Accord Values with two Accord Commissioners and the three members of the delegation that would be going up to the visitors' ship:

Katherine Le Seaux, Andrew Chen, and Kenneth Okwanko.

'This is a great moment for the Accord,' said Captain Dravid through the headset. 'A great moment.' He was slim, dark, and recently promoted. Unlike Captain Odilli, he was friendly to me. Possibly this was because I'd been promoted overnight to Lieutenant Commander.

'The sky's the limit from here, Burns—literally,' Captain Dravid said. He looked out of his window at the sea rolling away to the horizon and then swung back to me. 'I think we can say the Accord's messages of fairness and diversity are about to travel out into the universe.'

'Yes,' I said. 'As long as the Romans agree with the values.'

'Why wouldn't they agree?' he said. 'The great worth of our values is self-evident. Look at what they've done for our own world since the Accord was established. Anyone can see that. Equality. Fairness. It's obvious.'

'Yes,' I said again. 'It's just that the visitors might take some convincing.'

'Call them Romans or intergalactic friends, Lieutenant Burns,' said Captain Dravid. 'We're not sure which name they prefer yet, so use either one till they make it clear.' Then he pointed to the sky. 'When you're up there in space.'

'Yes, sir. The Romans,' I said. 'They might not immediately take to our ideas.'

'Whose to say they haven't adopted them already?' Dravid said. 'It's only natural that an advanced civilization would have arrived at the very same values. It's inevitable. The Romans probably adopted

T.E.D millennia ago.'

'Yes, sir. It makes sense,' I said, but I had my doubts. I had seen the blue beams and the pile of steaming blue sludge on the parade ground back at AONS Harmony. It hadn't seemed like a display of acceptance and appreciation for diversity. It seemed just the opposite. It was display of aggression and power—no doubt about it.

I trusted the Accord Commission's wisdom, of course, but I couldn't help but think the Commission was too eager to trust the Romans. What did the Romans really want? Why meet behind the moon and not on Earth? Why request four unimportant people to be the messengers? And why me?

And once again there was the question that seemed to bother me alone, the question no-one dared to ask for fear of 'othering' the visitors: What if the visitors turned out to be monsters—hideous dangerous monsters?

Bad thoughts, Burns. Bad thoughts. There are no such things as monsters. There is only diversity and greater diversity.

But I still felt uneasy.

'Coming up now,' said the pilot's voice in my headset. Captain Dravid and I strained to see what he meant. From our side windows we could only see the endless sea stretching away north and south.

But a minute later, we could see the ship.

The AONS Accord Values was an impressive sight, an aircraft carrier of six thousand crew and a main deck over four hundred yards long, like a great piece of the Accord itself. It bristled with Slingshot jets just like a real ship of war, except that it had never been deployed for anything other than goodwill.

'That's your launching place, Burns,' shouted Captain Dravid. 'From there to the stars.'

It was an inspiring vision and I could hardly contain my excitement at the thought of it. But when the chopper landed, and Dravid and I had stepped onto the deck, I sensed something wasn't right.

A Navy commander stepped forward. She, or maybe he saluted Dravid, received my salute, and then said, 'Welcome to AONS Accord values.' The name patch read De Soto.

'What's going on?' said Dravid.

'I'm here for Lieutenant Burns, sir.'

'I'm ready,' I said. 'What's first? The pre-mission briefing?'

'Change of plans, Burns,' said De Soto. 'The personnel assigned to the mission has changed. I'm sorry Burns. You're out.'

16

Next morning, the morning on which the Roman shuttle was to arrive, I walked onto the windy deck of AONS Accord Values. Arranged along the great ship's flat bow were the crew members assigned to welcome the visitors. There were Marines and sailors in Service Dress Blues, various admirals and generals, and no less than two members of the Accord Commission itself: Commissioner Daniel Genet, and Commissioner Rowena Martin.

The Commissioners and the other VIPs stood on a podium while photographers and videographers bobbed and circled around them. The Commissioners' broad smiles were sincere. This meeting with visitors from another world would be a career highlight. No doubt about it. Forever after, they would be linked to this great leap forward for Accord values and influence.

My own career felt like it had reached a low point. Since I had arrived onboard, I had been treated as a pariah. No de-briefing. No contact with senior command. No explanation. Nothing. If they didn't want me on the mission, why put me to the trouble of coming out here?

A commissioners' aide called Onslow came up to me. She was accompanied by a Navy captain I had never met.

'You heard the change of plan, Lieutenant Burns,' said Onslow. 'The Commissioners have decided you're not right for this mission.'

'Yes, ma'am?'

'You have a problem with that.'

'No, ma'am.'

'You know why, of course.'

'I'm afraid I don't, ma'am.'

'You're not diverse enough. You're too straight, too male and your family descends on both sides from the pre-Accord West. You will set a bad impression to our galactic friends regarding our values. Captain Paine told me you knew that already.'

'No, ma'am. I mean yes, the Captain mentioned it, but I thought I was still to go.'

'You're also too tall, Burns.'

'Too tall, ma'am?'

'The Commission believes your height will threaten the visitors.'

'Yes, ma'am,' I said. 'If that's what the Commission decides.'

'It's what the Accord believes, Burns.'

'Yes, ma'am.'

I saw the emissaries who were still going on the mission. They came onto the deck and saluted the Commissioners, the generals, Admiral Zhou and Captain Paine. I recognized the slim female in the Army BDU as Katherine Le Seaux, and the Asian man beside her as Andrew Chen. The third, Kenneth Okwanko wasn't there. Instead, there was a new guy, a slim dark guy in a grey suit.

'May I ask who is replacing me?' I said.

'We're going with someone inline with Accord diversity policies. We're sending a civilian named Mohammad Ahmad. He's from a minority people that were oppressed for centuries by Western pre-Accord imperialists in AONT Eurabia. He's a more appropriate fit. He's also partially abled which makes the delegation even more diverse, so that's even better.'

I looked at Ahmad. He looked lean and healthy. I noticed he had no cane, nor wheelchair. Maybe he had a prosthetic limb.

'Yes, ma'am,' I said. 'The Commission knows best.'

'Of course it does.'

'But a question, ma'am.'

'Make it fast, Burns. It's getting near time.'

'The Romans requested the four envoys by name. Might we be provoking them by not sending exactly who they requested?'

'Are you saying the Commission is wrong, Burns?'

'No, ma'am.'

'Are you saying you know better than the Commissioners?'

'No, ma'am, definitely not.'

'Then shut it and do as you're ordered.'

'Yes, ma'am. Tolerance, diversity, equality.'

'Tolerance, diversity, equality,' said Onslow.

Now the Navy captain beside Onslow spoke. The name patch read Teixeira.

'Burns.'

'Yes, Captain.'

'Orders from Captain Paine. You're now demoted back to O-2 grade, instead of full Lieutenant Commander. You are to return to AONS Harmony at twelve hundred today. Once you arrive on AONS Harmony, you will resume your previous orders.'

'Yes, ma'am.'

'As a special consideration, I've requested AONS Accord Values Captain Bunyasarn to allow you to watch the arrival of the Roman shuttle. You will stand on the deck with personnel of equivalent rank in his crew.'

'Thank you, Captain.'

'Dismissed, Lieutenant.'

I saluted. The Captain and the aide called Onslow walked away, leaving behind a Lieutenant Commander, whose name patch read Nagoya. Not thirty seconds ago we had been the same rank. Now she was my superior, and she was not friendly.

'Change your uniform back to a plain, blue NWU, Burns,' she said. 'Report to Lieutenant Commander Alaoui. She'll arrange for the uniform and then give you orders on where to stand when the Romans arrive. That's her over there by the Accord flag. Any questions?'

'Yes, ma'am. Just one.'

'It's sir.'

'Sir, what happened to the fourth member of the greeting party, the one the Romans requested— Okwanko, the civilian from AONT Africa? I don't see him.'

Captain Nagoya looked at me sternly, as if I should know Okwanko's whereabouts. She blinked a few times. 'Civilian Okwanko took his own life earlier this morning, Burns.'

'Took his own life? Oh, no. Surely not.'

'Do I sound like a liar to you, Burns?'

'No, sir.'

'His body will be repatriated to the Accord branch in AONS Africa tomorrow. It's part of Accord civilian law for people to take their own lives if that's what they choose, Burns. He should have obtained Accord approval, of course, but the circumstances were extreme.'

'Yes, sir.'

'You got a problem with that, Burns?'

'No, sir. No problem here, sir.'

'Don't they instruct you in sensitivity at AONS Harmony?'

'Yes, sir.'

'They do or they don't?'

'They do, sir. It's a mandatory course.'

'Sounds like you better take it again, Burns.'

'Yes, sir. My apologies, sir. I was surprised by the news.'

'Now report to Lieutenant Alaoui and stay out of the way. Your mission is over.'

17

At the appointed hour, dressed in an NWU with a new name patch and fewer stripes, I followed Lieutenant Alaoui who pointed to the rows of crew members standing out in the breeze on the ship's vast deck.

All ranks were represented in the formation, even the crew from the ship maternity ward. I was four rows back, anonymous, just like the rest of the sailors.

The clock ticked toward eleven, the rendezvous time. The breeze ruffled the collars of the sailors in front of me. The ship's engines groaned quietly astern, keeping the ship's position at 18°49'23.7"N, 116°34'14.2"E

One of the sailors in my row leaned forward and looked my way. She was a tall cadet with a wisp of dark hair escaping her cap and falling over one eye. She smiled and mouthed the word, 'Hi,' followed by a raise of her eyebrows and the word, 'Later.' I looked away. I didn't want to jeopardize what remained of my career.

At five minutes after eleven, we were still standing. There was no sign of any ship. Whispers came along the row that nothing had been sighted by the monitoring stations in Hawaii and Fiji, and the telescope on AON sub-territory Canary Islands hadn't seen the visitors' ship itself, let alone a shuttle.

So we waited. The ship's crew stood at ease, their hands behind their backs, silent. The VIPs waited on the podium, looking at the sky, then down at the deck and occasionally shrugging to one another. The four emissaries stood at ease in front of them. They mostly looked at the deck.

Then, at ten past the hour, more whispers came down the line. The shuttle had been located. It was traveling at great speed from behind the moon, and, based on its current speed, it would arrive here in a matter of minutes.

Everyone looked to the sky, waiting for the shuttle to burst through the clouds.

'T.E.D.,' said the Lieutenant beside me, a young male whose patch read, Park. 'It's a great day for the Accord,' he said. 'Our message is going to the universe at last.'

'Sure is,' said someone behind me.

'Atten-shun!' called a voice over a loudspeaker. We all snapped our heels together, put our hands by our sides and raised our chins. Then, we raised our eyes to the sky. A dark, nebulous shape loomed behind the low, cloud.

Then, the shape grew darker and larger.

And larger.

'How big is this galactic friendship vehicle?' said Park.

Then, the shuttle pushed its way through the clouds —black, huge, bigger than the AON Accord Values, and shaped like a zeppelin or an enormous cigar.

There was a gasp around the Accord Values and some of the crew actually took a step back as the great object's black bow came towards us, like a monster sliding from a grey den.

'May the values protect us!' someone said.

This was no shuttle, I thought. That was the wrong description completely. Shuttles were supposed to look harmless, meant only for taking passengers between places. This ship looked military—a huge, dark warship.

As it moved closer, the shuttle cast a rippling shadow the size of several football fields. The shadow moved darkly over the surface of sea, as if there were a twin monster spaceship underneath the water, moving in parallel.

Together, these two dark shapes converged on AONS Accord Values, like silent and enormous predators.

'The Romans, our galactic friends…' said Park, trailing off. He apparently didn't have anything more to add, but then managed, 'they must be very diverse.'

'Too diverse for me,' said one of the other sailors. She broke from the formation and ran aft. 'This is oppressive,' she said as she went by. No-one stopped her.

The shuttle came to halt about thirty feet from the AON Accord Values' starboard bow. The sun was behind it, so the shuttle's shadow fell across the deck, stealing the light so that we were in half darkness. The water lapping against the ship's side was now audible as each splash echoed off the monster's hull, creating a weird sensation of intimacy.

What now?

The Accord anthem began playing over the loudspeaker. The emissaries looked grimly at the shuttle's bow. One of the Marines stepped forward to escort the Admirals and Commissioners down from the platform.

But the Admirals and Commissioners didn't move. They didn't take a single step forward. They just stood there, looking at one another.

Commissioner Genet spoke to Admiral Zhou who dismissed the Marine, and then turned and spoke to one of the aides at her side. The aide then stepped down from the platform and walked forward to where the three emissaries waited.

Katherine Le Seaux saluted. Chen and Ahmad nodded. They listened intently for a few minutes, looked back at the VIP platform, and then the three of them began walking slowly towards the shuttle, by themselves. Le Seaux walked on the left side, Ahmad in the middle, Chen on the right.

Halfway there, they seemed to lose heart. No port had opened. No welcoming figures stepped out. No space suits for the journey had been proffered (and none were provided by the Accord). Nothing. There was only the enormous, silent mass of the ship.

When they within twenty feet of the shuttle's bow, they stopped. Le Seaux looked over her shoulder. Admiral Zhou nodded, urging her on. Le Seaux turned back to the shuttle and took a couple of slow steps further into the shadow.

Suddenly, a gunport opened in the shuttle's bow. A thin blue beam shot out straight past Le Seaux. It hit Mohammad Ahmad in the chest. Everyone gasped. No-one moved. Ahmad didn't so much as explode as melt, the same as the Lieutenant on the parade ground of AONS Harmony. The blue beam stayed lit for ten seconds and then snapped off. The gunport closed, and everything returned to silence just like before.

Except that something had now changed. Mohammad Ahmad was now a pile of sludge on the deck—blue colored and about the size of a small backpack.

At the sight of it, more sailors broke ranks from the formation and ran either aft. The Lieutenant Commander in charge of us said nothing. Maybe he was too shocked. Even the guy called Park beside me rushed away. 'It's very diverse,' he said.

This was not a great display of bravery by the Navy.

Now, more discussion took place among the group of VIPs. Eventually, they began nodding to each other. Then, Captain Nagoya shouted at one of her lieutenants. The lieutenant, turned and came striding across the deck towards the assembled crew of the AON Harmony.

She stopped in front of us.

'Burns!' she shouted. 'Where's Lieutenant Burns?'

Everyone looked around, left and right.

'Here!' I shouted.

'Who said that?'

'Me, sir. I'm Lieutenant Burns.'

She saw me and shouted. 'What are your preferred pronouns?'

'Sorry, sir. I didn't hear you.'

'I said what's your preferred pronouns.'

'Sir, he and him,' I said.

'Captain Nagoya orders you to report to her right now.'

I stepped out between the remaining sailors and walked over to the platform, keeping an eye on the shuttle. The three emissaries stood motionless in front of it, looking at the steaming pile that had been Mohammad Ahmed.

'Yes, Captain,' I said, saluting.

'The Commissioners, through Admiral Zhou, have reinstated you to the mission. Get over there with Le Seaux and Chan. Don't worry about your kit, just get over there.'

'Sir? Er ma'am?' I looked at her face. Was she shaking? I looked behind her at Captain Paine, Admiral Zhou, Commissioner Martin and Commissioner Genet. They looked frightened.

'Did you hear me, Lieutenant?' the Captain said.

I turned and looked at Le Seaux and Chen. They were looking back at me wondering what was going on.

'Now, Burns!' said Captain Nagoya.

Suddenly I felt a change—something hard to describe. Call it a sense of having the upper hand. Something was calling me on. It was the strangest feeling, like my ancestor from the dream whispering in my ear.

'I'm waiting, Burns,' said Captain Nagoya's furious face. Her teeth were actually bared.

'My rank, Captain,' I said.

'What?'

'I'd like my rank restored to Lieutenant Commander.'

'Not now, Burns. Get over there.'

'No,' I said. 'Promote me back to Lieutenant Commander.'

This was unthinkable insubordination. Career-ending insubordination. Yet I had said what I said.

Captain Paine stepped forward. 'What's the problem?' zee said.

'Just a small matter of insubordination,' said Captain Nagoya.

'He won't go?' said Captain Paine. 'Is that the problem? He won't go?'

'He wants his rank reinstated.'

'Whatever, Burns,' said Captain Paine. 'For the Accord's sake, get over there.'

'You're giving him the promotion? Just because he asks?' said Nagoya.

'If it'll get him onto the shuttle. We can't afford to make our visitors wait.'

'I want it entered in the ship's log,' I said.

'We don't have time, Burns. Haven't you noticed what's going on?' said Captain Paine.

I looked over at the emissaries, still frozen before the shuttle. Then, I looked back at Captain Paine. Admiral Zhou had leaned in, frowning.

'What's going on?' said Admiral Zhou.

'The log,' I said.

'No,' Captain Paine replied. 'There will be no log entry.'

As soon as zee said this, the enormous shuttle edged forward and banged against the bow of the AONS Accord Values. The ship lurched. The engines groaned. Everyone had to take a step forward to maintain their footing. Then, the shuttle edged back, as if it had made a point.

'OK, Burns,' said Captain Paine. 'We'll put it in the log. But not Lieutenant Commander. You'll get full Lieutenant, O-3, the equivalent rank of Captain Le

Seaux in the AON Army.'

A sailor came running back from the bridge carrying a large red logbook. The Navy used electronic logs but still kept manual ones. The sailor passed the log to the Captain who showed it to the Admiral, and then turned and showed it to me. There was the entry, nice and neat and official.

'OK, Burns?' said Captain Paine.

'Yes, sirra,' I said.

'We'll sort this out when you return. In the meantime, your orders, Burns, are to convey the Accord values to the visitors, along with Le Seaux and Chen. Then you are to present the Accord's gift. The gift is currently with Captain Le Seaux and will be presented by Captain Le Seaux only. Following that, you are to hear the visitors' requests and report them to us. If possible, have them televised to us. Then you return. Nothing more. Nothing less. You are representing the Accord, Burns, so conduct yourself properly. Got that?'

'T.E.D.,' I said. Then, I saluted, turned and walked down the steps and across the deck to Le Seaux and Chen.

'What was that all about?' Le Seaux said. I noticed she had green eyes, and she spoke with an accent from AONT Eurabia, sub-territory France.

'Quiet,' said Chen, tilting his head at the shuttle looming over us. 'It's listening.'

As he said this, the outline of a large rectangle appeared on the shuttle's bow. It wasn't the gunport with the laser. It was port with a gangway inside it. The gangway laid itself onto the steel railing of the ship, buckling the railing as if it were plastic. Inside the port was a passageway with dark walls leading into a darker interior.

'Here we go,' I said.

'Wait!' said Le Seaux.

She turned and faced the Accord flag and fired off a snappy salute.

I turned a beat after her and made a salute of my own—way too slow. Captain Paine was shaking her head.

'Let's just get on board,' said Le Seaux.

We stepped from the deck onto the gangway.

'Deiseil a-riamh,' I said.

'What?' said Chen. 'What's that mean?'

'I don't know,' I said.

'Then why'd you say it?'

I was going to answer that it seemed appropriate somehow, but before I could speak, Le Seaux was talking.

'Come on,' she said. 'Before it closes.'

I walked up the final few feet of the gangway. I couldn't help but turn around one last time to look at the scene. Back there lay the deck of the carrier, the assembled crew, the admirals and commissioners on the raised platform, all watching, all waiting.

Two days ago, I was languishing on shore duty, years away from being ordered to sea. Now, I was on the threshold of the most important mission of the Accord of Nations Era.

'Burns!' shouted Chen. 'Come on.'

I turned back towards the entranceway to the shuttle. Then I stepped from the half-light of the AONS Accord Values and into the gloom.

Part 2: The Mission (1)

PROTOCOL

'All cultures are equal and must be tolerated equally without exception.'

Accord Of Nations Constitution

18

The great shuttle's gangway began to rise, dragging the twisted metal railing with it. The metal scraped and moaned and hung on until it was cut through by the gangway's sharp edge. Then it flung itself back, waving madly as if warning us not to go.

Then, the port cover slowly closed off the view. It blocked out the deck of the AONS Accord Values, then the welcoming committee, and finally it blocked the sky itself, sealing the three of us into darkness and silence.

No going back.

After a few seconds, Le Seaux said, 'Move up this passageway. Our visitors will have provided somewhere safe for us to sit in harnesses for the ascent.'

'Shouldn't we wait a moment, Captain?' I said. 'We're in the dark with no way of knowing what's inside this thing.'

'It won't be dangerous,' said Le Seaux's voice. 'The Romans are our galactic friends. We are their guests. Do you think they would expose us to danger?'

'I don't think we can be so certain,' I said. Then, I shut my mouth. Not thirty seconds into the mission and I was already arguing with Le Seaux. Toxic masculinity was leaking out of me, just as Captain Odilli said.

'Well, I think we *can* be certain, Lieutenant,' said Le Seaux, coldly. 'And I am the one who has been briefed on the mission. Not you.'

'We are of comparable rank,' I said. 'An Army captain is the same as Navy lieutenant. A Navy captain is equal to an Army colonel.'

'I know that, Lieutenant,' said Le Seaux, 'but I am the one who the Accord designated to lead this mission. You are to respect the Accord's wishes.'

Chen's voice cut in. 'You know it's possible,' he said, 'that they're here in the dark too.'

His words caused an immediate ceasefire between Le Seaux and myself, and for several seconds, no one said a word. We listened quietly for the slightest sound.

'Who?' said Le Seaux. 'Who's here in the dark?'

'Them. The visitors. The Romans.'

'Don't call our galactic friends "them," Mr Chen,' said Le Seaux's voice. 'We are guests here, and you are othering our friends with your words. You were briefed the same as me about the importance of language on this mission.'

But Chen's statement had made an impact. We were no longer in the familiar world of the Accord but in the realm of alien visitors, and no matter how much reminded ourselves to be tolerant and to admire diversity, we might still be shocked if the visitors showed themselves. Or even more than shocked.

Terrified, maybe. None of us knew what they would look like.

'You're right,' said Chen. 'I apologize for othering the visitors.'

We waited as if expecting a reply from the void, but we heard nothing but our breathing in the thick silence. Not even the deck sounds from the Accord Values reached inside.

My imagination began to work. Was anything actually creeping or padding on soft feet in the dark? Or sliding down from the bulkhead above, or slithering along the deck?

Crazy thoughts.

I commanded myself to kill them and replace them with self-control—the same self-control I'd learned through having to keep my head during all the dressing downs by superior officers.

Chen broke the uneasy silence.

'I don't think we've been introduced properly,' said his voice. 'I'm Andrew Chen.' He had a smooth AONT USA accent. 'I'm from AONT China, sub-territory Hong Kong, but I went to school in AONT USA, sub-territory Utah. I've met Captain Le Seaux and poor Ahmad back there, but I haven't met you.'

'Lieutenant Burns,' I said. 'AON Navy, based in AONT USA.' I almost held out my hand for him to shake but remembered he couldn't see it. I had also forgotten that Navy Spirit had banned handshakes between men not one month before. Men were now only allowed to shake hands with women. It was an initiative to further remove all gestures of the patriarchy.

'Ever been to AONT Hong Kong?' Chen asked.

PROTOCOL

'Only in combat simulations,' I said. 'And for short periods.'

'Well,' said Chen. 'When we get back, you'll have to come and see it for real. You could stay at one of my places.'

I noted the 'one of my places.' No-one in the Accord was supposed to own their own home let alone several 'places.'

'I'm Captain Katherine Le Seaux,' said Le Seaux on the other side of me. She pronounced 'Seaux,' like 'sew.' 'My preferred pronouns in English are zee, zir, and sir, but for this mission, I will use the traditional pronouns of she and her.'

I silently breathed a sigh of relief.

'As I said,' continued Le Seaux. 'I'm the leader of this mission. Just so you are clear, Lieutenant Burns. Are you clear, Lieutenant?'

'Yes, Captain.'

'My pronouns are just the old ones,' said Chen.

'Same here,' I said.

'Good,' said Le Seaux. 'Are you also clear about your orders?'

'Yes,' I said into the dark. 'We ride up to the flotilla in this shuttle. We meet the Romans, our galactic friends. We describe the values of the Accord. We emphasize tolerance and diversity. Then, we present them with the Accord's gift, and hear their reply.'

'You have forgotten that we must also use the appropriate pronouns,' said Le Seaux.

'Yes,' I said. 'Of course.'

'I've read your Navy Spirit file, Lieutenant Burns, and I've heard the Accord's views on your participation on this mission. You are not sufficiently diverse, and

102

you have not reached a sufficient level of training to overcome your toxicity. You are only included because the visitors wish you to be, not because the Accord desires it. Just so you know.'

'Yes, Captain. I'm aware of the Accord's views as well.'

'I have also read about your attitude, Lieutenant. Before we go any further, I want you to understand that I won't put up with any mansplaining. Clear?'

'Yes, Captain.'

'I'll be reporting all that happens to Navy Spirit.'

'Yes, Captain.'

'What about you, Mr. Chen? Are you clear?'

'Like I said in the briefing,' replied Chen. 'You're the military. I'm the civilian.'

'Thank you,' said Le Seaux. 'Yes, I am in the military, but I am also a believer in our Accord values. In my experience, the values are more useful than any military training.'

'Sure,' said Chen. 'You're in charge.'

'All right,' said Le Seaux. 'Now, I order you both to move up the passageway.' She brought out her handheld, switched on its torch, and shone the light on my face, then on Chen's face, and then away into the darkness. The beam penetrated no more than ten feet, intensifying the dark and the silence.

'Captain,' I said. 'I really think we should wait a few minutes first.'

I heard Le Seaux slowly inhale and then say, 'I will give you one opportunity to state your opinion without asking, Lieutenant Burns, just this once.'

'Thank you.'

'So tell us why we should wait?'

'It's because we don't know our galactic friends yet. Their values might not be the same as ours.'

'You are othering them again, Lieutenant Burns.'

'With respect, Captain, I saw what they did at AONS Harmony. They destroyed buildings and killed hundreds of personnel. We have to be mindful of that.'

'That's logic I can agree with,' said Chen.

I heard Le Seaux breathing slowly in the dark— breathing with great patience, like a teacher keeping her cool in front of an unruly class.

'As you would know if you had been briefed, Lieutenant, the use of blue beams is part of the visitors' culture, which we must respect in accordance with our values of tolerance, equality, and diversity. Once we have explained the values to the visitors, they will understand our views about the blue beams. If you had been in the briefing, you would understand that. The values are the most powerful force in the universe and once they are communicated to the visitors, we will be in a state of harmony.'

Le Seaux swung the torch toward the gloom. 'So,' she said. 'Move out.'

But before we could take a single step, the shuttle jolted violently, as if someone had thrown it into reverse gear.

And we began to accelerate back and up.

19

The jolt was followed by a shudder as if the hull were complaining about this sudden jump into action and the new distribution of weight.

The shuttle's three human passengers were slammed against the port entrance.

'I told you we should go down the passageway,' said Le Seaux. 'Now we are without harnesses as well as light.'

'Too late now,' I said. 'We're on our way like it or not.'

The shuttle continued to rise and accelerate, pressing us harder into the cold hull. The G-force increased so rapidly, I could not lift my head.

Beside me, I heard Le Seaux wince and Chen groan. 'Why didn't they put this in the briefing?' he said.

'At least we can breathe,' I said.

'We must trust our galactic friends,' said Le Seaux with effort. 'T.E.D.'

'Maybe they don't know that humans can break,' I said.

We continued to rise upward, trapped in the dark

without seats, without harnesses without anything, except the Accord values, which at the moment weren't any help.

The ship did not rotate as it rose. I imagined the great black vessel backing into the sky away from the Accord Values, like a video played in reverse, or as if the shuttle wanted to keep the AONS Accord Values in sight until the last minute.

But then, inevitably, the rotation began, and we found ourselves sliding along the bulkhead.

'Why didn't they warn us?' said Chen again.

'Be quiet, Mr. Chen,' said Le Seaux. 'You are representing the Accord.'

'But is the Accord representing us?' Chen replied, quickly followed by. 'That's not what I mean.'

'Just hold on,' I said. 'The force is leveling out.'

This was true. After the initial shock, the G-Force had not increased, not to the point where we might be injured, even though we were still pressed hard against the hull.

After a while, Chen's voice said, 'This would be easier if we weren't in the dark.'

Le Seaux said, 'Do either of you have any ideas as to how to get the lights on.'

'We could ask,' I replied.

'Why would that do any good?' said Le Seaux.

'It might,' I said. This ship…this shuttle seems to be either intelligent or to have intelligence controlling it. You saw how it reacted to Ahmad back there.'

'What do you suggest?' she said.

'We could ask it,' I replied.

'Ask it?'

'Yes. Just ask.'

'I don't want to offend our hosts.'

'I'll make it very polite.'

'No, Lieutenant. Not you. I'll make the request. It should come from the senior representative of the Accord here.'

'OK.'

'Could we have some lights, please?' she said.

Nothing.

'To our galactic friends, the Romans, could we have some lights, please?'

Nothing.

'Worth a try,' said Andrew Chen. 'Proper business etiquette to request lights.'

'This is not a business meeting,' said Le Seaux. 'It is a goodwill mission. We must be respectful.'

'Perhaps we could try the Latin word for lights?' I said. 'The visitors wrote their messages to us in Latin. Maybe that's the way to communicate…or the language the shuttle might respond to. Maybe they set it up that way for us.'

'I have a handheld,' said Chen, 'with a translation app, but I can't move my hand to get it from my pocket.'

'Your handheld probably won't work anymore,' I said. 'Not till we get back.'

'Really? Well, there goes the call to my girlfriend,' said Chen. 'I mean my partner.'

'Captain,' I said to Le Seaux. 'Do you know the Latin —for lights?'

'I know the French,' she replied.

'Might be worth a try.'

Le Seaux was quiet for a moment, then called, 'Lumiere, s'ill vous plait!'

Nothing.

She called again, 'Pouvons-nous avoir de la lumière, s'il vous plaît?'

Still in the dark.

'Could lumiere be similar to the Latin word for lights?' I said.

'I don't know,' she said.

'French is from Latin, right?'

'I said I don't know, Lieutenant.'

'You know, lumio, maybe. Luma, lumo, lumina?'

At the sound of the last word, something happened.

The shuttle continued to rocket upward away from the Earth, but lights came on, one by one, first above our heads, then running down its length, like the dividing lines on a highway. They ran on until they reached the passageway's end, way over on the far side of the shuttle.

We were soon blinking at each other, and at the awkward tangle of our limbs against the bulkhead, the green and brown of Le Seaux's uniform, the blue of mine and Chen's dark shirt and brown slacks.

'Mr. Chen, move your leg, please,' said Le Seaux.

'I wish I could,' he replied.

So for the moment, we were still stuck against the bulkhead, but at least now we could see the shuttle interior.

We were in a passageway that ran from port to starboard across the ship's nose, a distance as long as a football field and as narrow as a truck. We could also see the color of the interior. It was a dull, functional grey, slightly lighter than the shuttle's slimy black hull, but just as lifeless.

But now the shuttle accelerated again and this time

we were flattened against the deck. The force was still so great we were unable to raise our arms.

'You ever done anything like this?' I said to Chen, my face flat on the cold metal.

'I'm strictly civilian,' he said, a businessman. I've only ever been in civilian planes, never anything military.'

'A businessman?' I said. 'You mean a manager of an Accord department?'

'No, a businessman. I'm from Hong Kong,' he said. 'It's the only place allowed to have a non-Accord system.'

'You don't mean capitalism, do you, Mr. Chen?' said Le Seaux. 'It's forbidden.'

'Capitalism? No way,' Chen replied. 'What we have is called a non-Accord exchange system,' said Chen. 'Only Accord Commissioners and approved civilians can participate.'

'Still sounds like capitalism,' I said. 'What's the difference?'

'Capitalism is uncontrolled,' he said. 'Capitalism is oppressive, patriarchal and indiscriminate. The exchange system in Hong Kong is managed so as not to harm anyone. It's restricted to a few participants who play fair.'

'Like who?'

'Like I said. Accord Commissioners and approved individuals.'

'So what do you do, Mr. Chen?' I said.

'Among other things,' he said, 'I make movies. You've probably seen some of my more famous ones. I might even make a movie about this mission—with the Commission's approval, of course.'

As he spoke, the shuttle's hull groaned again, and we accelerated a third time.

'How long does this take?' said Le Seaux.

'Well,' I said. 'I'm no engineer, but it takes only a couple of minutes for a rocket to leave the atmosphere —a pre-Accord rocket, I mean.'

'You have access to pre-Accord experiment data?' said Le Seaux.

'No,' I said, 'but my Slingshot instructor had limited access to it. He'd been an engineer in the Slingshot factory.'

'Only the Commissioners have access to pre-Accord information,' said Le Seaux.

'Some other people have access to it as well,' groaned Chen. Then he said, 'This is getting painful. I can't breathe properly. It's not going to be like this all the way to the other side of the moon, is it?'

'No,' I said. 'It'll probably change when the shuttle slows down after it leaves the atmosphere.'

'So, when will that be?' he said.

'I don't know,' I said.

'Make a guess,' said Le Seaux.

'The first part, the bumpy part's almost over,' I said. 'It'll only be a couple of minutes.'

'Until what?'

'Until we reach the Earth's outer atmosphere and then space. The ride will smooth out. Then hopefully no more jolts all the way to the visitor's flotilla.

The sound of the word flotilla caused us all to fall into silence again. The other two were probably thinking what I was thinking. In my mind I saw the image of a giant spaceship, or a collection of spaceships the size of a town, all floating beside the moon. I also couldn't help but wonder again about what would be waiting for us on that spaceship or spaceships when we got there and the black port opened.

'T.E.D.,' whispered Le Seaux.

'Feel that?' said Chen.

'I can feel your boot under my knee,' I said.

'No,' said Chen. 'Something else.'

The force on our bodies decreased. The shuttle must have slowed down. It also appeared to have cleared the Earth's atmosphere.

Now, instead of being squashed against the cold, gray deck, we found ourselves slowly rising upward.

20

The change caught Le Seaux by surprise. She flailed her arms wildly, as if she were falling, or drowning.

'Don't touch me,' she said, even though neither Chen nor I had made a move.

'I am fine,' she added.

But she was not fine. She reached and kicked, trying to grab hold of an anything to steady herself, but because the hull and the bulkheads were smooth, the only thing she managed to catch hold of was me.

'Let go,' she said.

'I'm sorry, Captain,' I said. 'But you grabbed me. Mr. Chen, please be a witness.'

'Yep. She grabbed you,' said Chen. 'It's true, Captain.'

'Get your hands off me,' Le Seaux shouted.

'Captain,' I said. 'Try to relax. You're not falling. I don't have hold of you.'

Le Seaux had now pulled my sleeve so hard that we were chest to chest, like dancers in an old pre-Accord movie. I was close enough to catch the scent of her deodorant. It smelled like lemons. I also saw her eyes properly. They were a vivid green. Very piercing. Very intelligent. Her face was actually small and slightly pixie-like, with high cheekbones and a ski-jump nose. She was pretty—a description which could earn me a Navy Spirit code violation if I spoke it aloud. But it was true. She was attractive. Very attractive. If only her hair wasn't cut so short she would be beautiful, especially those eyes.

But at that moment, those eyes were vivid with fear and anger.

'Sorry, Captain,' I said. 'I'm not trying to pull you close. Hold on to me if you have to, but please understand, I didn't reach out to grab you.'

'Let me go,' she warned. 'Get your toxic masculinity off me.' She struggled even more. In the process, she managed to knee me in the groin.

'Let me go,' Le Seaux said. 'Now!'

'I'm not holding on to you,' I repeated as the pain swelled. I held out my arms to show her. 'See.'

She looked at each of my hands, realized her mistake, and shoved me away. The force of the shove sent her sailing away from me, outward along the passageway. And her flailing began all over again.

I pushed off from the port and followed her. I came to a stop forty yards in. Chen came swimming up beside me. He apparently had no trouble with weightlessness.

'Will she be OK?' he said.

'Along as she doesn't hit anything hard—harder than me, I mean.'

At the passageway's far end, Le Seaux calmed herself. She stopped flailing and began making her way back towards us, pushing from one bulkhead to the other. She wasn't saying anything, so I guessed she was OK.

But halfway along, something happened. As Le Seaux placed a hand on the dark material on one bulkhead, a large panel silently opened, rising upward.

The panel's motion spun Le Seaux around, and she found herself rotating vertically, arms and legs spread wide like a parachutist spinning in free fall.

Chen and I swam down to her.

'Don't help me,' she warned as we approached.

'No problem, Captain. We're just coming down in case anything happens.'

'Nothing will happen. I am in control. Keep your toxicity to yourselves.'

But when we finally arrived, we weren't looking at Le Seaux any more. We were looking at the place in the bulkhead where the panel had been.

'What is it?' said Le Seaux.

'I wish I could tell you,' said Chen.

In front of us yawned an enormous space, the cavernous interior of the shuttle. In the dim lights, this vast space appeared to be as immense as the largest aircraft hangar in the Accord. It looked big enough to contain the AON Accord Values itself with room to spare.

'Look at the size of it,' said Chen. 'It's like a massive soundstage.'

'It's a hold of some kind,' I said.

'Who needs a hold this size?' he said. 'And for what?'

'And why send such a huge vessel just for three people?'

We stared into the vastness of the space, listening as our words came echoing back to us as whispers, almost as if someone were repeating them.

'Must be for transporting huge equipment,' I said. 'Or huge numbers of personnel.'

'Or equipment for building on new planets?' said Chen. 'Mining maybe.'

'Might be,' I said. 'Or it could be for something else, something military.'

'Like what?' said Chen.

'Like transporting an army with vehicles and jets or whatever they use during a…' I was going to say "military operation," but Le Seaux cut me off.

'Burns, shut it,' said Le Seaux. 'That's an order.'

She was right. I held my tongue.

'Just amazing,' said Chen.

As he did, we found ourselves dropping from the air and kneeling on the slippery deck. After a minute, we were more or less our usual weight.

'Anti-gravity technology,' said Chen. 'What next?'

We stood up. Then walked up and down, feeling our own weight again.

Le Seaux said, 'How long now till we arrive?'

'I can't tell,' I said. 'I don't know how fast we're going. The moon is about 240,000 miles from Earth. So to reach it even within a day, we would have to be traveling at a huge speed.'

'How fast?' said Chen.

'I don't know, but the Romans got here across the galaxy, and from the moon to the Earth in quick time,' I said. 'So, they must have some way of traveling extremely fast…faster than we can imagine.'

'What's your guess?' said Le Seaux.

'We could arrive today,' I said, 'Or tomorrow.'

'Tomorrow,' said Chen. 'What are we going to eat?'

'Maybe something in there,' I said, stepping into the

PROTOCOL

vastness of the hold.

'Burns,' said Le Seaux. 'Stay where you are.'

I stopped a few yards inside the great cavern. The deck was scuffed and scoured with the kind of lines something heavy might make. In the distance, I could see what looked like large seats. Very large seats for very large occupants.

'Don't touch anything,' called Le Seaux. Her words echoed around the huge space.

After I had gone about a hundred yards in, I turned around and looked back. Chen and Le Seaux watched me from the entrance. Then, I noticed that above the entrance three enormous screens were mounted. Each blazed with moving images.

'Take a look at this,' I said.

Le Seaux came through first, followed by Chen, both of them hesitant, looking left and right. When they reached me, they turned and looked back at the entrance.

'Talk about wide-screen,' said Chen.

On one of the screens was a picture of the Earth. It was blue, swirled in clouds, and receding. The other showed a view of the moon ahead, looming large and light gray.

'Their TV screens are better than our TV screens,' Chen said. 'Look at how sharp those images are.'

We all stood silently watching. This was like nothing we had seen on Earth. The quest to understand or explore space was considered an oppressive, colonialist pre-Accord activity. The Commission banned it long ago. Now, not even the Accord Space Administration studied space let alone ventured out into it.

'Where are the stars?' said Chen.

'They are there,' I said, 'but they don't appear because of the sunlight. Something like that.'

'How do you know so much about this stuff?' said Chen.

'I don't,' I said, 'I only know what I read in Slingshot training.'

'Sounds like you read beyond the course material.'

'What is that object?' said Le Seaux. 'That dark shape —is that Mars?'

'Where?' I said.

'That dark mass.'

She pointed at the dark shape behind the moon.

'I don't think so,' I said.

'What's the next planet after Mars?' said Chen. 'Is it Jupiter or Saturn?'

'They actually have new Accord names,' said Le Seaux. 'The planets are named after Accord social justice scientists, as you should know, Mr. Chen.'

'They're the scientific names,' said Chen. 'We still use the old ones where I'm from—names like Jupiter and Saturn.'

'Who's we?' I said.

'The Accord people I know,' said Chen. 'In Hong Kong.'

The dark mass behind the moon grew larger.

'What is it?' said Le Seaux. 'It can't be the galactic visitors' ship, can it? Their flotilla of ships?'

'I think that's exactly what it is,' I said. 'The flotilla. Although now that we're this close, it looks more like a single ship than a flotilla or convoy.'

'But we're almost there,' said Le Seaux. 'It can't be possible. Exactly how fast are we going?'

'And how big is that thing?' said Chen. 'They said it

was about the size of a large town.'
   But it looked bigger than that.
   Much bigger.

21

The dark shape of the Roman ship grew larger, sucking away the light and filling the giant screen.

'Strange shape for a spaceship,' said Chen. 'Looks like a stack of pipes.'

I thought it looked like a bunch of flat, dark purple grapes. I also thought it wasn't a flotilla, either. It was a ship made from many other ships, all connected together into one mega vessel.

'I can't see any lights,' I said.

'You're othering them again, Lieutenant,' said Le Seaux. 'They mightn't need light, and that's perfectly fine.'

No need for light? That makes them pretty 'other,' I thought, but I kept my mouth shut.

We all stared at the image of the ship on the screen.

'Look,' Chen said. 'On the underside. See?'

No lights had come on, but on one of the grapes, a port slowly yawned open.

'What if it's a gun port for one of those beams?'

'Mr. Chen,' said Le Seaux.

'I think that's where we're going to dock,' I said.

Chen looked at his watch.

'I can't believe it's only taken us an hour to reach here,' he said. 'How long did your Slingshot instructor say it took to reach the moon in the pre-Accord era? Must have been days, right? Right, Burns?'

I was thinking fast about something else, something about to happen.

'Oh, no,' I said.

'What's wrong?' said Chen.

'We've got to move before it's too late.'

'Move where?' said Chen.

'Captain,' I said to Le Seaux. 'This time, I think you're right. We better get into some kind of restraint. You saw what happened to us before, right, when we were thrown against the hull? Well, now we're going to have to slow down again.'

'Won't it be the same as on the way up?'

'It might be,' I said, 'but look at how fast we're coming in towards the ship. There won't be time to slow down gradually. They're going to brake hard.'

'How hard?' said Chen.

'Hard enough to squash us like bugs,' I said.

'Return to the entrance port,' said Le Seaux. 'We were safe there.'

Instead of arguing with her, I turned and walked deeper into the hold towards the giant seats. If they were for Roman troops, they could work for us too. Maybe.

'These might have harnesses,' I said. 'Whatever they are.'

Le Seaux was standing with her hands on her hips again. 'We're going back to the entrance port, Lieutenant Burns.'

I ignored her.

The hold was so large, the seats were even farther away than I thought, and much bigger. Whoever used them must have been huge, well over seven feet.

I sat down in one of the rows of seats looking aft, since that would mean when we slowed down I'd be forced into the back of the seat, not flung from it. The buckles and straps were way too large, so I quit fooling with the buckles and tied myself in, using a neat reef knot.

Then, I looked over my shoulder and called 'Here! This is how you do it. Come on.'

Chen wavered between Le Seaux and me and then, after shrugging, came over to where I was sitting.

'How big are these guys?' said Chen. 'They must be twice our size.'

While Chen fiddled with his straps, the ship decelerated. I guessed thrusters had been fired. Both Chen and I were pressed hard against the backs of our seats.

The deceleration ceased momentarily. I got up and looked for Le Seaux. She had been flung to the deck and then all the way back to the entrance. I ran over to her, hoping to get there and back before the next burst from the thrusters.

Le Seaux was standing up when I came over. 'Come on, Captain' I said, 'Trust a sailor on a ship.'

'What makes you think the Navy would be in charge of spaceships? This isn't the sea. And you've never been on a mission.'

'Thank you for the reminder,' I said. 'Come on, Captain. It will be safer this way.'

Luckily, she had come to her senses because she

turned and strode into the cavern, following me all the way back to the huge seats. Then she sat down and started trying to buckle the harness.

'Captain, the straps are too large to buckle tightly. A reef knot might be best here. They're easy to undo in a hurry,' I said. 'I can show you,' I said.

But she had tied her own knot. Just in time too. The shuttle fired its thrusters again, this time with much more force. We were flung violently backward into our seats.

'You're right,' said Chen. 'This is worse than the take-off.'

'How close are we?' said Le Seaux.

'I wish I could say, but I can't turn my head to look at the screens.'

So the three of us sat there in the giant seats, pressed flat against the seat-backs, saying nothing, gritting our teeth against the forces. It was hard to concentrate on anything but enduring it, but I guessed we were all thinking the same thing: What would be waiting for us when we docked and the hatch opened?

When the shuttle had slowed down enough, I untied and took a look at the giant screens. One showed a distant Earth, blue and white and small. The other screen showed the curved shape of the huge Roman ship, going away into the gloom. Our shuttle must now be one of the 'grapes.'

'Twice is too many times for this stuff,' said Chen. 'I'm going to need my masseuse to work overtime.'

'Your masseuse?' said Le Seaux. 'Masseuse?'

'My massage person,' Chen replied.

'I wasn't referring to your improper use of gender,' said Le Seaux. 'I was referring to the fact that services such as massage are illegal.'

'What can I say?' said Chen. 'It's different where I live. How else do you think we get to make the movies?'

We waited several minutes in the silence, expecting an announcement or an instruction, but there was nothing. Only silence.

'We will wait another minute,' said Le Seaux. 'Then we will return to the entrance port.'

Chen said, 'Before we go, there's something I meant to ask on the way up. Maybe you military guys know the answer.'

'What's that, Mr. Chen?' said Le Seaux.

'Why us?' he said. 'Why are we on this mission? Why not the generals and admirals and commissioners? Why us? I mean I'm not even military. I'm not government either. I'm a businessman and a civilian. The guy from AONT Africa was a civilian as well. So why us? They didn't even tell us in the briefing.'

I looked at Chen properly for the first time. He looked to be about six inches shorter than me, just under six feet. He had a mischievous grin and dark eyes. He wore his hair cut short with a side part. It was almost a military haircut, but not quite. Too long on the top. His clothes were practical rather than fashionable. Sensible pants. Shirt with a collar. And sports shoes, perhaps to signal that he wasn't totally serious about his appearance either. But there was something else about him that I had just put my finger on, an impression that he didn't regard the Accord with the same reverence as everyone else.

'So why?' Chen said. Why us?'

Le Seaux was about to answer his question, when

there was a bang and crash amidships.

'Oh great,' said Chen. 'More trouble.'

'We're attaching to the side,' said Le Seaux, sounding knowledgeable all of a sudden. 'Mr. Chen, Lieutenant Burns, let's stand at the entrance to greet our hosts.'

The bang on the side was followed by the sound of metal creaking. Then after several minutes of groaning and banging, everything went quiet. On the screens, the views of the Earth and the mothership had disappeared, replaced simply by space.

We stood in the void wondering which direction the port would open.

'Now what?' said Chen.

Then, with another round of creaking metal, a great section of the hull opened up, a panel, the width of an apartment building. It rose up slowly, like a gigantic garage door, revealing the gleaming black metal of the mothership's hull.

'What about air?' said Chen.

'What?' I said.

'If there's no air on the other side, we're going to be sucked out, right?'

He was right, but it was too late to do anything. The second port began opening. We braced ourselves for whatever might happen next: a great rush of air, a blue beam.

Or something worse.

But nothing happened. The seal with the mothership had been complete. The second port had opened and all we could see on the other side of the doorway was darkness.

For the first time, I wished I had a weapon with me. No, it wasn't T.E.D. thinking. It wasn't fear either. It was just an honest reaction. Carrying a weapon doesn't mean you can't be tolerant.

'Approach slowly,' said Le Seaux.

We walked around the deck to the door's great dark mouth. We halted at the edge and peered across the seam.

Nothing but blackness, emptiness, the smell of metal, distant murmurings or whispers that might have been from machinery—or not. It was like a tomb in there, a giant dark tomb. No welcoming committee waited. No official greeting came forth.

No monsters.

It was at this moment, I realized how reckless the Accord had been. They hadn't prepared for our safety at all, not even going so far as to ask about air or food. It wasn't that they had no regard for us. It was that they believed that tolerance would somehow make everything better. Also, they believed that if they asked these question of the Romans or visitors, they would risk hurting their feelings—and respect for feelings was at the heart of Accord values.

Anything to avoid being called xenophobic.

'Hello!' I called across into the dark. Nothing came back, not so much as an echo.

'Latin,' said Chen. 'What's the Latin for hello?'

'I don't know,' I said. 'What's the French?'

'It's hello too,' Le Seaux said, 'Or hallo, as we pronounce it. Or you can say bonjour.'

'Is it hail?' said Chen.

'I don't know,' said Le Seaux.

'At least there is breathable air,' I said. 'So far.'

We waited on the threshold for another minute, half standing, half at attention, expecting someone or something to step forward and greet us, but no-one did.

'What now, Captain?'

'I will step aboard first,' she replied. 'Then you, Lieutenant. Then you, Mr. Chen.'

She raised one Army boot, ready to place it across the seam. Then suddenly withdrew it.

'We have forgotten something,' she said.

'OK, Captain,' I said. 'Our mission. It can't hurt to remind ourselves. We greet the Romans, our galactic visitor friends. We tell them the values of the Accord. We hear their response. If possible we televise…'

'No,' said Le Seaux. 'The gift.'

'What happened to it?' said Chen.

'It's at the entrance. The first entrance, Lieutenant,' she said.

'I'll get it,' I said.

I turned and jogged across the deck, all the way through the doorway beneath the giant screens and out into the passageway. Le Seaux must have dropped the gift at the door when we entered zero gravity. I could see it at the far end lying at the base of the port. I jogged to the end, picked the gift up, then turned and ran back— actually ran from that lonely section of the ship. Just being alone in it only for a few seconds gave me a bad feeling and reminded me of how far from safety we were.

'All right,' said Le Seaux. 'Let's move onto the ship and wait there. And remember, when we meet our galactic visitors, I am the one to speak first. No one else. Understood?

'Understood,' we both said.

'Tolerance, equality, diversity.'

'Tolerance, equality, diversity,' I said.

'Tolerance, equality, diversity,' said Chen.

We all paused a moment to feel the power of the values stated aloud. Hearing them was like putting on armor or picking up a weapon. Whatever happened, the values would somehow protect us. Le Seaux and Chen even closed their eyes, drawing in slow, deep breaths, presumably so that they could concentrate on the words. They each smiled serenely as they did so.

But I wasn't so reassured.

When Chen and Le Seaux re-opened their eyes, we each glanced at each other one last time, then we stepped across the seam and into the Roman ship.

22

I had imagined a great moment in history was about to take place, but our entry onto the Roman mothership was an anti-climax: lonely, silent and intimidating.

The synthetic soles of Le Seaux's and my boots made no sound. Chen's civilian hiking boots made a cartoonish squelch.

'Sorry,' he said.

'Hello,' Le Seaux called out. 'Hello.' Her breath frosted in front of her face. 'Hello,' she said once more.

No reply.

'They must know we're here, right?' Chen said.

'Of course they do,' I said. 'How could they have missed our arrival? Somewhere on this ship there must be a bridge with crew members. They're probably monitoring everything going on in the space around them, especially their shuttle returning from Earth.'

'Maybe we're not a priority,' said Chen. 'Maybe they have a lot of other things going on.'

'Whatever the case, Mr. Chen,' said Le Seaux, 'we will respect their culture.'

'Captain,' I said. 'If they're not here, we could at least

explore a little.'

'It's more respectful to wait.'

I had already switched on the torch in my handheld. The beam penetrated only ten feet into the thick darkness, revealing more black-gray walls.

I switched off the torch. 'Should we try for lights again?'

'Yes, Lieutenant, we can try for lights.'

'OK,' I said. 'Lumina!'

No lights came on.

'Lumina,' I said quietly.

Nothing.

But then there was something. Lights came on above us and in front of us. They snapped on in a series, going away from us and either side of us, like the dividing lines on a highway, just as they had done on the shuttle.

'It worked,' I said.

'No, it didn't,' said Chen. He was standing next to a large box covered in switches just inside the entrance doorway. He was standing there with his handheld. 'Maybe their technology isn't as advanced as we thought.'

'It's strange that they're not here to greet us,' said Le Seaux. 'It must be a cultural difference,' she concluded, then added, 'Which, of course, is totally fine.'

'Maybe they're still preparing for us,' said Chen. 'Maybe they have a different concept of time. For them, our seconds might be as long as weeks. They could be making their way to us right now and think they're punctual and not keeping us waiting.'

'Whatever happens,' said Le Seaux, 'the Accord requires us to respect our visitors' culture.'

'What about this Roman thing?' said Chen.

'It's their choice,' said Le Seaux.

'I know, but why name yourself after an ancient pre-Accord people?'

'As the Commissioners told us in the briefing,' said Le Seaux, 'the galactic visitors know we call their planet Rome. They've simply assumed the name to make it easier for us.'

'Isn't that a form of cultural appropriation?' he said.

Le Seaux said nothing, but I knew the answer to Chen's question from hours of courses back on AONS Harmony.

'It's not considered cultural appropriation,' I said, 'when the former Western culture is appropriated by any other culture.'

'Exactly so,' said Le Seaux.

'Isn't that unfair on the Western culture?' said Chen.

I knew the answer to this question too.

'It is impossible to be either racist or oppressive to the West and its descendants,' I said. 'Didn't they teach you that in Hong Kong?'

'Of course,' said Chen. 'I just forgot.'

We spent the next minute peering at the corridors either side of us and in front of us, all of them lined with the same slimy dark material as the shuttle. They each seemed to lead nowhere, but the passageway directly ahead was punctuated by a series of heavy doors.

'Captain, permission to explore,' I said.

'No,' said Le Seaux. 'We wait for our hosts.'

'We can always say we went looking for them,' I said. 'That we were eager to meet them.'

'No,' said Le Seaux. 'Not when we've just arrived.

Your aggressiveness, Lieutenant Burns—it's coming out again. I remind you to keep it under control. We must trust our guests and our Accord values, and wait.'

I couldn't help but think that the Accord values weren't any help when it came to doing things, and the blasphemous idea popped into my mind that the values actually restricted action rather than encouraging it. They stifled initiative and restricted behavior.

'Yes, Captain,' I said.

'Good,' said Le Seaux, putting her hands behind her back. 'Let's just wait. Mr. Chen, you too,' she said. 'Our hosts will be along any minute, now. T.E.D.'

We waited in a respectful line by the entrance.

But suddenly, a noise came from somewhere along the passageway in front of us.

'Listen,' I said.

The noise came again.

'Sounded like a groan,' said Chen. 'Like someone's being sick. Or in pain.'

'Maybe that's a greeting,' I said.

'Or something we shouldn't be prying into,' said Le Seaux.

'Permission to inspect,' I said.

'Absolutely not, Lieutenant. Stay right where you are.'

But then the groan came again, louder this time, like a call for help, painful and horrible.

I had an idea.

'Permission to render assistance,' I said.

Le Seaux looked at me with her green eyes narrowed.

'It might be a way to help our hosts,' I said. 'That

might be the person sent to greet us. Perhaps they're in trouble. Or perhaps we are meant to move forward to meet our hosts rather than wait.'

Le Seaux thought for a moment, probably testing all the possibilities for consistency with Accord values. Then she said, 'OK, Lieutenant. Proceed slowly and with caution and respect. Never forget you are representing the Accord. Mr. Chen and I will remain here. Do not do anything without reporting to me first, and I mean anything, Lieutenant.'

As I moved down the passageway, the black material seemed to draw me into the darkness. Once again, I wished I had a weapon with me, a PQ47 rifle, or even a pistol.

Bad thoughts, Burns.

Ten yards in, I passed by the first of the heavy doors. It was at least ten feet high and fortified with rivets around its edges and a large handle—a large handle for very large hands. Or claws.

I passed several more doors, each the same. Which one was the source of the groan? When I was fifty yards down, I turned and looked back at Le Seaux and Chen. They stood way back at the entrance, the yawning cavern of the shuttle behind them.

Then, I heard the groan again.

It came from one of two doors on my right. From the first door, a crack of light could be seen. I turned to Le Seaux and mimed opening the door. She signaled by lowering her hands as if she were closing a car trunk. It was a military gesture that meant proceed with respect and caution.

So I knocked on the door and when no reply came, I gently pushed it open.

Inside was a room about the size of a basketball court. There were shelves running along each wall, like those in a library. One section of the shelves held books. The rest of the shelves held something like black bottles. In the center were giant desks and chairs.

Some books were open on one of the desks. I was about to proceed further into the room when I heard steps outside and the squelch of boots.

'Don't touch anything,' said Le Seaux coming into the room.

I walked to the shelves to check out the books. They looked like they could have come from Earth, but not recently. The bindings were old leather, faded and ragged. The books themselves were in several languages. There was a volume of the complete works of William Shakespeare, and a volume of Edward Gibbons's *The decline and fall of the Roman Empire.*

'These are PAE books,' said Le Seaux. 'Forbidden.'

'Take a look at this,' said Chen from the desk in the centre of the room. Le Seaux and I walked over to him. He held up a book. The cover read *An Introduction To The Latin Tongue.* It looked very old. 'Published in 1790,' said Chen. 'What's that in Accord era years?'

'Put it down, Mr. Chen,' said Le Seaux.

'When did they get hold of this?' he said. 'Were they on Earth once before?'

'Maybe they got them from Earth on the visit two days ago,' said Le Seaux.

'Doesn't look like it,' I said. 'These didn't come from any Accord Bookshop.'

'A library then?'

'But what library? No-one is allowed to look at books from the PAE, and no library would let such old books get into this condition.'

'Look!' said Chen. 'The Latin book has marks all through it.'

'How wonderful that they took the time to study the language,' said Le Seaux.

Chen put the Latin book down. I went over to it and turned a few pages. He was right. Marks all through it, including a page with the word Hyacinth underlined. Blue for Earth.

'What about this one?' said Chen. 'This one will really open your eyes.'

He held it up. The book's title was *Fashion In The Twentieth Century*. It was a modern book compared to the others, but its age was still in the hundreds of years.

Chen flicked through the book's pages. A series of faded photographs fanned by. Each one featured a woman dressed in strange clothes and wearing a bizarre hairstyle.

'This is real pre-Accord decadence,' said Chen.

He held up the book and flicked the pages. Women's names flashed by. I saw the names Anne, Elizabeth, and Caroline. They were all first names that hadn't been used for centuries. The poses too were something we never saw in our lifetimes. The women smiled and stood in unnatural positions. Some had turned their backs to the camera. Others drooped in mock swoons.

But it was the clothes that were the most striking. People who identified as women in the Accord always posed in military uniforms or sports clothes or Accord unisex smocks; they never wore the pre-Accord clothing article known as a dress or anything that accentuated the female form.

Le Seaux frowned so severely, two creases appeared between her eyebrows. 'Obviously, these women were totally oppressed by pre-Accord thinking,' she said. 'Here, hand the book to me.'

She took the book from Chen, turned to the front page and flicked through the following pages slowly, shaking her head.

'See how they are suffering,' said Le Seaux. 'I sense their pain. Even now, I can feel it.' She felt their pain so much that she flicked through the pages all over again, pausing regularly to examine the oppressive clothing in detail. 'Thank goodness for the Accord,' she said.

'That looks like you,' said Chen, nodding at a page on which a tall, fair-haired woman stood wearing a gown of some kind. Then, realising his mistake, he said, 'No. No, she doesn't.'

At first, Le Seaux looked with new interest at the photograph. She brought the book closer to her face and for the tiniest fraction of a second, the creases in her forehead relaxed and she might possibly have smiled.

But then ideology, like an ever-vigilant guard, rushed in to put an end to the pleasure. Le Seaux snapped the book closed, tossed it onto the desk and walked over to Chen, her face furious, her green eyes aflame. 'What did you say?'

'I'm sure Mr. Chen was only making a harmless observation,' I said.

'I don't think he was,' said Le Seaux, her hands at her sides, her fists balled. 'Were you?'

Before Chen could answer, a terrible wail came from outside. 'Urrrf,' it sounded. 'Urrrrrrrrrrrrrrrffffff.' This was followed by heavy snuffling breaths and then,

'Urrrrrrffffffffff!' once more.

I walked out of the door and into the passageway. 'Urrrf,' came the groan again. Chen and Le Seaux followed.

'In there,' I said, nodding at the next door next along.

'Respect and caution,' warned Le Seaux. 'Tolerance above all.'

I knocked on the door. No response except for an extended 'Urrrrf,' and heavy labored breathing. I tried the door's handle.

'Careful, Burns,' said Le Seaux behind me, but the handle had already swung down, and the door slowly opened.

'Too late,' I said.

A dull glow seeped out.

'Do not enter, Lieutenant Burns,' said Le Seaux.

But I had already seen inside.

23

The room was a quarter the size of the library next door. The bulkheads were the same black, slimy material. The dull lights were suspended low over a table in the center of the room. The table was as high as my chest, and on its top, someone or something lay groaning.

My first thought: it's a monster. Not even years of Navy Spirit courses on acceptance could stop me thinking the word.

Monster.

'What's the matter?' said Le Seaux.

'What's the smell?' said Chen.

'There's someone strapped to a table,' I said.

Le Seaux pushed through the entrance. 'We are sorry,' Le Seaux said. 'We apologize if we have disturbed you.'

From what I could see, being disturbed was the least of the troubles.

On the table was a creature roughly twelve feet in length and covered in shaggy black fur. It had long arms and short, muscular legs, with long claws on each extremity. The legs and arms were strapped down so that it couldn't move. Its face was covered with a black cloth. And its stomach had been opened up revealing brown and red viscera.

'Urrrrf,' the creature groaned.

'What the hell is that?' said Chen.

'Mr Chen,' said Le Seaux. 'Please respect our hosts.' Her hand was on her mouth.

'Is it an operation?' said Chen. 'They haven't stitched it up.'

'It might be a special therapy,' said Le Seaux. 'We shouldn't question our galactic friends' culture.'

There were instruments on a short extension table: long, curved blades, clawed forceps, pliers, saws, drills. Was it an operation?

'Please excuse us,' said Le Seaux, stepping forward. 'We are the emissaries from the planet Earth. We are invited here by Admiral Octavia.'

'Urrrf,' groaned the creature, snuffling under the face cloth. 'Urrf.'

'We'd like first of all to extend the warmest greeting from our planetary governing body, The Accord of Nations,' said Le Seaux.

'Urrrrrrff,' groaned the creature, struggling against its straps. Its enormous furry legs thrashed. Its claws clenched and unclenched. Its viscera glistened in the light and slipped back and forth.

'Should we help it?' said Chen. 'Sorry,' he said. 'I meant them, or him, they—this individual?'

'Would you like us to help you?' said Le Seaux. 'We don't understand what you're saying, but we value tolerance. If you would like us to leave, just say so.'

'Urrrrrrrrfffff,' said the creature.

'I think he might be a prisoner,' I said. 'These rooms are cells. And this...this...is not for the individual's health. I think it's for something else.'

Le Seaux's eyes flashed. 'Lieutenant Burns...' she warned.

But she was unable to finish.

The room suddenly shuddered violently. The ceiling light swung back and forth; the instruments fell off the table in a clatter and the creature groaned even louder. 'Urrrrrrrrfffff!'

Le Seaux fell against me yet again, right into my arms. I caught her and held her upright.

'Are you all right, Captain?' I asked but she shoved me away.

'Let's leave this person in peace and return to the entrance,' Le Seaux said. 'We can ask Admiral Octavia about the situation when we meet. Sorry to have disturbed you,' she said to the creature.

The room shook again as we lurched into the passageway.

'Are we moving again?' said Chen.

'That's my guess,' I said. 'The ship is moving to a new position. It's taking off, raising its anchor.'

We left the stricken creature and rushed back into the passageway, then back to the point where the shuttle buttressed against the rest of the ship. We went back inside 'our' shuttle and looked at the large screens. One now displayed a star field. The other showed the Earth again, this time with the Earth receding.

'We're moving further into space,' I said.

'I can see that, Lieutenant,' said Le Seaux.

'This wasn't part of the mission,' said Chen. 'We're only supposed to tell them the values, then get the hell out, right, and get back to our lives and businesses? Not go on a space tour.'

'It might be part of their greeting ritual,' said Le Seaux, but her voice didn't have its usual certainty.

'So what do we do?' said Chen, looking and me and then at Le Seaux. 'No-one's here to meet us. We can't contact The Accord. And even if we could, they wouldn't be able to help us.'

The three of us stood there looking at the screens, wondering what to do. Should we go further into the ship, or should we wait to see what happens?

Then someone spoke.

'You can witness our battle,' said a deep female voice behind us, and in an accent that sounded like a voice from a pre-Accord movie. It was slow and certain and pronounced each syllable of each word with precision.

We turned all at once and looked. I expected the monster might have gotten off the table, sewn up its chest, and come bounding along the passageway, claws bared, teeth and eyes shining.

But the sight that greeted us was something totally unexpected.

Standing there was a woman. She was about Le Seaux's height and age, perhaps thirty years old. She wore a white, full-length flowing robe, draped from over one shoulder down to the dark gray deck, concealing her feet. Her hair was blonde-red and, swept up into a kind of bun shape, like the styles worn by the women in the book in the library: *Fashion In The Twentieth Century.*

But most unusual of all was that she looked like one of the women in the book. I couldn't remember the name of which one, but she was striking, unlike any woman on the Accord. Perhaps it was the make-up she wore, the shade on her eyelids, the color of her lips. She was captivating.

She regarded us calmly, her eyes moving from Le Seaux to Chen to mine, where they lingered.

After several seconds, Le Seaux snapped to attention. 'On behalf of the Accord of Nations,' she said, 'we would like to greet you and to inform you of our values of…'

The beautiful woman interrupted her. 'That's not what I meant,' she said. 'I meant you can witness the battle.'

'Battle?' said Le Seaux. 'I don't understand?'

'It's quite simple,' the woman replied. 'The battle is about to begin.'

We heard movement, boots on the decking, boots thrumming unseen but coming nearer.

The woman turned her face to me. 'I am Drusilla, the captain of these vessels.'

'On behalf of the Accord…' Le Seaux began again.

'That can wait,' said Captain Drusilla to Le Seaux. Then she returned her attention to me. 'In the meantime, the battle.'

'The battle?' repeated Le Seaux.

'Yes,' said Captain Drusilla. 'You're in the military. You know about battles and fighting, don't you?'

24

Fighting. Battle. War.

The sound of the words made my heart race—and not just because it had been spoken by a beautiful woman dressed in a flowing white robe on—a spaceship.

Fighting, combat, battle—all of them were forbidden by the Accord. They were used only in the most extreme cases—fighting anti-vegans for example. Or clubbing down the fascists who said there were only two genders, or that men weren't responsible for climate change.

There was never an actual battle. There was never any conflict like the conflict I had trained for in the simulator, and in the courses of Naval tactics.

Now here was someone calling on us to witness one.

'What battle, Captain?' I said.

'Why, the one we're about to conduct,' said the woman. 'The battle against the Goths.'

'Honorable Captain,' said Le Seaux, interrupting. She held the gift from the Accord in front of her. 'I'd like to address you further, but I feel we should wait until

Admiral Octavia is here. I hope you don't mind the use of the pronoun "you" for the moment, but first I must ask which pronouns you prefer…in order not to cause offense. I notice you are speaking to us in an Accord language, for which we are grateful. I also notice you appear to identify as a female, which is of course, completely fine. It's just that you have gone so far as to dress like an ancient pre-Accord female, conforming to gender stereotypes of that time period, which again is absolutely fine, but which, as you know doesn't necessarily mean that you must be addressed as a female. You tell us how you want us to…'

Captain Drusilla looked down at Le Seaux without expression.

'Step back,' she commanded.

'What?' said Le Seaux, her eyes blinking.

'Step back.'

'But it's essential that I use your correct preferred pronouns.'

'Step back,' Captain Drusilla said once more, 'unless you want to be crushed. Move over there away from the port.'

She turned and walked away to the side of the entrance with a motion so smooth and captivating that both Chen and I did not even look toward the source of the approaching rumble.

Instead, we floated behind Captain Drusilla, as if we were hypnotized. Le Seaux, still astonished at the rebuttal she had just received, held out for a few seconds longer, then followed as well. I could imagine what she thought about it: how could someone not want to hear the values of the Accord? Especially someone from an advanced society. It didn't make sense.

Meanwhile, the rumble grew louder and louder until it was like the thunder of an approaching buffalo stampede, as if dust clouds would soon come billowing through the port.

'If you'd just let me know your pronouns, Captain,' said Le Seaux, to the woman's profile.

'As I said, my name is Captain Drusilla.'

'I'm Captain Le Seaux. My preferred pronouns are…'

Captain Drusilla looked at Le Seaux, silencing her. 'My pronouns are "she" and "her," she said, 'in your language.' And then in response to Le Seaux's gaping face, she spoke again. '"She,"' she said. 'And "her."' And then, she added. 'And "miss."'

'Yes, of course,' said Le Seaux, nodding over and over. 'Absolutely fine,' she said, nodding more, but I could tell she was horrified at the word 'miss' and all that it meant.

'They're taking this Roman thing all the way,' whispered Chen to my left. 'Have you ever seen a woman dressed like that? With hair like that? Displaying her figure like that? No smock? No floppy uniform? Make-up, jewelry—have you ever?'

He knew as well as me that the answer was no.

The first troops thundered through the entrance and curled off to the left towards the shuttle stern. They were followed by more ranks of troops, all moving in unison. They were so closely packed in black armor that they looked like the scales of a giant and furious snake, slithering out of a cave.

Each soldier was one and a half times my height, human-shaped but wearing thick black armor and helmets with blank, opaque face guards, so that we couldn't tell what lay behind them. Were they the male versions of Captain Drusilla? Or were they something else? Their height made me think they must be the second. Something else.

All the troops jog-ran, carrying riles across their chests. The rifles were fitted with cubed magazines on top—or what I thought were magazines. I wondered what kind of ammunition they fired. And I also wondered about the danger of firing a weapon inside a vessel in the vacuum of space.

And what kind of enemy would they be firing against?

The troops all assembled in the middle of the enormous hold, filling the void. The seats that we had seen earlier were retracted. The troops stood to attention in rows.

'Here are your weapons and armor,' said Captain Drusilla. Three troops had broken off from the main group and were now standing behind her. Each held out a weapon and a folded black suit.

'Take them and put them on quickly,' said Captain Drusilla. 'There is not much time.'

'With respect, Captain Drusilla,' said Le Seaux. 'We can't be part of any combat. We're here in peace on behalf of the Accord Of Nations.'

'If you don't use the equipment,' said Captain Drusilla, 'the Goths will sense your organs and attack you first.'

Le Seaux persisted. 'Captain Drusilla, I'm sorry but we can't be part of any…'

'Suit yourself,' said Captain Drusilla. She signaled to another soldier. He brought over a light, armored breastplate which Drusilla placed over her robes. It made her appear even more captivating.

Then, the entrance port slide closed and sealed itself. The metal strained and groaned, and the shuttle lurched. Seconds later, it began accelerating, causing all three of us to fall to the deck.

'Guess we're not going back to Earth just yet,' said Chen.

I looked up at the two big screens. The first displayed the many glistening hulls of the mothership, now slowly receding. The other displayed a different ship in the distance. It must have been the enemy vessel, the one in which the 'Goths' were waiting, whatever they were. It was also black, but of a completely different shape. It had one long hull, like a submarine—one with many ports.

The screen showed a flash of light on the Goth vessel's port bow. Within a second something had hit the shuttle, and we were thrown to the deck all over again. A second flash of light appeared, then a third. The shuttle was banged and thumped and thrown about.

'What are we going to do?' said Chen.

'Captain,' I said to Le Seaux. 'I think we should protect ourselves.'

Before Le Seaux could answer, I got to my feet and walked over to the three soldiers with the armor and weapons. I lifted a set from his outstretched hands. 'Thank you,' I said peering into the dark of his helmeted face.

'No!' shouted Le Seaux. 'Put it back, Burns. Wearing armor is considered an aggressive act. Stay where you are.'

At that same moment, the ship hit something hard.

Even some of the troops in the hold were knocked sideways from their places. Within seconds they were upright again and moving on the double to the far side of the hold where another large port exit began sliding upwards.

'Permission to speak,' I said.

'Save it, Lieutenant. We're not using weapons. We're not putting on armor.'

'That port over there is going to open,' I said, 'and something very nasty might be waiting on the other side of it. So, for the sake of saving your own lives, let's put the armor on at least. The Romans are testing us or playing a game, but that doesn't mean we can't protect ourselves—for the mission. We can't recite the Accord values if we're dead.'

'What?' said Chen. 'I can't hear you.' He wasn't kidding. There was a terrible roar coming from the other side of the door.

'It's now or never,' I yelled.

'No,' said Le Seaux, green eyes ablaze. 'I order you to leave that equipment where it is. Using it is not consistent with Accord values. It will be a display of intolerance to these other galactic visitors.'

'Captain, we're making a mistake,' I said. 'The Accord values won't protect us if we're attacked.'

'That's for me to decide,' said Le Seaux. 'Until we know more, we're operating strictly to Accord values. We are going to stay out of this conflict, whatever it is, whatever happens. Got that, Lieutenant?'

'Yes, sir,' I said, but I was thinking that Le Seaux knew nothing about war. Nothing about danger. Nothing at all. Not that I knew much myself, apart from the simulation exercises and marksmanship training, but I knew enough to know that an Accord value wouldn't stop a bullet from smashing through your chest.

'The Accord knows best, Lieutenant,' Le Seaux warned.

But I had my doubts, and they grew with each second of the mission.

On the far side of the shuttle, the troops formed several ranks. Then the first rank knelt on one knee. Behind them, troops in a second row raised their weapons and aimed them at the doorway.

I recognized what was going on immediately. It was classic pre-Accord infantry tactics. It was what used to be called volley firing. But why would they need it? Surely their weapons were automatic and rapid firing.

No time to think about it. With the troops poised with their rifles, the port opened all the way up. Bright light flooded in. Shortly after came the next nightmare vision for that morning.

The Goths.

'This can't be real,' I heard Chen say. 'I'm a civilian guy from AON sub-territory Hong Kong. I know twelve Accord commissioners. This can't be happening to me.'

Le Seaux said something in French.

I thought of the words 'Deiseil a-riamh,' even though I still didn't know what they meant.

Captain Drusilla said, 'Unfortunately, we did not enter your part of the galaxy alone. We were pursued by our enemies. We must repel them before we can complete our mission.'

The Goths came through the port like a tsunami of fur, teeth, and claws. Maybe 'avalanche' might be a better description because they seemed to fall onto the waiting Roman troops. It was a horrible sight, not to mention a horrible sound with their battle cry being in the form of hundreds of animal roars.

'It's the same,' said Chen.

'What?' I yelled.

'It's the same,' he yelled back. 'The same creatures as on the table back in that room.'

Despite the troops' formation, the Goth creatures were faster. The first row of squatting troops was overwhelmed by the onslaught, falling before they could fight back, their chests were torn by claws and teeth. Their armor was obviously not as strong as it looked. The volley firing troops behind got off a blaze of the shots or rays or pulses or whatever they were, but these had limited effect. While some of the Goths were knocked down, they weren't killed. They kept up their attack on the front row of troops, clawing, tearing off arms and heads, ripping apart bodies. It was carnage.

'How can we get out of here?' said Chen.

'We can't,' I said. 'I think we have to put on the armor.'

'No,' said Le Seaux. 'We must show them we're not from Rome. We must show them we're about acceptance and tolerance.'

'I don't think they'll understand, sir. Better to protect ourselves first and talk about tolerance later. We can't be tolerant if our heads are being torn from our necks.'

'That's a Navy Spirit code violation, Lieutenant Burns,' said Le Seaux.

Across the hold, the Roman troops were fighting back. The fallen front row had been mauled and

PROTOCOL

trampled, but rifle fire was having an effect. Goth creatures were beginning to fall from the fire.

It took at least three hits from each blast to kill or at least disable a Goth soldier. Once knocked down, each of these wolf-bear creatures rolled to the side, and piled up like smoking cattle carcasses. Several twitched, jerking their legs in the air. Others bit at their own limbs where the shots had hit, like animals caught in traps.

'More are coming through the door,' shouted Chen.

I wasn't listening to him because four of the Goths had broken away from the main mass and bounded, wolf-like or bear-like, towards the far side of the shuttle. Then they fanned out around the stern bulkhead, sniffing, snuffling, throwing equipment aside, looking for something—or someone.

'We must put on the armor,' I said. 'There are three Goth creatures coming this way.'

'OK by me,' said Chen, sensing what was to come.

'No,' said Le Seaux. 'We can't be involved. Our mission is to convey the Accord values and nothing more.'

'If we don't,' I said, 'those four breakaways down there will tear our limbs off like Captain Drusilla warned. They're looking for the creature we saw earlier. And we probably have his scent on us.'

'You don't know that, Burns,' said Le Seaux beside me. 'By putting on the armor and holding a weapon you'll be declaring yourself a combatant. You'll also be othering these new galactic neighbors. We're not at war with them. Waging war is against Accord values.'

We faced off against each other, Army Captain to Navy Lieutenant. 'Is allowing yourself to be killed also against Accord values, Captain?'

It was already too late to argue. The four Goths ceased their snuffling, looked up, sniffed the air some more, then focused in our direction.

They were coming.

I watched them come, filled with a sense of purpose I'd never experienced before. There was no question what had to be done. Any minute now it would be life or death—them or us. A more primal, natural sense of action took control. Ignoring Le Seaux, I stepped back to the guards holding out the armor and the weapons.

'Lieutenant!' shouted Le Seaux. I slid the breast plate over my over my torso. As soon as it was roughly in position, it form fitted itself to my chest and back, hardening as it did into the same black material from which the shuttle was built. The leggings did the same. The helmet snapped tight by itself. Then, I weighed the heavy alien rifle.

'Burns, I'm ordering you to put that down,' shouted Le Seaux, standing now.

'When was the last time you fired a rifle?' I said.

Le Seaux yelled a reply, but I couldn't hear. My guess was that she hadn't fired a weapon since her training, and the training would have been minimal.

So, I turned away from her and toward the advancing monsters. They were no longer scenting the air. They had made up their minds about us, and they were stalking towards us with ever more urgent lunges.

Getting ready to run.

I raised the Roman rifle and leveled the muzzle, just as I'd done hundreds of times against advancing enemies in the simulator and with the Navy PQ47 rifle.

The alien rifle was heavy—impractically heavy for humans, but obviously not for the tall Roman troops.

I expected it also had a massive recoil.

The monsters were now running our way, leaping over the rows of seats, teeth bared, eyes shining. I sighted in front of the first attacker, allowing for the distance it would cover before the shot arrived. I wanted to make sure I hit the creature's face or shoulder, and not the hull.

'No, Burns,' said Le Seaux, placing a gloved hand on the muzzle and trying to force it down. 'I can't let you,' she said, 'for the Accord.'

But it was too late. I pulled the trigger. The heavy weapon bucked in my arms, rearing up and throwing Le Seaux to the side and me backward. I saw the bolt hit the first Goth in the chest, knocking it over, its claws raking the air. But it didn't slow it down for long. It was on its feet and again in seconds and charging, the other two coming behind it.

With Le Seaux climbing to her feet to stop me a second time, I fired again, aiming low and in front. The shot hit the same Goth in the same part of its chest. This time, the Goth yelped and fell sideways, its shoulder no longer working. It thrashed on the deck, biting itself.

I looked over at the far doorway where the original surge of Goths took place against the Roman troops. The carnage continued. I looked back at Le Seaux and Chen. They appeared to be stunned, unable to act.

'Grab a weapon!' I shouted. They did nothing. They just stood there paralyzed with fear or in Le Seaux's case, paralyzed by principles. Would she really allow herself to be killed before she dared 'other' the Goths?

Did she really think she would hurt their feelings by defending her own life?

I chose not to think about it. I was following a deep, old, instinct. It wasn't self-preservation. It wasn't a sense of professional duty either. It was something else. The image of my ancestor on his ship flashed in my mind—the image of him standing calmly on the quarterdeck in his great blue Navy coat, unafraid.

Deiseil a-riamh.

I had to be like him.

The other three Goths were still coming. The leader forked off, on course to run at Le Seaux. I aimed, allowing for distances and motion. It was more difficult this time because I was on an angle.

I fired. The shot missed. I was thrown back. I clambered to my feet, put the weapons into a firing position, aimed and fired when the Goth was just twenty yards from Le Seaux. The shot smashed its muzzle, knocking it sideways. The creature thrashed on the deck, its claws driving it around in a circle.

The remaining two Goths were just a few bounds away. I could get one last shot at one of them before they landed on us. I also knew I would be too late.

Better to die on your feet, as I imagined my ancestor might have said, and I raised the heavy rifle again.

But just as I was about to fire, one of the Roman troops stepped between the two rampaging Goths and the three of us. This particular soldier was not as tall as the others, he was about Le Seaux's height, but the way he stood there radiated courage and defiance.

He took up a staggered stance and fired, hitting the lead Goth not just in the face, but in the maw, knocking its head back, blowing off the top of its muzzle and actually throwing it back into the next Goth who was just behind.

Then the troop took up his stance again and prepared to fire a second time. This time, the remaining Goth was already in the air, teeth bared, claws out. It hit the troop full in the chest. The two of them crashed onto the deck beside me. The Goth slashed at the troop's neck and chest— a sickening sight, like something from the Nature Channel on Unity TV. Horrible and primal and bloody.

The troop pushed back, just managing to hold the Goth's slavering jaws away, delaying the final claw or tooth or blow.

I raised fired the heavy weapon anyway, aiming as far away from the troop's head as I could. I pulled the trigger and hit the Goth in the ear, knocking it to the side. The weapon's recoil flung itself from my grip. It clanged on the deck behind me. I looked back at the troop. He was still prone on the ground. The Goth was bleeding badly from the side of its head, and it was looking my way with furious, shiny eyes.

'Burns!' I heard Le Seaux call out.

The Goth turned and snarled at her, then it turned back to me, and to my utter disbelief, it actually said something to me. It wasn't a snarl; it was a series of words, spoken while the creature looked steadily in my direction.

It rose on its feet and walked, not jumped. It actually stepped on the chest of the fallen soldier to get to me. Then it drooped onto all fours and was on me before I could react, shoving me onto my back. All the better to rip your armor off, I imagined it saying. All the better to pull your ribs open and claw out your heart.

The stench was powerful: wet dog, bad breath, sweat, leather, blood—all of them. The weight of the thing was shocking. I felt a rib crack as it settled one of its enormous paws on my chest. The other was raised for the slash at my neck. Here it comes, I thought. Here it is—finally. What would follow? Pain, yes, but what then? What waits for me after life?

The Goth hesitated. It peered through the helmet cover at my face, narrowing its eyes. Then, it seemed to make a decision, as if saying to itself this is a strange one, or I haven't slashed the face of one of these before, but I'm going to really swing hard and get the claws in deep.

The great arm came down, claws like fruit knives. I shut my eyes. Then I heard the blast of a weapon, then a second blast and then a third. The Goth's head snapped away from me, then further away. Then it dropped, and the whole horrible weight of the creature collapsed on me with gurgling breath. The breath rushed through the opening at the base of my helmet, up my neck and into my nose. After a final great foul exhalation, the horrible creature lay still, wheezing.

Le Seaux and Chen dropped down beside me. Both were open-mouthed and stunned, like they'd been slapped. It was as if it were both of them and not me who had just been smothered by a twelve-foot, giant wolf-bear creature.

'No-one told me there'd be this kind of shit,' said Chen. 'I'm just a businessman. Are you all right, Burns?'

Le Seaux was not as remorseful.

'This isn't in the mission,' said Le Seaux. 'You've compromised us before we could even start.'

But for the moment, I wasn't thinking about the Accord.

I was thinking how wonderful the experience of battle had been. How exciting it felt. How right it felt. How right.

Two of the soldiers came and pulled the carcass off me. The soldier who'd been attacked watched on from the side. His armor had a great slash across the breast where the fruit-knife claws had raked. The collar beneath his helmet had been completely slashed, revealing a pale, slender neck.

'Did you fire those shots?' I said. 'Thank you. You saved me.' Then, when the soldier didn't move, I said, 'You can understand me, right?'

The soldier removed the dark helmet, lifting it slowly with two gloved hands. As the helmet rose, long light-red hair fell down and flowed out, falling onto his shoulders. Then a human face, a woman's face appeared—one even more beautiful than Captain Drusilla's, if that were possible. Maybe it was a little older too. She saw me looking and smiled. It was a smile that made me gasp, which was really saying something because my ribs were in agony.

'I'm Admiral Octavia Caesar,' the woman said.

Before I could answer, Le Seaux stood up, turned to her and saluted. 'Admiral,' she said. 'I'm Captain Le Seaux of the…'

But the admiral ignored her and kept her blue eyes on me. 'I know who you are, Alex,' the Admiral said. 'I thank you in return for saving me.'

For a few seconds, I couldn't get the words out. 'It was just…' I began. 'It was just my….

My what? My role? My calling? My duty? The role I

had been waiting to play all my life? To serve, to defend, to be brave and to fight.

Instead, I said, 'I reacted the way anyone would react...considering the situation.'

'He means he acted to help our galactic friends, Admiral,' said Le Seaux.

The Admiral turned to look at her.

'Admiral Octavia, my name is Captain Le Seaux,' she said again. 'My fellow emissaries and I are here on behalf of the Accord of Nations of Earth to bring you a...'

Octavia held up a hand, silencing Le Seaux. She turned back to me.

'No, Alex,' she said. 'It's not exactly like anyone would react.'

'No?' I said.

'You are like him.'

'Like who?' I said.

'I think you know,' she replied. 'Maybe taller, and your hair is fairer.'

Now I was beginning to feel self-conscious.

'Admiral, I don't understand,' said Le Seaux. 'May I ask you what you wish from us?'

Admiral Octavia spoke while keeping her eyes on mine.

'Everything will be explained at the testimonies.'

'The testimonies, Admiral?'

'Yes, Captain, the testimonies.'

25

'Lieutenant Burns, you have a question,' said Captain Drusilla.

It was the aftermath of the attack. The Roman soldiers were carrying away their dead and wounded. The Goth dead were piled by the sealed doorway. I guessed they would be flushed into space. Some of the wounded twitched, others wheezed, some were actually smoldering. Everywhere smelled like burned fur.

Meanwhile, Le Seaux, Chen and I awaited instructions from Drusilla who stood, as before, in her white robes and breastplate, pure and beautiful amidst the carnage and filth.

'No, Miss Drusilla,' I said, feeling Le Seaux's hot gaze on me as soon as I had uttered the unutterable word 'miss'. She probably wanted me to keep using 'sir,' or 'ma'am' or 'captain,' but Drusilla had made her preferences clear. She didn't mind being addressed as either Captain or miss, so I was only respecting her culture, but for reasons of mission harmony, I addressed her by the military title from then on.

'I am just thinking about the battle,' I said. 'It was a very courageous display by your Marines—if that's what we should call them.'

'It is their duty to be courageous, Lieutenant. That is why they serve,' she said. 'But that is not the question you wish to ask, is it?'

'No, Captain.'

'Then, ask it.'

'I'm wondering why you chose not to pursue the Goth ship once it had retreated.'

'Why do you think?' she said.

'Could it be,' I said, 'because the enemy ship is more maneuverable and faster than your own ship, like one of our Earth frigates compared to a much larger carrier ship?'

'Well-observed, Lieutenant Burns,' said Drusilla. 'We can't catch them in our cruise ship nor this shuttle,' she said. 'Not if they are determined to evade us. Their tactics are guerrilla in nature. They ambush and they retreat, evading pursuit and any pursuing laser beams.'

'You've fought them before?'

'For centuries, Lieutenant. We know their tactics. They are always the same. Sneak, attack, retreat.'

'If you don't mind me asking another question, Captain,' I said, 'why did you decide to board the Goth ship instead of firing on it from a distance?'

'I think Captain Drusilla has more to worry about than your questions,' said Le Seaux who had been standing nearby, rainbow wrapped package under her arm.

I kept quiet and rubbed a sore rib, thinking about the battle.

One of the Marines lumbered up to Drusilla and

saluted. Like all the rest of his comrades, he continued to wear his helmet closed, concealing his face. He spoke a strange growling language.

'Excuse me,' Drusilla said. 'I will return in a moment. Then we will leave.' She glided away.

'What now?' said Chen. 'When are they going to hear what we have to say?' he said. 'So that we can get out of here.'

'I guess we'll find out at the testimonies,' I said, 'whatever they are.'

'Yes, but our mission is still the highest priority,' said Le Seaux. 'The sooner we explain the Accord values to our galactic friends, the better,' said Le Seaux. 'I will also request to communicate with the Accord back on Earth.'

'Seems like they have more important things on their minds,' said Chen. 'Fighting these bear-wolf creatures, for one. Why come to visit another part of the galaxy when you bring your own enemy along?'

'Maybe they couldn't avoid it,' I said. 'Seems like they're always fighting them.'

'Who the hell are the Goths, anyway? All of this makes less sense than it did on Earth,' said Chen.

'Maybe this was a display,' I said. 'To show us how effective their troops are.'

'These big freaks were unstoppable,' Chen said. 'I don't know much about the military, but wouldn't they make mincemeat of our fighting forces?'

'Stop,' said Le Seaux. 'We are not here to speculate on our friends' military strengths. Nor on the strengths of their enemies. Our galactic friends have their own reasons for their militarism. We in the Accord are fortunate enough to live in peace.'

'Sure,' said Chen. 'You're right. The Accord knows best.'

So we were always told, but I couldn't help but wonder if beings on other planets would all think the same way, especially if they had enemies.

Drusilla returned with an escort of four Marines. 'We must walk a short distance to our transport,' she said. 'We will travel far across the ship.'

'Yes, Captain,' said Le Seaux. 'We're ready.'

'How are your ribs, Lieutenant Burns?'

'I'll live, Captain,' I said.

'Then, please follow me.'

We walked back out into the passageway, leaving behind the troops and the pile of slain Goths. My ribs complained with each step, but I didn't care. I was thinking that we were at last going to see inside the rest of this enormous spaceship, and the technology it contained—the navigation systems, the engines, and the weapons.

We followed Drusilla to a large door that rolled upward revealing the entrance point to what looked like a train station platform. A single rail rolled away under lights along a dark passage whose end we could not see.

'Put these on, please,' said Drusilla.

The soldiers handed helmets to Le Seaux and Chen. Le Seaux was about to protest.

'Please,' said Drusilla. 'We will be passing through an area in which the ship's atmosphere is no longer breathable.'

'How about you, Captain?' said Chen.

Drusilla only smiled.

In the distance, a small train carriage came gliding

into view and stopped in front of us. Doors rolled back.

We stepped inside along with Drusilla and the escort. The doors closed and the carriage began to move into the tunnel, traveling smoothly and silently.

'Linear induction?' said Chen to Drusilla. His voice came through the speaker in my helmet.

'I don't know what that is, Mr. Chen.'

'Magnets,' said Chen. 'It runs on magnets, right?'

'You know technical things, Mr. Chen.'

'Just curious,' he said. 'We had them on Earth,' he said. 'Long ago, but not any more.'

We rode in silence as the carriage glided deep into the ship. I calculated that there must be at least fifty of the enormous shuttles joined together to make the one enormous ship. That was fifty Accord aircraft carriers, at least, each of which carried five thousand troops. This was not counting other vessels we couldn't see, such as the smaller teardrop shaped ones that had attacked AONS Harmony two days before.

The carriage came to a stop, rotated ninety degrees and then glided down a new passage. I guessed it had reached the central spine of the ship. Now, it moved along its length, probably towards the bow.

Le Seaux clutched the package in its rainbow-colored wrapping. 'We're looking forward to explaining our values to Admiral Octavia and yourself,' said Le Seaux.

Drusilla's face remained expressionless. 'You have said this several times, Captain Le Seaux.'

Le Seaux was undaunted. 'Yes,' she said. 'But we believe an understanding of our values is important for any interaction with the people of the Accord of Nations.'

Drusilla smiled a very small smile.

The small carriage began slowing down and stopped at another station. The doors slid open. The escort stepped out and stood in pairs either side of the door.

'Through there,' said Drusilla, pointing at a doorway leading from the platform to another passageway. The escort peeled off and marched away. We followed them.

At the door, Drusilla stopped and turned around. She pressed a button and then looked back at us, smiling.

'You may now remove your helmets.'

Which we did. Le Seaux leaned over to me.

'We're going to meet them formally now. You are not to speak without my say so.'

Drusilla signaled to the escorts. Two of the soldiers stepped forward and into the passageway, leading. The other two remained behind.

'Please,' said Drusilla, motioning us to move on.

The passageway opened out onto a vast, high-ceilinged cabin, although it might properly have been called a stateroom. The inevitable black material lined one side, but the other side offered a view that was truly startling: a cinema-screen view of space. The blackness was crystal clear, the stars in the distance glittered whiter than they did on Earth. But most striking of all was the view of the moon, gray and huge, and in the distance, the blue and white of planet Earth.

In the stateroom's center, forty or more crew members gathered. Most were dressed in dark blue uniforms, all human-sized, not Marine-sized. Not Goth monsters. And all were female—or at least female in form. The twelve in front were dressed in the same white robes as Drusilla.

And standing regally in front of them stood the most startling view of all.

Admiral Octavia Caesar.

26

The escort peeled off and stood either side, like a gauntlet. We followed Drusilla through, walking towards Admiral Octavia. When we reached within twelve feet, Le Seaux called out, 'Attention!' The three of us stopped. Le Seaux and I snapped our heels together and saluted. Chen stood with his hands by his sides and made a small bow.

Octavia did not salute back. She stood wearing a white, Roman robe, the same as Drusilla's. But there was a difference between the two of them. Octavia was more striking. Much more striking. She wore her strawberry hair swept upward into a bun like one of the women in *Fashion In The Twentieth Century.* She wore makeup too, also like the women in the book. Her eyelashes were extended, her skin tone even and glowing, her lips a pale flesh color. Her eyes almost cerulean blue, the color of the laser beams.

The effect was unnerving. I could barely stop myself from opening my mouth and gawping at her. She was a fantasy woman, unlike anything I had ever seen on Earth. It was as if she had been created by a computer

—created to look exactly how Accord men daydreamed women could look—something they never saw in reality.

As if waiting for Chen and I to pick up our jaws, Octavia nodded slightly. Her neck was so slender, so fragile.

'Salvete,' she said. 'Tibi grata sint omnia.'

There was the pre-Accord accent again, the same as Drusilla's, but even more refined. It sounded like something from an Accord instructional video about pre-Accord decadence. It was confident, polished. It didn't sound like any of the accents from AONT USA that I'd heard.

Chen exhaled beside me. Or was it a whistle. I couldn't tell if he was impressed that she had greeted us in Latin, thereby keeping up the Roman persona that fascinated him, or the way her mouth formed the word 'omnia.'

After a few moments, Le Seaux cleared her throat. 'Admiral Octavia,' she said, 'in the spirit of tolerance, equality, and diversity, and on behalf of the Commissioners of the Accord Of Nations, I would like to thank you for welcoming us aboard the...' she was about to mention the name of the ship, but we hadn't heard one, '...your mighty vessel,' she said, 'which on Earth we are calling The Friend Ship.' She said looked around for smiles. There were none.

'Lieutenant Burns,' said the Admiral, ignoring Le Seaux. 'How are you feeling?'

'Much better, Admiral,' I said

'You displayed bravery in the face of danger.'

'You are kind, ma'am,' I said, realizing I was speaking as if I were someone from the pre-Accord era greeting a queen. 'Your soldiers…your Marines were far more courageous. They faced the greater danger, and suffered greater losses.'

'It is their duty,' she said, echoing Drusilla's comment from the shuttle. 'Surely you understand, Lieutenant.'

'Yes, Admiral. I understand. On Earth, we also value duty,' I said, but of course, I was not referring to duty in battle. In the Accord, duty meant always seeking an equality of outcome for every Accord member on the Oppression Hierarchy.

Octavia smiled and nodded slowly. 'Did Captain Drusilla inform you we repaired your ribs while you were unconscious?'

'No ma'am,' she did not. 'Thank you.'

The Admiral then turned her gaze upon Chen, who was already flushing pink.

'Mr. Chen,' said Octavia. 'You are interested in the technology on the ship, are you not?'

'Yes, Admiral,' he said. 'The ship's construction, materials and workings are fascinating.'

The Admiral nodded approvingly. Then, she turned to Le Seaux. 'Captain Le Seaux, you wish to say something.'

'Yes, Admiral. Firstly, the Accord Of Nations Commission would like to present you with this welcoming gift.' She held out the package in its rainbow-colored wrapping. One of the uniformed officers stepped forward, accepted the gift with a deep bow, and walked back to her place in the ranks. The gift remained unwrapped.

'Thank you, Captain,' said Octavia.

'With your permission,' said Le Seaux. 'I would like to read a message from the Accord of Nations

Commission. But first I would like to make sure I am using the correct pronouns for yourself and your officers.'

'Before you begin, Captain, I would like to name my officers,' said Octavia. She turned to the twelve women either side of her.

'These are Captains Aurelia, Liviana, Domitia, Fausta, Flavia, Decima, Cassia, Aquila, Vistillia, Fabia, Horatia, and Aelia. They are each a captain of one of the many vessels that make up our main ship.'

'We salute you,' said Le Seaux.

The Captains bowed in return.

'May I ask your pronouns, now, Admiral? Or at least read the Accord's message?' said Le Seaux. She was almost smiling for the first time in the mission. 'Our commanding officers and the Accord Commissioners are eager to know that we have done so. If it is possible, Admiral, we would also like to arrange a broadcast to the Commission, or at least for the reading of the message to be recorded for transmission later.'

'No,' said Admiral Octavia. 'Your message must wait.' Le Seaux's smile faded. 'First, we will hear the testimonies.'

Le Seaux blinked several times, unwilling to let go. 'Naturally, we respect your culture, Admiral,' but the message is most important to the Commission. It contains our values of…'

'No, Captain. The testimonies.'

'The testimonies?' echoed Le Seaux, her voice a mixture of respect and disbelief.

Octavia looked to her left at the officer named Fausta, who turned and growled a command. Almost instantly, a large door slid open in the bulkhead to their right, and in came four uniformed women, each pushing a hovering cart on which a glass case was mounted.

'What next?' whispered Chen.

Three of the cases contained ancient weapons from the PAE: a chipped and rusty broadsword, a rusted battle axe, and a knotted wooden club. The fourth case contained something very strange.

'Is that a cannonball?' whispered Chen.

I ignored him. I had an uneasy feeling about what would happen next. If the battle with the Goths had been strange, this procession of relics from pre-Accord was going to be stranger still.

Three of the Captains left their ranks behind Octavia and walked to the glass cases. Octavia pointed to the fair-haired woman standing beside the first case, which contained the sword.

'Captain Le Seaux,' she said. 'This is Captain Aurelia, as you know.' Le Seaux and Captain Aurelia bowed slightly to each other. 'In 1805 in your so-called pre-Accord years,' said Octavia, 'Captain Aurelia was a mere midshipman in our fleet. She met your ancestor who was a soldier in the army of your famous general, Napoleon, in the land now known as AONT France, Eurabia. Your ancestor used this sword to slice her neck, causing intense pain, physical damage and requiring her to abandon her mission and return to our ship before it was complete.'

Le Seaux's mouth slowly opened.

Octavia now pointed to the next officer, standing by the axe. 'Mr. Chen, this is Captain Vistillia.' Chen followed Le Seaux's lead and made a slight bow, but a far more uncertain one. Captain Vistillia responded with a small bow of her own, her face expressionless.

Octavia spoke again.

'In 1825 an ancestor of yours, Chen Lai Min, was a soldier in the palace guard at the Imperial Palace in present-day AONT China, sub-territory Beijing. On duty one night outside the palace walls, he used this axe to cripple Captain Vistillia, who was then a lieutenant, by hitting her sideways on her knee, breaking it and causing her leg to bend at a forty-five-degree angle. He then clubbed her on the back of the head, knocking her to the ground.' The Admiral raised one perfect eyebrow. 'Very hostile, Mr. Chen. Very violent. Captain Vistillia was also unable to complete her mission.'

Octavia then turned to the third officer. 'This is Captain Liviana. Mr. Okwanko, who regrettably is not here, had an ancestor who made an attack on her with a club in AONT Africa, sub-territory Nigeria. Since he is no longer here, we will speak no further of this incident.'

I watched all this with amazement. The injuries were horrible, sure. I'd never seen anything like them on Earth, not even in the simulator, which kept the detail of slain soldiers to a straightforward fall to the ground. But surely these injuries Octavia described were understandable in the case of war—or invasion.

What was it all leading up to? Revenge? Would we have to suffer the same injuries? And how could we believe these same captains had been alive for so many years?

Octavia moved to the cannonball and looked at me. I guessed what was coming. My ancestor, my great grandfather, twenty-eight generations ago. Captain

Alexander Burns had used his ship to fire on the Romans. I waited to see which of the captains would step forward. Yet, no one did. No one came forward to stand in front of the glass case and the rusty object within it.

'Why are you looking that way, Lieutenant Burns?' said Octavia. 'Why do you shake your head in that way?'

'Whatever my ancestor did,' I said, 'whatever any of our ancestors did is surely not a crime committed by any of us here.'

'No,' said Octavia, a hint of a smile on her impossibly beautiful face. 'None of you actually committed the crimes. That is true. But, Lieutenant Burns, is it not the case that in your Accord, entire groups of people living today are penalized for the actions of their ancestors centuries before?' She turned to Le Seaux. 'Am I correct, Captain Le Seaux? Some of you are said to unfairly benefit from the privileges of your ancestors' actions and also to bear the shame of them. Everyone who is descended from pre-Accord Europe is required to bear this shame. It is fundamental to your education. Am I wrong in this perception?'

'No, Admiral,' said Le Seaux. 'That is what we believe in the Accord, but it only applies to descendants of the pre-Accord West.'

'But other peoples on your planet were equally violent, equally oppressive. They were equally intolerant of other peoples, and in many cases, even more so—much more so, and they continued to be so long after the West, as you call it, banned certain practises.'

'We are not taught about these other people,' said Le

Seaux. 'We believe that in the pre-Accord era, it was only the West that oppressed others. No one else.

'Well, then,' said Admiral Octavia. 'I return to my original question.'

'Yes,' said Le Seaux. 'If that is what you are asking. I am willing to accept the punishment for the actions of my ancestor.'

'Truly? Even though you yourself have done nothing wrong, nor benefit in any way from this action?'

'Yes,' said Le Seaux. 'That is…that is consistent with Accord beliefs.'

'You too, Mr. Chen?'

'I, well, it does seem… it…I'm not descended from the pre-Accord West.'

'We will all accept responsibility for what our ancestors did,' said Le Seaux.

'And you, Lieutenant Burns?' said the Admiral. 'Do you also accept responsibility for the actions of your ancestor?'

I felt Le Seaux's hot gaze on my cheek. I knew what she and the Accord wanted me to say.

'That depends on what did my ancestor did.' I said. 'And to whom he did it?'

Le Seaux interrupted me. 'Lieutenant Burns will also accept responsibility for the actions of his ancestors,' she said.

Octavia looked at all of us. 'I think you are all under a misunderstanding. We are not going to punish you. We are going to commend you.'

'Commend?' said Le Seaux.

'Yes, we congratulate your ancestors. We congratulate them for defending themselves.'

The three captains beside the cases bowed deeply.

Le Seaux said nothing.

Chen said nothing.

When the three captains stood up again, Octavia said. 'Aren't you wondering about your own case, Lieutenant Burns?'

'Yes, Admiral,' I said. 'I am very interested to know what my ancestor did.'

'As it turns out,' Octavia said, the blue eyes looming. 'It was me who met your ancestor. His ship was called HMS Morgause, a warship that saw action in the same Napoleonic war in which Captain Le Seaux's ancestor fought.'

She stepped closer to me. The cerulean eyes blazed, the icy white robe flowed, the skin on her bare shoulder glowed so clear. 'The ship was commanded by Captain Alexander Burns of the Royal Navy.' She stopped two yards from me. 'A most fearsome warrior,' she said, 'though early in his career at the time.'

I looked deep into those amazing eyes and did my best to hold their gaze and not flinch.

'What did he do, Admiral?' I said. 'Did he fire on you with cannons from his ship?'

'As it turns, out Lieutenant, he did.' She moved closer. I could now smell the scent from her hair, 'but firing on me is not his crime.'

'No?' I said.

'No, Lieutenant. He did worse than fire his cannons.'

'And what was that?'

'He broke my heart.'

27

With a nod from Admiral Octavia, Captain Drusilla dismissed the assembled officers and crew.

Le Seaux and Chen were invited to rest in two cabins somewhere else on the ship. I was requested to stay behind. Le Seaux asked once more if it were possible to read out the Accord's message straight away. The Admiral said they would convene again in eighteen hours. She said that by then it would be daytime at the AON Commission headquarters in AONT Los Angeles, which would make a more appropriate time for the message to be read. Le Seaux then asked when we would be returning to Earth. Admiral Octavia said she would tell us tomorrow. When Le Seaux asked if the Admiral might give an indication of what she wanted from Earth, the Admiral also said that this too would be revealed tomorrow.

Tomorrow, it seemed, was going to be a signature day.

An aide carrying two helmets appeared beside Le Seaux and Chen. Then they were invited to follow her back down the same passageway through which we had entered.

But Le Seaux was not ready to leave. 'Admiral,' she said. 'I would like permission to speak with Lieutenant Burns.'

'I would prefer if you did not, Captain Le Seaux,' said the Admiral. 'I wish to talk with Lieutenant Burns alone…about his ancestor.'

'Admiral, I would prefer it if all your communications were made through me.'

'To you? Are you saying I may not speak to your fellow visitor?'

'No, Admiral. Pardon me. I only meant that I would prefer if I were present when you speak to Lieutenant Burns. It's the wish of the Accord Commission. It is not meant to be disrespectful.'

'I see, but I wish it otherwise. I think it will promote greater harmony between our two worlds. Don't worry, Captain. We'll only talk about history.'

Le Seaux was silent. She looked about to say something more. She blinked five times. Looked at me. Frowned. Turned. Turned back. Bowed to the Captains. Opened her mouth. Closed it. Then followed the aide and Chen back through the door.

I was left alone with Admiral Octavia and the twelve captains.

Octavia turned to me with a look of conspiracy, as if to signal how good it was the adults had left the room.

'Would you like to see some of the ship, Lieutenant?'

'Yes, Admiral. Thank you. I would, but I am sure Captain Le Seaux and Mr. Chen would also like to see the ship, especially Mr. Chen.'

'They will see it later.'

She raised her chin slightly. Drusilla instantly

snarled an order. The captains bowed and filed away toward the door at the far end of the stateroom. No sooner had they left when four more women filed in. They also wore blue Navy uniforms with short jackets and small caps. Beneath the caps were a range of hairstyles, also from *Fashion In The Twentieth Century.*

Two of the women wore long hair swirled under the caps. The other two wore their hair cut short but not short like Le Seaux's hair or Captain Paine's. It was cut to a length just above their white shirt collars.

The four women filed up to Octavia, saluted and then stood at attention, their faces blank, their gazes directed up into the distance.

'Thank you, Drusilla,' said Octavia.

Drusilla smiled, turned and walked from the stateroom.

'Walk beside me, Lieutenant,' Octavia said.

This was easier said than done. I waited for her to lead off, but she stood motionless, as beautiful and imperious as a statue. So, awkwardly, I crossed the few yards between us and stood beside her. She placed her arm through mine and stood closer—close enough for me to once again register the caramel scent of her hair. Now, I also felt the curve of her hip against my thigh.

'Ready?' she said, and we began to stroll along the enormous viewport. Our reflections in the glass revealed a beautiful woman in a white robe, a hulking sailor in a blue camouflage Navy Work Uniform, and four women in blue uniforms of their own, all walking as if this were the deck of a pre-Accord luxury passenger liner and not a spaceship from the far side of the galaxy.

'You can relax, Alex,' said Octavia. 'The formalities

are over.'

'Thank you, Admiral.'

'You are walking so rigidly, Alex. Is it because you are so tall and muscular, or is it because you never escorted a woman on a walk?'

'Not a walk like this one, Admiral.'

'Women on Earth prefer not to be escorted—is that so?'

'Lieutenants don't offer their arms to Admirals.'

'Civilians, then—civilian women prefer not to be escorted.'

'The Accord believes women shouldn't have any reliance on men.'

'Not even during courtship, or to show affection while walking?'

'The Accord believes that courtship is a pre-Accord ritual that oppressed women. The Commission discourages it, as they do marriage and families. Accord women—those people who identify as women —follow that advice strictly.'

'Affection, then?'

'Affection is also considered a pre-Accord concept.'

'That leaves nothing but loveless sexual encounters or perfunctory coupling to procreate. Am I right, Alex?'

Her intonation was disarming. I hadn't actually heard many pre-Accord women speak because the archives of film and audio recordings were mostly forbidden. But in the few movies about the PAE that I had seen, some of the women spoke this way, in sentences with old-fashioned grammar. It was one more beautiful and intriguing thing about Octavia.

'Alex, you are suddenly silent.'

'Apologies, Admiral. I was thinking…about your

question.'

'And?'

'The encounters aren't always…loveless.'

'You speak from your own experiences?'

'It's more from the many courses and study I've undertaken in the Navy—those and my observations.'

'Your observations? What do you mean?'

'Only that humans…people have drives stronger than any lesson can override. It's not all loveless in the Accord. But it's what the Commissioners would like it to be. I'm sorry Admiral. I'm not expressing myself very well.'

'Call me Octavia.'

We walked through an arch-shaped opening in the bulkhead and emerged into an even larger stateroom than the one we had just left. The view of the stars was even more spectacular. The window was twenty yards high and extended almost the entire length of this section of the ship, which I guessed to be the same size as our shuttle. It gave the sensation of actually being out in space.

'Impressive, no?' she said.

Octavia's dress swished as she walked. I was conscious of her body moving inside it. Her hip continually brushed against me as we moved along the window. Don't forget, I told myself, that she is a visitor from another planet. Who knows how she really looks? Her sandaled feet might suddenly turn into claws. Her beautiful face might actually be a furry snout.

Then I reminded myself not to other her.

And I remembered my ancestor's warning in the dream.

'My apologies, Admiral,' I said when one of my

boots nearly trod on her feet. 'I was watching the stars instead of where I was going.'

'Call me Octavia,' she said again.

We reached the end of the long window. Octavia stopped and turned. The escort of four women stopped also. They were about ten yards behind us.

'Do you know that star, Alex, the brightest one out there?'

'I'm not sure which one you mean?' I said.

'I'll help you,' she said. She growled something at the four escorts. The one in front with a dark fringe withdrew a device from her pocket and twisted it. Instantly, the lighting inside the room dropped and we found ourselves in almost total darkness. The only light was from the stars themselves.

'Now do you see?'

'The bright star over there?' I said.

'Exactly.'

'That's Polaris,' I said. 'Or what we call Polaris. It's one of the stars all sailors know for navigation, along with Sirius. They're the most important, although we don't actually use the stars anymore.'

'No,' she said. 'Your technology has advanced since the days of compasses, sextants, and clocks.'

'Like my ancestor, Captain Burns?' I said.

'Yes,' she said. 'Like your ancestor, Captain Burns. He was a brilliant navigator. Or so he seemed.'

I could tell it was time to talk about my ancestor and whatever he had done to Octavia, which must have been serious, at least from Octavia's point of view. A broken heart—it sounded so un-warlike, and so out of place in the context of aliens and spaceships and voyages across galaxies.

A strange thought entered my mind: could it be that Octavia was mad. This beautiful, sophisticated woman beside me—could she be illogical and reality-challenged, as the Accord doctors described some conditions?

I looked at her profile. She looked back at me. Her beauty was astonishing, especially in the starlight, especially so close.

The air thickened. I spoke quickly to fill the silence.

'How well did you know him?' I asked. 'My ancestor, I mean. You must have known him quite well when you were here to…'

'Your ancestor certainly liked the way I looked.' She was now almost in front of me, not beside me. Her breasts were against my arm. She turned her face to me. 'You really are very like him, Alex.'

'I never heard of him until today.'

'Only today?'

'Yes, when you mentioned him. We're not allowed to know our ancestry in the Accord, except that we were part of a group.'

'But that's not true, is it, Alex?'

'What's not true, Admiral?'

'You have seen your ancestor before, haven't you—in your dreams?'

'How do you know that?' I said.

'There is a lot I know about you, Alex—everything from where you were born to your career in the Navy —even very private things, such as your lack of advancement, your frustrations, even your romantic life—or your lack of a romantic life. And that's despite all the attention you receive from young cadets, like Frank.'

'How?' I said. 'How do you know?'

'One kiss to remind me,' she said. 'Of *him*.'

'What?' I said, not believing what I had just heard.

'One kiss,' she whispered.

It's not possible I thought. It must be a test or a trap, a setup to either humiliate me or compromise the Accord. If she knew so much about me, she would also know how dangerous it was for Accord men to approach women, let alone for an emissary from the Accord to go kissing the admiral of a visiting nation's Navy.

'Now, Alex.'

I looked at the four escorts. I could see them in the starlight, watching on with blank faces. I had to change the conversation. I took a step back from Octavia, but her hand was still on my arm, her grip strong.

'Admiral, I can't.'

'Don't worry about them. I'll send them away.'

'It's not that.'

'Your Accord rules? The sexual harassment rules? I give you my consent, Alex, if that's what you need.'

'With respect, no, Admiral,' I said.

'You don't find me attractive?'

'No, Admiral. I mean, yes. You're very attractive.'

'Just attractive?'

'Beautiful.'

'How beautiful?'

'More beautiful than anyone I've ever seen.'

She smiled. 'Then, hurry up, Lieutenant. Don't keep a lady waiting.'

'No, Admiral,' I said. 'I'm sorry. It would not be permitted by the Accord. My duty is to the Commission. I can't, no matter how much I might want to.'

'Are you mad, Alex?' she said. 'Look at me. There's no-one on Earth like me.'

'Even so, Admiral. I can't.'

'You mean you won't,' she said.

'It comes to the same thing.'

'One kiss to remind me of your ancestor, Alex. It's a very small thing. Think of it as redressing the wrong he did.'

'No, Admiral,' I said again. 'With respect.'

It was the strangest situation. If Octavia had simply reached up and kissed me herself—surprised me, it would have been over. No harm done. But instead, she commanded me, making it into a test of conviction to the Accord, or a test of my will to resist her. I wanted to kiss her. No doubt. A face like hers. It was a fantasy. She was beautiful.

But I resisted—foolishly or not.

And now Octavia was angry.

She turned to the escorts and growled. The escort with the dark fringe stepped forward and withdrew a weapon from her pocket, a large pistol, gleaming of the same black metal as the hull.

'This steward is called Calpurnia.'

'There's no need for violence, Admiral.'

'Oh, but there is, Alex.'

'Admiral, I'll comply with almost any request…in the spirit of harmony. There's no need to shoot me.'

'I didn't mean you, Alex. I mean Ensign Calpurnia. She will shoot herself the moment I order her to.'

I smiled at her as if she were joking. I wanted for them all to drop the pretense and start laughing. Any second now.

But everyone stayed as they were. Ensign Calpurnia stood with the pistol at her side. Octavia looked me in the eye. The stars watched on from outside. She raised one beautiful eyebrow.

'No, Admiral,' I said again.

She growled something again. The ensign instantly raised the pistol and fired. The side of her head exploded. Flesh whacked against the window. Whatever blood these creatures contained, streamed down it, ruining the flawless picture of the stars.

The weapon clattered onto the deck. Octavia growled. A second ensign stepped forward and withdrew a similar pistol from her uniform and stood ready.

'So much bloodshed for such a small thing.'

'I can't, Admiral.'

Octavia's features twisted in annoyance.

'This is not a test, Alex, if that's what you're thinking. I don't want to know how dedicated you are. I don't want to test your loyalty to the Accord. I've been waiting for centuries. Don't worry about the reaction on Earth. They'll just think it's part of our culture.' She smiled. 'Or even better, if you don't kiss, me, I'll tell them that you sexually harassed me. Sexual harassment, Alex. It'll be consistent with what's in your file already. Given the way I look, it would only be natural for you to assault me. You weren't able to control yourself. They'll believe me. And then, I will tell them the worst thing possible in the entire Accord Of Nations.'

She leaned in close and whispered.

'I'll tell them you were racist towards me.'

She looked at me with a triumphant smile.

'Now, for old time's sake.'
'Admiral, I represent the Accord Of Nations.'
'Then, I have no choice.'

28

The situation would have been ludicrous if it hadn't been so dangerous. I was two hundred and forty-thousand miles from Earth, orbiting alongside the moon in an enormous spaceship with a beautiful, dangerous and powerful alien furious at me for not kissing her.

I couldn't have imagined this scene even if I'd tried.

And for a just a brief passage of time, I had a moment of clarity. Of just how dangerous it really was. If she chose, Octavia could use the weapons of this ship to attack Earth. The troops, the lasers and whatever else could be deployed with a simple nod.

She wasn't interested in harmony between nations from different planets. She had some personal vendetta to work out, based on being spurned by my ancestor. It just didn't make sense. How could any nation put someone so unpredictable in charge of such destructive power?

Unless the nation itself suffered from a similar kind of madness.

Suddenly, I felt afraid. Not just for me, but for the

Accord and all the people on Earth.

But more revelations were to come.

Octavia turned and raised her chin at the three remaining escorts. One reached into her jacket pocket and brought out a small handheld device and clicked it. A portion of the great window lit up with a view of the Earth. It tracked in closer, going through the clouds to AONT USA, then sub-territory California and finally to a city and then down to streets of a typical suburb.

I recognized my mother's house.

'Is this the night Kresta and her friend perform their yoga?' said Octavia, smirking.

'Admiral, please,' I said, suddenly thinking of a way out of this mess. 'Could we wait until this diplomacy stage is over? Then perhaps I can meet you as a civilian. We could meet up after the formalities. I could show you some of Earth. At the moment, I must think of the Accord first.'

'The Accord,' Octavia said. 'The Accord, the Accord, the Accord! It's all you and your thin-lipped comrade can say. The Accord, the values, the pronouns. If only you knew how deluded you are. How stupid it sounds! And how stupid it really is.'

She was working herself up.

'You call yourself citizens of the Accord. But nothing could be further from the truth. You don't even have democracy. Citizens? Don't make me laugh. You're not citizens. You are slaves. Slaves to the Commissioners who exploit you. Slaves to an ideology that will keep you slaves until you rise up and smash it, which you never will.'

I kept quiet.

'I'm not surprised you stand there, saying nothing,

but I know what you are thinking, Alex—that I'm mad, that I don't know what it's like. That I have no understanding of the wonders your government brings. But you couldn't be more wrong. I've seen it all before.' She held out a hand to the three escorts. '*We* have seen it all before. And we thank the stars we've banished it to history.'

'Admiral, I think it's time I joined Captain Le Seaux and Mr Chen.'

'I'm sure you do, but I don't want you to leave just yet. Maybe, Alex, I never want you to leave—never want to be apart from you again.'

She nodded at three remaining escorts. The one in the middle of the group said, 'The laser beam port is open, Admiral.'

Octavia looked back at me.

'You think we want harmonious relations with such a government? Oh, I guess we could use them to keep everyone under control. The Commissioners are as deluded about the ideology as everyone else. Like you and Miss Le Seaux, they believe that up is down, that ignorance is strength, and all the other nonsense they teach you. It has made the whole planet blind and your military as useless as a neutered bull. So, yes, we could use the Commission, but they irritate me so much that I think we'll try it another way.'

She watched me as her words began to sink in.

'That's right, Alex. We're not here to shake hands, wave flags and indulge your government's foolishness. You think we would bring a ship this size just for that? Look out there.' She pointed at the edge of the great window where the black hulls of the various connected ships rose and fell like distant hills.

'What do you think we carry in all those?'

Then she nodded at the three petty officers.

'Admiral,' one of them said. 'The beam is fired.'

'Admiral, no.' I said. 'Please. My mother is down there. She's not part of this.'

Octavia said, 'The beam takes about four seconds, Alex.'

'Then, I'll do what you want. Switch if off. Cancel it.'

'There'll be time later,' she said with a singsong, flirtatious voice. 'Lots and lots of time.'

On the window, the image of the street filled with dust.

Octavia stepped closer to me, leaned near and whispered in my ear.

'The really tragic thing, Alex, is that your Commissioners will just put it down to cultural differences, all in the name of tolerance.'

I said nothing.

'I never told you the name of this mighty vessel, as Miss Le Seaux described it, did I? It's not called a friend ship, Alex. Far from it. It's called The Excidium. I won't translate what it means. They tell me you're a natural with Latin.'

29

The next morning we gathered for Le Seaux to read her message from the Accord Commission.

Over two hundred personnel were present in the stateroom, including a hundred of the enormous Marines dressed in their combat uniforms and armed with the same heavy weapons.

Le Seaux and Chen were already there when I was brought into the room. Overnight, I'd been billeted in one of the other shuttles. The petty officers had taken me to a cabin furnished in pre-Accord-era style with a bed that had a canopy and four posts. The three petty officers warned me not to leave the room. 'No oxygen will be outside,' they said. 'You will die.'

I hadn't slept, which meant I had no opportunity to return to the windy deck of HMS Vengeance to ask serious questions of its captain. Instead, I'd spent a long night mourning my mother, and of thinking through what had to be done.

'Where did you go last night?' said Chen, winking. 'Last we saw, you were alone with Octavia, Drusilla, and the all-female Roman cheer squad.'

'You didn't say anything about the Accord did you, Lieutenant?' said Le Seaux, her green eyes accusing.

'Listen, we're in danger,' I whispered.

'Who is?' said Chen.

'The three of us, the Accord, the Earth.'

'What?' said Chen.

'The Romans are not what they seem.'

'They were OK yesterday,' said Chen, 'after all the Goth stuff.'

'No,' I said. 'They are not OK. We're going to be invaded,' I said. 'We've got to warn the Accord.'

Le Seaux looked at me as if she had been expecting something like this.

'No,' she said. 'We're going to speak about the values, Lieutenant. That's our mission. That is the first and last most important thing. Not only that, we're going to live those values, right here and now on this spaceship with our new allies.'

'They don't care about the values,' I said. 'They know all about them anyway. They know all about our system of government, our history, everything.'

'Address me properly,' said Le Seaux, 'or you'll have yet another Navy Spirit code violation to add to the pile.'

At that moment, I couldn't care less about Navy Spirit. My mother was dead. An invasion was threatened. Octavia was mad and wanted to imprison me. Worse, no-one else realized it. Not Le Seaux, not the military command, not the Commission.

'OK, sir,' I said, humoring her. 'They don't care about the values. The Admiral told me herself.'

'Keep your mouth shut, Lieutenant,' said Le Seaux. 'Until we get back to the Accord, you are to talk about nothing except Accord values and how much you admire them.'

'We've got to get off this ship and warn the Commission,' I said. 'We've got to get our forces ready to defend ourselves.'

'Warn them? About what?'

'An invasion.'

'Lieutenant.'

'I'm serious. Admiral Octavia told me last night. This is not a case of using more tolerance. Tolerance will just end up in our defeat. We can't tolerate the intolerable.'

'Lieutenant,' said Le Seaux again. I could tell she was fighting to remain calm. She wanted me to shut up, but she knew she couldn't shout with so many others in the room.

'OK, Lieutenant,' she said. 'Your concerns are noted. But we must wait until the Accord values are read. Then we can talk about what happened to you last night.'

I could see there would be no convincing Le Seaux. All that mattered to her was the recitation, but as I was concerned, the values were increasingly becoming the problem, the impediment, the obstruction making us vulnerable and stupid. I would have to find a way of my own to either make the Accord listen, or to prevent Octavia from acting on her plans—if that were even possible.

At the other end of the room, Octavia, Drusilla and the officers assembled on a platform. They wore their robes again. Octavia looked across at me once without expression. She was back to being Admiral Octavia, the stateswoman, not Octavia the madwoman on the viewing deck.

A section of the giant window flickered. Up came an image of the Accord Commission chambers. The chamber was an amphitheater with seats for representatives of all the six hundred nations of Earth. A podium in the center represented the centrality of the Accord values. The letters T.E.D were emblazoned on a plaque above it.

The Commissioners waited in their rainbow smocks. When they saw Octavia and Drusilla in their flowing robes, they almost gasped, especially the Commissioners who identified as female. The commissioners who identified as male were expressionless.

'This is going to make a great movie,' whispered Chen.

Admiral Octavia spoke to the Commission. The Chief Commissioner, Daniel Genet, responded. The Commissioners applauded.

Then, Le Seaux stood and read out the values. She mentioned tolerance, diversity, and equality. She stated the quest to share prosperity among all the peoples of the Earth, and finally to welcome new, like-minded peoples such as the Romans, our new galactic friends, who would enhance the diversity of the Accord even more, because diversity is our strength.

When Le Seaux had finished, she saluted both the Accord and Octavia's podium. Then she walked back to where Chen and I stood. Her face was beaming, her task completed at last. Everyone applauded. It was a great moment for intra-galactic harmony. All would be well from now.

Then Octavia stood and addressed the screen.

'On behalf of my people,' she said, 'we acknowledge

the values of your Accord of Nations.'

More applause. Commissioner Genet responded with an invitation to visit Earth and join in the Accord Establishment Day celebrations in AONT sub-territory Hong Kong, in two days' time.

'We would be very pleased, Commissioner,' said Octavia.

More applause. Longer applause.

When all the clapping finally died down, Octavia said. 'Now, Commissioner Genet, with your indulgence, we would like to conduct a ceremony of our own.

'Certainly,' said Commissioner Genet.

'The ceremony will be what we call our punishments.'

'Punishments, Admiral?' said Commissioner Genet.

'Yes, Commissioner. We would like to punish Mr. Chen, Captain Le Seaux and Lieutenant Burns.'

'Forgive me, Admiral, but punish them for what?'

'For the crimes committed by their ancestors against members of our crew on previous visits to your planet.'

The Commissioner was confused. 'Are you being humorous, Admiral? Are you making a joke?'

'No, Commissioner. I am serious. We tried Mr. Chen and Lieutenants Le Seaux and Burns yesterday for their ancestors' crimes. They were all guilty.'

The Commissioner said, 'Admiral, naturally we would like to do all we can in the interest of tolerance, but...' He was interrupted by someone behind him. The sound cut out. Then he came back to the screen and said, 'What is the nature of the punishment, Admiral? If it's some light form of fun, then perhaps we can agree...so long as it's in the interests of tolerance and respect for our two cultures.'

Admiral Octavia's face was blank. 'The penalty for the crimes, Commissioner, is death.'

Commissioner Genet's mouth opened wide without a sound coming from it. It stayed that way for several seconds. Then it closed and opened again. The rest of the Commissioners in the chamber ceased moving, as if the picture on the screen had frozen.

'Death, Admiral?' he said.

'Death, Commissioner.' She turned to her right. 'Captain Drusilla.'

Drusilla turned to a crew member, a woman with dark hair in the blue Naval uniform, the first lieutenant, perhaps. Drusilla growled an order. The first mate saluted and then growled an order of her own at high volume.

Instantly, four of the large Marines marched our way.

Le Seaux said, 'But Admiral, I thought we were not responsible for the actions of our ancestors.'

'You thought wrong,' said Drusilla.

'You told us.'

'Yes,' said Octavia. 'I know I told you. I was lying. No-one attacks our nation without punishment. Not the filthy Goths and not you.'

'But you just heard the values of the Accord. You heard Commissioners Genet's assurances regarding tolerance and diversity. You applauded them.'

Octavia stepped forward and looked stood opposite to Le Seaux, her white robes against the Army green. Her beautiful pre-Accord face against Le Seaux's modern one.

'Those values, Captain Le Seaux, are the values of slaves.'

Drusilla growled at two Marines who stepped forward and grabbed Le Seaux, Chen, and me by the shoulders and shoved us towards the back of the room.

The Marines pulled Le Seaux and Chen to one side. Two others brought forward two black frames. Le Seaux and Chen were clamped to them, their hands behind their backs. Then the Marines stepped back, leaving Le Seaux and Chen standing against the frames, their expressions ones of total astonishment.

Like prisoners about to face a firing squad.

Another Marine came forth and held out one of the large rifles we had used the day before against the Goths. He held it in two hands and thrust it towards me.

I looked at the rifle, then at Drusilla and Octavia, who stood to the side smiling. On the screen, Commissioner Genet was speaking, but making no sound.

'You can't be serious,' I said.

'Oh, but we can, Alex. We have decided that Le Seaux and Mr. Chen will be executed for what their ancestors did.'

I looked at the rifle being held out to me.

'Is this something to do with last night?' I said.

Octavia looked at me, her beautiful face expressionless. 'I don't know what you mean, Lieutenant Burns.'

'Yes, you do,' I said.

Drusilla said, 'The court has decided, that you, Lieutenant Burns, shall be imprisoned on the Excidium at the Admiral's pleasure.'

'What court?' I said. 'What court?'

But Octavia ignored me.

PROTOCOL

'In the interests of intra-galactic harmony,' said Octavia, 'we are not going to perform the execution ourselves.'

'What does that mean?' I said.

'We are going to have you perform it, to execute yourselves.'

'What?' said Le Seaux.

'What?' said Chen.

'Take the rifle, Lieutenant Burns,' said Drusilla.

'No,' I said. 'No one's firing any rifles. No-one's doing any executing.'

'So bold all of a sudden, Lieutenant,' said Octavia. 'It's as if I can hear your ancestor speaking and not you.'

'No one's doing any executing,' I said.

'There it is again,' said Octavia. 'What happened to you overnight? A bad dream?'

'What are you trying to achieve, Admiral? Even the Accord Commission's tolerance won't extend this far.'

'I think you're wrong, Alex. I think the Accord will accept anything as long as I say it's part of our culture. All cultures are equal, after all. It's written in your constitution.'

I put the weapon on the deck and stepped forward to Le Seaux and Chen. I reached for cuffs on Le Seaux's wrists. 'Do you believe me now?' I said to her.

But before I could begin to untie her, a Marine grabbed me by the shoulders and with astonishing strength, lifted me up and dropped me back at where the rifle lay on the deck.

'I'm not doing it, Admiral.'

'Well, I thought you might say that, Alex,' she said. 'So, to help you overcome your reluctance, I have an incentive. Look up at the screen, please.'

A second screen appeared on the window. This one showed a rural scene, a village somewhere in the tropics. It looked to be a town square. People were assembled for the Accord Anthem.

'This is the village of Manning,' said Octavia. 'It's named after one of your so-called social justice warriors.'

Here she stopped and nodded to Drusilla again, who growled at a uniformed staff member beside her.

'We have just fired a laser at the island,' said Octavia. 'Allowing for the distance from our position here beyond the orbit of your moon, the laser should be landing just outside the village in a few seconds... about... now.'

On the screen, the image of the village remained as it was. Then the laser hit, sending up plumes of earth and dust.

Octavia said, 'If Lieutenant Burns fails to execute his colleagues, we will fire exactly one hundred beams all over the territory and its three million people.'

The officers all turned to look at me, as must have the members of the Accord Commission.

'Take the weapon,' said Drusilla.

When I didn't reach out for it, she said. 'You have ninety-seconds.'

I still told myself there was no way I would be an executioner, no matter what.

Octavia said, 'Commissioners, do you give Lieutenant Burns permission. His action will save the life of millions of people. Just signal with a thumbs up or down.'

On the screen, the Commissioners turned and spoke

rapidly to each other. Arms were waved. Heads were shaken. Hands were held out in exasperation. Then, there was a raising of hands from what looked like a third of the Commissioners. Then a raising of hands from about half of them.

Then Commissioner Genet's face came back on the screen, his face grim. Then he raised his thumb.

Octavia allowed herself a smile. 'Lieutenant Burns, you have fifty seconds to execute Captain Le Seaux and Mr. Chen, or the beams will be fired.'

On the screen, the image changed to a street scene in Manning. People were running, children crying.

'Thirty seconds,' said Drusilla.

'What are you trying to do?' I said to Octavia. 'What does this prove?'

She said nothing.

'Twenty-five seconds,' said Drusilla.

I looked at the screen and the panicking crowds. I looked back at Le Seaux and Chen. 'Do it, Lieutenant,' Le Seaux said. 'Shoot me first. That might be enough. Spare Mr. Chen.'

Chen was too shocked to speak.

I looked at the rifle, felt the weight in my hands. Closed my eyes. How could this be happening to me? It was an impossible situation to put someone in. Two deaths against a million. And there was no doubt that Octavia was mad enough to actually send the beams.

'Fifteen seconds,' said Drusilla.

I'd wanted a mission. Now I'd got one. And it had turned into the worst nightmare I could imagine. How could I decide? What would my ancestor do? How could I stop Octavia, this mad, evil…

'Ten seconds,' said Drusilla.

I raised the rifle and aimed at Le Seaux. Leveled the sights on her forehead. She looked directly back at me, brave and resolved, a true believer to the end. The Marines stepped back.

'Five seconds.'

Then I quickly swung the rifle at the group of officers, fixing the sights on Octavia.

And I pulled the trigger.

30

Nothing happened.

No blast.

No recoil.

No deaths.

I pulled the trigger again.

Nothing.

Just a click of the trigger mechanism, nothing more.

I looked up from the sights at Octavia. She smiled down at me, eyebrows raised, enjoying watching me reach the terrible conclusion.

'Times up,' said Drusilla.

'Oh dear,' Octavia added.

I looked down at the rifle and up at Le Seaux and Chen.

'You can't be serious,' I said

'Totally series,' said Drusilla.

'But there's no need. It's…it's inhuman.'

This time, both Drusilla and Octavia smiled, two non-humans enjoying the human squirm.

I looked at the screen. The Accord members were still. Several held their hands to their mouths. I saw one Commissioner crying. But others in front nodded slowly.

'Hurry up, Lieutenant,' said Octavia. 'Millions of people's lives depend on you.'

'Too late,' said Drusilla. And then, over her shoulder, she called something in the weird Roman language. My guess: ready the laser for a second blast.

'We're waiting, Alex,' I heard Octavia say. 'All of us are waiting. We'll give you thirty seconds more.'

I walked slowly toward Le Seaux and Chen. Le Seaux's face wasn't nobly resigned any more. Chen's face was twisted with panic as he struggled against his restraints.

'Don't take too long,' said Octavia.

I stopped in front of them. Could I really do this? Could I raise the rifle and smash the stock into Le Seaux's face?

'You have to,' whispered Le Seaux.

That was when I heard a terrible and ear-shattering snarl. It sounded like a command to stop. So I lowered the rifle and looked around. Three Marines were restraining someone at the entrance to the room. Everyone had turned to see what was happening.

Then, there was an almighty explosion at the back of the stateroom, right beside the troop formation.

Pink mist and pieces of flesh thwacked onto the deck beside us. Smoke billowed all around. Several of Octavia's officers were on the deck. Confusion everywhere. I had been knocked down with the rifle still in my hands.

I looked up.

The snarl must have been from one of the Goths.

A Goth wearing explosives.

31

With my head thumping, I climbed to my feet.

'Here's our chance!' I shouted to Chen and Le Seaux.

'What?' said Chen, cocking an ear. 'Can't hear anything. Just ringing.'

'Never mind,' I shouted. 'Stand still.'

'What?' said Chen.

'Wait, Lieutenant!' said Le Seaux. 'Don't touch Chen. Don't touch me, either. Don't do a thing.'

'We've got to get out.'

'I said wait.' Le Seaux was glaring at me. 'That's an order.'

'You want to stay tied up, Captain?'

'That's what the Accord Commission commanded, Lieutenant.'

Her face was resolute. Her eyes clear. Her brow creased. She meant it. She was totally serious. She was prepared to die for the Commission and the Accord.

'Sorry, Captain,' I said. 'Not this time.'

I got behind Chen and examined the clamps on his wrists. They looked like they could be undone with a blow from the rifle on their mountings. I picked up the rifle and raised it, stock downward.

'What are you doing?' said Chen.

'Calm down,' I said. 'I'm freeing your hands. Think of it as a great scene for your movie.'

'Burns, wait!' Le Seaux repeated.

I looked away and jammed the rifle butt down on the mountings of Chen's wrist clamp.

'Burns!' Le Seaux shouted.

'I'm disobeying you, Captain Le Seaux,' I said, raising the rifle again. 'I'm disobeying you because I think you are traumatized. Navy Spirit code allows an officer to assume command when his superior has lost their wits. Totally understandable after what you just went through.'

'I've never been more clear in my life,' said Le Seaux. 'If you undo those restraints, you're disobeying an order, which as you know will mean the end of your career.'

I smashed the rifle down into Chen's other restraint. It broke and freed up his wrist.

Around the great room, the chaos was slowly coming back to order. Marines climbed to their feet, but no officers were snarling out commands. Their attention elsewhere.

Not on us.

I stepped over to Le Seaux's frame and raised the rifle butt over the clamps holding her wrists.

'Burns!' said Le Seaux.

'It's time to grow up, Katherine,' I said.

'How dare you call me that,' she replied. 'What do you mean it's time to grow up? If anyone needs to grow up, it's you, Burns.'

'It's time to grow up for all of us. It's time to stop

being treated like children by the Accord.'

The two Marines who had tied up Le Seaux and Chen were also climbing to their feet. They looked in bad shape. Their bodies had taken the force of the blast, shielding us from it. One was staggering towards me, arms out. The second was about to follow.

I stepped back while Le Seaux and Chen climbed away from the frames. Then I faced the first of the two Marines—all ten feet of him.

'You two go,' I said over my shoulder.

'What?' shouted Chen.

'Go!' I shouted.

'Go where?' said Le Seaux.

'To one of the shuttles.'

'No!' shouted Le Seaux. 'We'll stand aside and wait till this is over. The Accord will sort this out with our galactic friends. There's been a misunderstanding. That's all. It can be fixed.'

'Doesn't look like a misunderstanding to me. Just look at this guy. You think he misunderstands?'

'You're presuming gender, Lieutenant?'

'I might be, Katherine, but do the Romans even have genders? Seems like they can be anything shape they want, be anywhere they want.'

'Which is exactly why you should never presume their genders.'

I didn't have time to argue. The tall soldier came at me, arms out, helmet beaver down, no eyes or features visible.

He held out his arms. He was going to grab me like a toy.

But I wasn't going to let that happen.

I swung the rifle butt at the outside side of his left

knee, ready to follow it with a kick to make sure the joint bent inward, tearing enough ligaments to ruin his mobility.

That's if these things even had ligaments.

Then, once he was immobilized, I would turn to his head, perhaps with an upper smack with the rifle butt to the underside of the helmet—if I could reach it.

I swung hard. The butt rifle hit his knee with a metallic whack that would have smashed a human knee as if it were a paper drinking straw. But the rifle simply bounced backward in my hands, jarring me all the way to my collarbone.

'Are you running yet?' I called over my shoulder.

'No,' said Le Seaux.

'What did you say?' said Chen.

'Get out of here!' I yelled.

The Marine kept coming. He was like a zombie. No pain. No fear. Obviously, this was a fight I was about to lose. I looked around for something else I could use. Saw that some of the Marines had dropped their weapons after the explosion.

'Grab one of the loaded rifles!' I shouted to Le Seaux. 'You're Army, right? Infantry? Weapons are your thing, right? So shoot him. Shoot him where there's no armor —in his neck, the gap under his helmet.'

'No,' shouted Le Seaux. 'It is against the Accord laws to attack a friendly nation.'

'They're not friendly. They just wanted me to murder you. You have a right to defend yourself.'

'A misunderstanding. It's their culture.'

'Oh for fuck's sake!'

'Disgusting patriarchal language,' said Le Seaux.

At that moment there was a crash—not an explosion.

The whole ship was flung backward as if something had crashed into it.

Everyone was thrown off their feet. Chen, Le Seaux, me. And the Marine.

'A Goth raid,' I said. 'Has to be. They've rammed this thing with their own ship. The suicide bomber was simply a distraction.'

'Where are they?'

'Don't know,' I said. 'Breaking open the hull somewhere.'

But now both Marines were coming for us.

'While they're still groggy,' I said. 'Let's go. Now!'

'Where?' said Le Seaux.

There were two entrances to the stateroom. The one we had entered into that morning and a second one—a closer one.

'There,' I said, pointing. 'Go to that exit first.'

I ran at the Marine. He wasn't quite on his feet. I launched an almighty kick to the underside of his helmet where his chin might be. It snapped his head back about one degree.

These guys were as tough as they looked.

Time to get myself out.

Through the smoke, I could see Drusilla shouting, trying to restore order. I didn't see Octavia.

I turned and ran after Le Seaux and Chen, or at least tried to run. My knee felt like a rusty hinge. It creaked all the way to the entrance.

'Your knee is all bloody,' said Le Seaux.

'Never mind,' I said. 'It's working.'

'Where to now?' said Chen.

'Let's go to any of the sections of the ship that can fly,' I said.

'Why?' said Le Seaux. 'What are you planning to do? Hide?'

'No,' I said. 'I'm going to fly us home.'

'You're going to what?'

'At least I'm going to try,' I said. 'How else will we get out of here.'

'We aren't getting out of here,' said Le Seaux. 'We're going to wait till order is restored.'

'No we're not,' I said. 'We're going to a shuttle.'

'You want to add theft to assault as well as disobeying orders and attempted murder?'

'It doesn't matter anymore. We're at war.'

'Really, Lieutenant? There's no war until war is declared, which won't happen.'

'I'm declaring it. So let's get moving.'

'Only the Commission can declare war, which it would never do.'

'That's the trouble,' I said.

'Where has this insubordination come from, Lieutenant? This swagger?' said Le Seaux. 'What's happened to you?'

I was about to answer when Chen said, 'What's that noise—apart from the ten thousand bells ringing in my ears?'

We stopped and listened. Thunder again. Hundreds of boots coming up a passageway.

'Get to the side!' I said.

Around the corner they came—Marines stampeding into the room like the herd of bison. They rolled past us to where Drusilla was standing. She ordered them into a formation facing the other entrance to the stateroom.

Then, I remembered the weapon Le Seaux had failed to pick up.

PROTOCOL

'Wait for me here,' I said.

'Hey where are you going?' said Le Seaux. 'Burns!'

I limped back into the hall, picked up an alien rifle.

Then, I ran back to Le Seaux and Chen.

'This one feels loaded,' I said.

'No shooting our galactic friends,' said Le Seaux.

'Your friends, not mine,' I said. 'Now come on,' I said. 'Let's find a shuttle.'

'Then what, Burns?'

'Then we'll work out what,' I said.

'You think you can fly a shuttle?'

'I'm the only one here with a pilot's license.'

'This is not a Slingshot. It's not a J-Pack. You can't just jump and push a button. This is space not some practice field outside AONS Harmony.'

'No, it's not,' I said, 'but I'll work it out. Can't be too hard.'

As I said this, the entrance at the other end of the great room became a mass of fur, teeth, and claws as the Goths burst in. The whole battle scene from the previous day was repeated with the bear wolves screaming their battle cry and the Roman Marines almost stunned by the ferocity of the attack.

'At least I told them our values,' said Le Seaux, defiantly.

'Yeah,' I said. 'And we heard what they thought of them.'

32

We ran along the passageway, the roar of growling goths and blasting weapons swelling louder behind us.

'Why do those freaks keep attacking?' yelled Chen. 'Won't they just get smashed all over again? They don't even carry weapons.'

'They've done us a favor,' I said. 'If they hadn't shown up, we'd still be back there.'

'Yeah, and you were going to beat our brains out with a rifle butt,' said Chen. His hearing or his senses must have returned.

I turned and hobbled off down the passageway, yelling 'Come on!' over my shoulder. Chen and Le Seaux came after me.

I guessed from the number of doors along the passageway, that we were still a long way from the outside shuttles—and that meant a long way from freedom. The only way to reach the outer shuttles was to keep walking going, however long it took.

When I reached the far end of the passageway. I looked behind. Le Seaux must have changed her mind about following me. She and Chen had stayed behind again. Le Seaux was talking at him and shaking her head, looking at me, then looking back at where we had just been.

It's like a death wish with her, I thought. That was the power of the Accord. Freedom or slavery. She chose slavery.

I was about to go back and argue with them when a giant Goth appeared in the doorway at the passageway's far end. It was rabid with fury, snuffling the air. Then it dropped to all fours.

Le Seaux stopped talking and started running. Chen followed behind. The Goth charged after them.

I raised the rifle, resting it on the jam of the doorway and aimed in front of the creature to offset the speed it was traveling, just like yesterday. But this time Chen and Le Seaux were blocking my line of fire.

'Out of the way, Chen,' I said. 'OUT OF THE WAY!' I yelled.

Too late! The creature had swung a paw and knocked one of his legs, sending him skidding to the deck. Then it was on him, its claws slashing his chest.

I fired once, hitting the creature in the neck. It reared up. Now I could hit in the face, but the recoil from the first shot had knocked me several steps backward and I had to climb back to the door jam and aim again. Chen by this time was clutching his chest silently with red hands.

I put the bear wolf's head in the sights of the rifle and pulled the trigger. When I was able to stand up again and look, I could see the blast had hit its neck a second time. Not a great outcome, but it would do the trick. The monster was on its back, roaring and clutching its throat from which brown fluid sprayed all over Chen, mixing with the scarlet of his own blood.

'Is he OK?' said Le Seaux.

'He got slashed in the chest,' I said.

When we reached Chen, he hadn't gotten up.

'I was nearly dead back,' he panted.

'Sorry about that. My shot hit a little close to your head.'

'What shot?' he said. 'I meant the freak,' he said looking at the twitching mass of Goth. Then he said, 'You shot at me? Again?'

'Show me your wound,' I said.

We opened Chen's shirt. Three scarlet streaks crossed his chest, like a sash.

'Deep but not dangerous. No arteries hit. Can you run?'

We helped him to his feet.

'Something not right with my knee,' he said.

'That makes two of us,' I said.

Suddenly, a new sound was added to the swell of growls and fighting coming from the stateroom, the groaning of metal, as if the entire ship was complaining.

'What's happening?' said Le Seaux

'I don't know,' I said. 'Maybe we're moving again.'

Then, the pandemonium in the main hall spilled out into the passageway. More Goth bear-wolves. More Marines.

'Come on,' I said. 'Let's go.'

We limped to the passageway's end and I slammed the door closed and dogged it shut.

Another long passageway lay ahead. Fortunately, no-one and no creature was in it? But the loud metallic groaning persisted.

'So where to?' said Chen. Le Seaux remained silent.

'I think all the pieces of the ship can fly,' I said. 'It's part of the ship's defense tactics. If it's boarded, they can split it up, and isolate the fighting. I think that's what all this metallic scraping might be.'

'And you know that from your tour of the ship?' said Le Seaux.

'No,' I said. 'It's just a guess.'

'What else did you discover on your tour?'

'Like I told you,' I said. 'Octavia's plans. Invasion, destruction, enslavement.'

She shook her head. 'Once this Goth attack is ended, I'm going back.'

I ignored her and looked at the passageway.

It was similar to the one we'd arrived in the day before, the one that was like a brig. Same black slimy walls, same heavy doorways either side. Then, I checked on Chen.

'You OK there?'

'Do I look OK?' he answered. His shirt was soaked red and black.

'Hold on till we get into a shuttle. Then we'll take care of it.'

'You keep talking about when we're in a shuttle,' said Le Seaux. 'How will we get moving? How will you fly a shuttle? How will you even operate it let alone aim it at Earth? How will you land it when you get there? And how far is it to the outside of the ship? Based on yesterday's train ride, it's miles. It would take us a day to walk there, even if you and Chen weren't both injured. What about the air? Will it be breathable? And for all we know, we're right in the middle of the ship itself, as far as possible from its outer edges.'

'I know,' I said. 'I know. But if we don't try something, we'll just end right back in some game for Octavia's twisted pleasure. And the Accord will be powerless to help us. Or worse, I added, actually endorsing whatever Octavia demands. You saw how they've already arranged for Octavia to be at the Establishment Day.'

'It's what the Accord Commission wishes,' said Le Seaux

'And did you see the sign they made, authorizing me to kill you and Chen?'

'I don't believe it.'

'Well, you should. They were willing to sacrifice us in the name of tolerance. It just doesn't make any sense. They're supposed to protect us.'

'They were in a difficult situation,' said Le Seaux. 'What else could they do?'

'Hey!' shouted Chen.

We both looked at him, his shirt soaked in blood, his panicked face.

'Go back or get moving,' he said. 'As long as we do something.'

We moved off down the passageway and into a shuttle, almost identical to the one that had carried us to this hostile ship not twenty-four hours ago. It had the same hold and the same enormous whispering void.

'Now, where's the bridge in this thing?' I said.

'Well, it's not here in this hold area,' said Chen.

'You're assuming that it has a bridge,' said Le Seaux. 'You're also assuming we are on the outside of the main ship. Which, clearly, we cannot be.'

She had a point. In the rush, I hadn't thought

PROTOCOL

straight. The shuttle looked the same, but it couldn't be the same one. We must have been in a similar shuttle, still deep inside the mothership.

But then I looked at the screens above the exit to the passageway near the bow.

'Check out the screens,' I said. They showed a view of the main ship. The Goth ship hovered by the main ship's side, like a wasp feeding on fruit.

Le Seaux said, 'What else did Octavia say to you last night?'

'Wait!' I said. 'Look.'

On the screen, the bunch of grapes was splitting. The Romans were isolating the Goths and sending the other sections away from the fighting, just as I'd thought.

'This shuttle's not going to be on the inside for much longer,' I said.

'Then what?' said Chen.

'Then we can get out of here,' I said.

'How?' said Chen.

'One step at a time,' I said. 'We just have to find the controls to this thing. Then we can work on flying it.'

'No,' said Le Seaux shaking her head. 'This has all been a mistake. We have to go back as soon as we can. The mission is not complete. We haven't heard the response from our friends. We're just angering them.'

'You're joking,' I said. 'They were speaking loud and clear when they said they wanted to kill us.'

'Wanted *you* to kill us,' corrected Chen.

'Same thing,' I said.

'We have to go back,' said Le Seaux. 'For better or for worse.'

Suddenly, the port entrance began to close. A section of the hull rolled slowly and heavily down toward the deck.

I turned to face Le Seaux.

'Too late,' I said. 'They're now splitting this shuttle off too.'

'I'm going back,' said Le Seaux.

'They'll just kill you if you do.'

'I'm willing to take responsibilities for my ancestor's actions if that's what it takes to demonstrate our tolerance and keep the relationship alive.'

'Think about it,' I said. 'The ancestor stuff was just a trick to mess with us. They don't care. You'll be wasting your life.'

'I think you're wrong,' she said. 'In the interests of the Accord, I must show them I will pay for my ancestor's shame—as should we all. You, Chen, me. We're all guilty.'

'No, we're not,' I said. 'We don't have any shame. We didn't do anything. You weren't there when your ancestor hit that woman. Chen, you weren't there when your ancestor swung his axe. Shame is just one of the things the Accord tells us so that they can keep us in line and make us do what they want. For all we know our ancestors weren't the only ones oppressing the world. There must have been others and worse. There had to be.'

'What has happened to you, Burns?' Le Seaux said. 'Listen to the way you're talking. You've gone mad. A couple of hours with Octavia and you're willing to throw out centuries of experience and become a traitor.'

I shook my head. 'No,' I said. 'It's not that.'

'You think that all of a sudden, you actually know more than the Commission?'

I looked across at the port entrance. It was halfway

closed.

'Not more,' I said, turning back to Le Seaux. 'It's that I'm beginning to see them for what they are, what the Accord is. Yes, it might have something to do with Octavia. She told me some things about them that…I don't know. But I just know it won't do anyone any good to go back and let them kill or imprison us.'

Le Seaux said, 'I can't be part of this.'

She turned and walked towards the exit. I followed. I reached out and touched her shoulder. Touching an officer. Another Navy Spirit code violation.

Le Seaux looked in surprise at my hand. I withdrew it. Then she turned to face me.

'Don't go, Katherine,' I said. 'It's not worth it.'

She shook her head. 'I feel sorry for you, Burns.'

'If you knew what I knew, you'd feel sorry for everyone in the Accord.'

'You have lost your faith,' she said. 'If you don't have the Accord, what have you got?'

'I've got plenty. I've got the truth—at least a glimmer of it. The strange thing is that it's taken this idiotic situation with Octavia and these aliens to reveal it to me.'

She shook her head. 'I don't hate you, Burns.'

Then she looked at the exit. It was almost shut.

She turned away from me, dropped to her knees and ducked beneath it. Her cap was knocked off as she went. We saw her legs and her boots on the other side.

Then we heard heavy footsteps, terrible snarling and growling. Le Seaux's face appeared briefly beneath the descending edge of the panel.

'I'm not what you think I am,' she shouted.

Then she stood up. The snarls and growls grew

louder. She took several steps backward. A weapon blasted. Le Seaux's feet were knocked up and off the deck.

I dropped to my knees and slipped my fingers under the panel. It wouldn't stop. Then, I stood up and looked for controls, first on the left side of the port, then on the right. But there was nothing but the slimy, black interior of the hull.

'Is she alive?' asked Chen.

'I don't know.'

'You saw what happened?' he yelled. 'You saw, right?'

'Yeah,' I said. 'I saw.'

'Why don't you do something?'

'I'm trying,' I said, searching the black metal for a way to reopen the exit.

'She could be lying there in agony.'

'I'm looking!' I shouted.

'And if she's alive, she'll be a hostage.'

I ignored him and kept searching either side of the exit port, but before I could find a control or a button or a panel, I heard a great groan of metal and felt the shuttle lurch sideways, detaching itself from the mothership.

Part 3: The Mission (2)

PROTOCOL

'Equality of outcome is more important than equality of opportunity.'

Accord Of Nations Constitution

33

'Now what?' said Chen.

'I'm thinking,' I said.

'Oh great,' Chen said. 'Ten minutes ago you were going to fly this thing. Now you're thinking. What about Le Seaux?'

'Just give me a minute,' I said.

Chen shook his head over and over. 'I should have said no to this whole thing, like Okwanko.'

'They didn't tell you?'

'Tell me what?'

'Listen. It's possible this shuttle is being flown remotely from the mothership, but like I said, it must also have controls somewhere, a bridge, a helm. Something.'

'Where?'

'I don't know, but we've got to find it first.'

'Then what?'

'I don't know.'

'You don't know? What about Le Seaux?'

'Just shut up and help me look.'

The large screens over the entrance to the hold

displayed the great bulk of the mothership coming into view as we drifted away from it. Beneath the screens, lay the entranceway leading to the same passageway we'd entered the day before.

'Let's try down there,' I said.

Once we were back between the passageway's canyon-like walls, I said, 'Can you see anything that looks remotely like controls?'

'I'm no pilot,' said Chen.

'You don't need to be. It could be a button, a lever, a panel, anything that might open up a bridge or a cockpit. You know what a plane's cockpit looks like, right?'

'I do a certain amount of traveling, yes,' he conceded in the same voice he used whenever he talked about his businesses.

'Must be in the bow,' I said. 'Wouldn't make sense for it to be at the stern.'

'Unless it's outside,' said Chen. 'It might be on a turret outside.'

'Could be,' I said. 'These aliens are capable of anything.'

We stood in silence for a moment, as if waiting for Le Seaux to correct me for using the word 'aliens.'

'Let's split up,' I said.

Chen checked to the port, me to starboard. We move along, prodding and pressing the grey bulkheads, but no panel clicked open and no secret doorway swung wide.

And then, to make everything even more difficult, zero gravity returned.

'I forgot about this part,' said Chen.

'It won't matter,' I said. 'Might even help us.'

'How?'

'Look up there.'

Chen looked up to the top of the canyon that divided the two bulkheads. From the floor to the top must have been a hundred yards. And three-quarters of the way up, there was a small rectangle in the forward bulkhead, about the size of an elevator's double doors.

'Could be a doorway,' I said. 'Let's check it out.'

'Doorway or hatch?' said Chen. 'Which is it?'

'Hatches go between decks,' I said. 'They don't go through bulkheads.'

We swam upward, bouncing from one side to the other until we were thirty yards above the deck, floating like scuba divers above the seafloor.

'They better not switch the antigravity on,' said Chen. 'Or we'll hit the deck and splatter like turnip cakes.'

'See this,' I said pointing out a groove in the wall. 'It's an entrance of some kind.'

'Not a hatch?'

'No.'

'Maybe it's an emergency exit from the bridge.'

'Well, how do we open it?' he said bobbing in front of me, blood droplets from his shirt floating around him.

'The same we got the lights on?' I said. 'The Latin word for open. It's worth a shot.'

'So what's the word? Without Le Seaux, we don't even have the French to go on.'

'Can't be too hard,' I said. 'Try changing a few English words.'

'Like what?'

'Porto,' I tried.

Nothing happened.

'Well, that went well,' said Chen.

'What's another name for an opening or windows or doors?' I said.

Chen thought for a moment. 'Fenestration,' he said. 'That's a building term.'

'Got any more?'

'Aperture,' he said, 'like in photography.'

'Aperturo,' I said, and watched the seal.

No response.

I opened my mouth to speak another variation on aperto, when Chen said, 'Wait! What's going to be behind that panel if we do get it open? Shouldn't we have a plan?'

'No time,' I said.

'And shouldn't we be quiet?'

'Right,' I said, and then whispered, 'Aperta.'

We watched the panel. At first, nothing happened, so we both returned to thinking of more words. Then, while we both had our heads down, Chen's surrounded by floating blood droplets, the panel slid quietly open.

We swam to the entrance to look inside. The good news was that it was the cockpit all right. It had a large window with a view of the huge bulk of the mothership, splitting apart. Beneath the window was the cockpit itself. There were two seats and a simple set of controls: a screen displaying position, a helm and twelve or so other glowing buttons on a touch panel.

The bad news was that the cockpit was occupied. Inside, seated at the controls was a pilot. He was dressed in the same armor and helmet as the Roman Marines, though human sized, not one of the giants.

But, of course, that didn't mean he wouldn't be dangerous.

I looked at Chen, who looked back at me and shrugged. How were we going to get the pilot out?

I brought up the Roman weapon. The first way could be to point the weapon at him and order him out to where we could tie him up. The danger was that he might not comply. He might fight back.

The other way was to shoot him. But to shoot the weapon might disable the cockpit, smash the glass or pierce the hull.

A bad move.

Another way might be to float up on him and try to strangle him from behind, which might be possible, given we had the element of surprise, plus I had the rifle to jam under his throat and pull.

But could these aliens be strangled? They apparently didn't breathe air. Unfortunately for me and Chen, I had forgotten all about that important fact when we began to work out a plan.

'Know any fighting techniques?' I whispered.

Chen instantly made several poses that resembled a pre-Accord cop directing traffic—surrounded by blood drops.

So, I decided it had better be me who attacked the pilot.

Bringing the rifle up, I pushed myself from the far wall and floated into the cabin, towards the back of the solitary figure at the helm. I could hear voices speaking into the helmet, and see another smaller screen that displayed the chaos inside the mothership.

The pilot's neck was protected by his armor, but it didn't protect him all the way down to his armor. I

PROTOCOL

could see a band of skin. If I could wedge the rifle into there I'd be able to put my feet onto the back of his seat and pull until I crushed his windpipe—a good plan, so long as he had a windpipe.

I floated up behind, the rifle in both hands. I raised it slowly over the helmet, then brought it down quickly. As I did, I brought my feet forward and put them on the back of the chair. Then, I pulled back hard. The rifle barrel hit the pilot's neck. The neck compressed. The guy's hands instantly shot to his throat, wrenching at the weapon, struggling in his seat, gurgling, just as any breathing mammal would.

So far, so good.

After struggling for around thirty seconds, the pilot seemed to give up. His hands dropped from his throat. His body went limp. He looked just like he was dead, or at least passed out. I kept the pressure on his neck, but I was confident the plan had worked.

Job done.

But that's when things began to get strange.

The pilot's head rotated on top of his neck, like a cap on a bottle. Rotated smoothly, slowly, the whole one hundred and eighty degrees from looking forward at the control to looking back.

Still pulling on the rifle, I found myself face-to-face with the blank glass of the helmet's reflective front. This slowly withdrew upward onto the top of the helmet. What I saw beneath was not a grizzled soldier's face, and not even a monster's face. It was the face of a young woman, one so striking and beautiful that she too could have come from the pages of *Fashion In The Twentieth Century*. The sight of her stunned me into silence.

'Bad move, Lieutenant Burns,' the woman said in a flirtatious voice, revealing even teeth. Then she raised an arm, and, despite her body facing the cockpit's window, she swung a fist forward and punched me hard in the face.

Then, things got really bad.

34

I felt my nose squash sideways as I shot backward out of the cabin and into the passageway, hitting the bulkhead opposite, the rifle drifting from my hands as I clutched my face. Before I could grab the rifle again, the woman dived through the door with her hands out in front of her. Her fingers found my throat. Her thumbs dug into my Adam's apple.

Her head rotated back to a normal position, facing me.

'You don't really know anything about our physiology, do you?' she said, smiling, digging her thumbs in harder. 'Not one of the subjects you discussed last night, was it?' Her eyebrows rising as if she knew all about last night. 'No, don't try to speak, Alex. Just relax. This won't take long.'

Her thumbs dug deeper still, squashing my windpipe, making it impossible to breathe. Her eyes smiled as if this were immense fun for us both. 'Excidium,' she called, smiling her beautiful smile. A response came growling from the speaker inside her helmet. She responded in the same growling language, obviously bringing the main bridge up to date. Then she spoke back to me. 'Don't worry, Alex,' she said. 'It's going to be all right.'

One thing about being strangled: no matter how good a grip your assailant has on your neck, it can still be evaded—if you know the right technique. Though I'd never used the technique in a real fight, I knew it well from hand-to-hand combat training.

Step one: don't panic. Step 2: don't try and pull your attacker's wrists apart. You won't succeed. Step 3: Instead, pull violently down on the attacker's wrists and duck your head through them and then emerge on the side of your attacker's arms. Then hit them from behind.

With the beautiful face leering at me, I prepared to make the move. What I hadn't factored into the move was Chen. He must have caught the spinning rifle because he was now floating beside us, holding it at his hip. The woman saw the direction of my eyes and turned to look. She saw Chen and the weapon, floating to her right, like a pre-Accord cowboy and his gun.

'Let go,' Chen said.

'Won't be a moment,' said the woman. 'Then you'll have my full attention.'

'Last chance,' Chen said.

'One moment,' the woman sang.

'Too late,' said Chen.

With her hands still around my neck, the woman flung a kick at the rifle. Chen moved aside at the last second and her foot whistled past him.

'No, you don't,' Chen said, but he hadn't counted on the kick coming again. The gun muzzle was knocked aside.

'Yes,' the woman replied. 'Oh, yes, I do.'

Chen fired anyway.

The blast hit the woman in the side with a sickening splodge.

'Awooooh!' she screamed. 'Awooooooohhhhhhh!' Her hands were yanked from my neck, and she went spinning away, clutching her side, banging into one bulkhead, then another.

Meanwhile, Chen had been flung by the recoil to the other end of the passageway, sixty yards to port, as if pulled by an enormous spring. Luckily, he had managed to keep hold of the rifle. Now, he raised the muzzle ready to fire again.

'Chen, don't!' I croaked.

'What?' he said.

I pushed off the wall and swam towards him. The ship by this stage seemed to be accelerating again, so I kept bumping against the rear bulkhead. I half swam, half crawled. It took me a full minute to reach Chen. By that time, the beautiful assailant had recovered enough to swim after me, and had somehow recovered from the blast to her side.

'Chen, throw me the rifle,' I yelled.

He floated, blinking, his eyes staring, his mouth open.

'What's the matter with you?' I yelled.

'I shot a woman.'

'No,' I said. 'You shot someone impersonating one.'

'Pretty convincing,' he said.

'What's wrong with your arm?'

'I think it dislocated when I hit the wall.'

'Not your day.'

'No,' he said, and then, 'Not yours, either.'

I took the rifle from his good arm and turned to face the advancing, swimming form coming at us. I set the iron sights first on her head and then about six feet in front, just as I'd done with the charging Goths.

'Get out from behind me, Chen,' I said.

'We shouldn't fire on our hosts,' he said.

'Don't fail me, now,' I said. 'Get the hell out.'

He moved away, clutching his arm.

I pulled the trigger. The rifle fired. The muzzle jerked upward and the recoil threw me back into the bulkhead, spinning me like a spindle in a blender.

Chen was horrified at the blast's effect. 'You shot her,' he said.

I struggled in the air until I was upright again and facing down the passageway. At the far end, the woman floated, immobile. There were pieces of the helmet suspended around her.

'Shouldn't have done it,' Chen said. 'No matter what happens, she is still one of our hosts.'

'Wait here,' I croaked, my throat still recovering from those gauging fingers.

I pushed myself down the passageway, my nose stinging and swelling. I poked my head into the cockpit and checked out the screens. One screen showed the mothership in the distance. The other screen showed the battle still raging in the great hall. By the number of shaggy bodies strewn across the deck, the Goths were losing, yet again.

At the far end of the passageway, the beautiful woman floated lifelessly among the detritus of her helmet. Despite the terrible blast, her face looked undamaged. There was no blood.

'Is she dead?' said Chen.

'She might be,' I said, 'but I doubt it.'

'Oh, this is bad,' said Chen. 'We're in deep trouble. Trouble with the aliens, trouble with the Accord. This is going to be bad for everyone.'

'Who is to say it wasn't always going to be bad?' I said. 'Didn't you hear me when I said the aliens are going to invade us? Why should we just let them without fighting back?'

'Yes, I heard,' said Chen, 'But it's not for us to decide what to do. We don't speak for the whole planet. The Accord,' said Chen. 'It's for them to say what's right and wrong. They would never authorize an attack on our new allies. And we've gone ahead and shot their crew and stolen a ship, and started who knows what?'

I ignored him, and swam up to the woman, keeping the rifle aimed at her. When I was sure she wasn't moving, I grabbed her arm and pushed her downwards, then followed behind, swimming, pushing off the bulkheads, shoving her down in front of me until I could get her all the way to the deck. Chen followed behind, propelling himself one-armed, trailing blood.

At deck level, I pushed the body out into the void of the hold, shoving her along until I reached the thick, wide machinery straps on the starboard side.

'What are you doing?' said Chen.

'I don't think she can be stopped for long—or even damaged. So, we've got to tie her up before she comes at us again.'

'You don't think she can be damaged?'

'No, I don't. Does that make you feel better?'

'Not really. I still shot her. That's the same as killing

someone.'

'Let's just tie her up and lock her in here. We might need her as hostage for the flight back.'

'Right,' said Chen, but without conviction.

I found a small chain and used it to tie the woman's hands behind her back. Then I pressed her against the hull, and ran two of the big flat straps across her chest and her legs. Then, I used the winches to tighten them until she was strapped in hard.

'Think that'll hold her?' Chen was beside me. I turned and looked at him. His left hand cupped his right shoulder.

'I don't know,' I said. 'But we've got to get going. They'll be coming for us—and they won't be friendly.'

'No,' said Chen. 'Why would they be?'

I looked around. 'Where's the rifle?'

'Don't you have it?'

As Chen said this, the limp figure in the straps came alive. Her face was back to normal, as was her flawless skin, her fair hair, her beautiful smile.

'Too late, guys,' she said. 'You are guys, right? I mean, you are males, aren't you? From our study of Earth, the whole gender thing is not what it used to be back in the old days. You two could be anything.'

'Why is it too late?' I said.

'Look at the screen, handsome,' she said. 'Go on. Turn around and look. I'm not going anywhere. That's it. Hey, how tall are you anyway?'

I looked at the screens above the door. One of them displayed the great hall on the mothership. Goth bodies lay all over the deck in various states of ruin. Roman troops were reassembling in front of a single figure, whom I guessed was Drusilla.

I looked back at the woman. Now she had changed again. It was now another face that looked at us.

'It's Le Seaux!' said Chen. 'She's OK.'

'The correct pronouns is ze,' said the Le Seaux figure in the same accented English. 'Ze! Got it?'

'It's not Le Seaux,' I said.

'Give it up, Lieutenant Burns,' she said. 'Octavia's already sending one of the fighters after you. It'll be full of troops angry about what you just did to one of our hosts. Better to surrender now and get what mercy you can. Our friends, the galactic visitors told me they'll be understanding if you give yourselves up. They won't retaliate…much.'

'What the hell?' said Chen.

'Ignore her,' I said. 'Let's get up to the bridge and get out of here…if we can.'

'She's changed again,' said Chen. 'Look who it is.'

'I'll sign that consent form now Alex,' said the womanly voice of Octavia. 'Come closer, so I can reach you.'

'What's she talking about?' said Chen.

'Come on,' I said. 'We don't have time.'

We swam across the expanse of the hold, back to the passageway, checking out the screens as we floated by. Octavia—if that's who the woman was— had been right about the fighter. The screen displayed a small craft leaving the mothership. It was one of the black, teardrop-shaped vessels that had attacked Earth.

'I don't like the look of that,' said Chen.

As we were about to go through the door, a voice called after us.

'Alex,' it called. 'Alex, how can you do this to me? How can you do this?'

'Who is it this time?' said Chen.

'Just keep going.'

'But who's voice is it doing?'

'That's my mother,' I said.

'Your what?'

'Don't ask.'

We swam back into the passageway and upwards to the panel leading to the cockpit.

A monstrous, prolonged snarl followed us. A deep, angry, howl that filled the void and rattled the bulkheads.

'What was that?' said Chen.

'I don't know. Don't look. Don't go back.'

'Forty-eight hours until the Establishment Day celebrations, Alex,' snarled the voice. 'All those commissioners in one place. All your military commanders too. Millions of people watching around the world. It's going to be a real party.'

And then she laughed long and hard.

'Do you know the word to close this door?' I said, meaning the entrance to the hold.

'No idea,' Chen said. 'Fermero!' he said. 'Close!'

'Let's just get moving,' I said. 'We'll work it out later.'

'You're invited to the celebrations too, Alex!' snarled the voice. 'Make sure to wear your Service Dress Blue uniform. You look so good in it.'

'Don't listen. Keep going.'

As we swam up to the opening onto the bridge, a long, terrible wail pursued us from below.

'We're going to have to do something about that,' he said.

'What? Flush it into space?'

'I was thinking of helping her,' said Chen.

'No,' I said. 'Don't backslide on me now. We don't have time to help her, and anyway, I think she can heal herself. You saw what I saw, right?'

'So what do we do?'

I was beginning to lose patience with him.

'Let's just get to work on the controls.'

We collected the rifle and then swam into the cockpit. Then we settled ourselves into the seats and looked at the controls and the two screens. There wasn't a helm, a wheel, or even a joystick. One screen showed Drusilla ordering the Marines. The other showed the teardrop-shaped ship slowly gaining on us.

'Well?' said Chen. 'You're the pilot. What now?'

35

Chen and I sat looking at the controls.

He was silent, still stunned by the act of firing the weapon. He had lost his swagger. All the talk of making movies and his powerful friends in the Accord had vanished, replaced by a panicked silence.

He could see the terrible reality of our situation.

I left him to it and tried to focus on the next step: to get the shuttle moving.

'Well?' said Chen, after two minutes of watching me stare at the panels. 'Why aren't we moving?'

'We're still standing off from the mothership.'

'So?' said Chen.

'So, that means our friend down there was piloting this ship herself. It wasn't controlled by someone on the mothership.'

'That doesn't help.'

'Yes, it does,' I said.

'How?'

'If she can do it, we can do it.'

'Then what? We go for a drive around the moon?'

'No, we can give the shuttle another heading.'

'As simple as that?'

'I don't know yet.'

'What about Le Seaux?' Chen said. He was cradling his arm. The guy had a ripped chest and now a dislocated limb.

'We have to get this thing moving first.'

'And when we do, shouldn't we rescue her? We can't leave her back there, injured or captured.'

I knew this question would come. Should we try to rescue Le Seaux or continue the escape? It was the big decision of the minute, the one that would have the greatest impact, the one that could decide the fates of everyone involved—ours, Le Seaux's, and maybe those of the Accord and the Earth.

I put a hand to my forehead.

I went over the situation again.

Le Seaux was dead or captured.

If we returned to the ship, we would be killed or captured too.

No question.

On the other hand, if we could find a way to get back to Earth, we could raise the alarm. We could try to convince the Accord about the threat posed by Octavia.

Which would be virtually impossible.

And would probably mean imprisonment.

No, not probably. It was certain.

We were damned either way.

But what else could be done?

The teardrop-shaped ship was still there on the screen.

The Roman Marines were marching from the stateroom.

Decision time.

I drew a deep breath, exhaled. Repeated. Then I turned to Chen and said, 'What's the Latin word for Earth?'

'Earth?' said Chen. 'We're just going to leave? We're just going to leave Le Seaux?'

'Yes,' I said. 'Le Seaux is either dead or captured. We can't help her now.'

'You're not serious.'

'What's the Latin name for Earth? We saw it somewhere.'

'What's the matter with you?' said Chen. 'You've changed. I've only known you a day and you've gone from being a loyal Accord Navy guy to a deserter, and a traitor.'

He nursed his wounded arm.

'Listen, Chen, we don't have time. Le Seaux is dead. Got it? You saw the blast. And if we try to go back to that ship, we'll soon be in chains again with orders to beat each other's brains out. You see that don't you? We can help everyone more by getting back to Earth and telling the Accord what we know.'

'The Romans said we'd be shown mercy.'

'Just think up the damn word for Earth,' I shouted.

Chen said no more about Le Seaux. I think he was glad someone had made the terrible decision.

'Earth-o?' he said. 'Terra?' His voice was lackluster.

'No,' I said. 'That's not it.'

'Then, I've got no idea,' he said.

'I saw the name in that Latin book when we first arrived,' I said. 'There was a page in that book in the library. Remember?'

'I didn't see it,' said Chen.

'Think! What was it?'

'What's that thing doing on the screen?' said Chen, nodding at the teardrop-shaped fighter.

'Ignore it,' I said. 'What was the word written in the margin in the book?'

'I don't know.'

'Look over there,' I said nodding at the view of Earth from the window. 'Look at it. Maybe it will jog your memory. Look at the white clouds, the blue sea, the whole thing looking like a blue marble.'

'We're never going to get there,' said Chen.

'It was mentioned in the briefing as well, way back in the Affinity Room.'

'I don't know anything about it,' said Chen.

Then, I had a memory flash of the Commissioner from the Accord Space Agency.

'It's hyacinth,' I said. 'Like the flower. Hyacinth! I yelled at the screen. 'Hyacinth.'

'It fired something,' said Chen, looking at the screen on which the teardrop-shaped fighter loomed. A streak of blue raced in front of us. They had fired a shot across our bows. It was something my ancestor might have done.

My ancestor! Captain Alexander Burns of HMS Vengeance. Brave, stoic and capable. The thought of him cheered me up. And 'Deiseil a-riamh,' too, whatever it meant. I'd ask my ancestor when I saw him again—if I saw him again.

'Hyacinth!' I yelled. 'Hyacinth!'

'That's not it,' came a deep, menacing voice from down below. 'That's not it, Alex. You're wrong again.'

But the great shuttle moved anyway, rotating until the blue and white of Earth came up into the window, directly ahead.

'Maybe Hyacinth is it after all,' said Chen.
'Not maybe,' I said.
Then we were thrown back into our seats.

36

The shuttle accelerated towards the distant blue of Earth.

On the screens, the image of mothership slowly receded. Its separated hulls looked like a swarm of black beetles hovering behind the moon.

Ten minutes later, we had passed the moon itself.

Time for some housekeeping.

'Hold out your arm,' I said to Chen.

'What are you doing?' said Chen drawing back.

'I'm going to put it back into place.'

'No, you're not,' said Chen. 'I'll wait till we can see a doctor.'

'You might have to swim first,' I said. 'Or climb out of this thing, or fire the weapon. It's better if it's back in,' I said. 'Now hold it out.'

Chen stayed withdrawn in his seat, guarding his arm.

'Have you ever done it before?' he asked.

'No,' I said, 'but I've had it done to me. My shoulder popped during hand-to-hand combat training. The instructor put it back.'

He shook his head. 'No thanks. I'll take my chances.'

'I'm not doing it for you,' I said. 'I'm doing it for us both. Now hold out your arm.'

He blinked a few times and then slowly, wincing, extended his arm. I took hold of it with one hand and placed the other beneath his armpit, like an archer drawing a bow. I kept one finger pressed into his shoulder socket.

'There will be a lot of pain,' I said, 'then no pain.'

Then, I gently, but forcefully pulled on his arm.

'There's plenty of pain now,' Chen said, his face screwed up. 'I can feel the damn thing moving in the socket. Let it go.'

But I kept up the force. Chen's shoulders swiveled to avoid the pain.

'Wait!' he yelled. 'Please. Stop!' He pushed at me with his left hand.

But I kept on pulling.

And then, I felt the bone slide completely over and back again on the other side of what I hoped was the socket.

Chen unscrewed his eyes and blinked at me.

'Pain and then no pain, right?' I said.

He bent and unbent his elbow. Then he did it again. Like he was discovering it for the first time.

'Right,' he said. 'You bastard.'

'I wouldn't go hurling any javelins yet,' I said. 'The ligaments will be torn or stretched. Takes months to heal.'

'What about your nose?' he said. 'It's bent to the side.'

'I'll cope till we land,' I said.

'Octavia won't fancy you anymore.'

Maybe Chen's humor was returning.

'I'll live,' I said.

On the screens, the Earth grew, and the alien ship, the Excidium, receded further. The fighter stayed in pursuit but was unable to close the gap. Or chose not to.

'How long?' said Chen.

'How long did it take us to get to the alien ship in the first place?' I said.

'About an hour. But even if we make it,' said Chen. 'How are you going to slow us down? How will you stop us crashing into a mountain? Or a city of people?'

'One step at a time,' I said.

'That's it? One step at a time? That's your plan?'

'The ship docked itself on the way out. It'll land itself on the way back.'

'You're trusting this great flying cigar?'

'Do you have a better plan?'

'Ha, ha, ha, ha, ha, ha, ha.' came a deep-voiced laugh from down in the hold. 'You guys are gonna die.'

Both Chen and I sat silent for a moment.

The voice spoke again. 'But if you like, I can help you. Let me go. Untie me. I can pilot the ship safely down to Hyacinth for you. If you don't, you're going to die.'

Ten minutes passed, then twenty. The fighter followed us but kept its distance. Now the moon loomed in the rearview screen, growing smaller, the gray craters and mountains less distinct.

Meanwhile, the Earth grew larger, spinning in the sun. We saw the green tropics near the equator, the deserts of AONT Africa, the mountains in AONT Asia, the white polar caps, and the deep blue of the oceans and seas.

'The Himalayas look very sharp.'

'The what?' I said.

'It's what AONMR Derrida was called in the pre-Accord days.'

'How come you know so much about the pre-Accord era?' I said. 'How do you know so many commissioners?'

Chen shook his head over and over as if to answer this question was dangerous, or forbidden—probably both.

'If we make it back,' he said, 'I'll tell you.'

Five minutes later, when the Earth filled the view from the cockpit, the shuttle changed course. It flattened its approach, turning its nose from the dusty yellow of AONT Sahara, and pointing east towards southern bulge of AONT Asia. It looked as if we would be returning to the same general area from which we had left off the coast of AONT China.

And down we went.

The view soon filled with blue, white and green. We plunged into high cloud. Our weight returned, and we dropped down into the seats. The shuttle shook and the instruments on the control panel spun as the temperature soared on the hull. Tongues of flame licked at the window's edge.

'This is it,' said Chen, tightening his harness. 'We're either going to gently touch down, or we're going go out in a blaze of fire and black metal.'

Then, the problem I had been dreading but not daring to think about suddenly reared its frightening head.

'Brace yourselves for landing,' growled a dark voice

behind us. It wasn't coming from the hold. It was close by.

I turned and there it was: the full nightmare, right at the entrance to the cockpit. The Romans, the galactic visitors, did not really look like humans, of course. Now, here was the truth about their appearance—or one of their appearances. In the entranceway was a huge and horrible face. Beneath it was sinuous neck that must have been attached to a body so large that it stood all the way up from the deck way below.

'What's the word for close?' I yelled.

'I still don't know,' said Chen. 'Ferma, shut-o.'

'How about *muerte*?' said the deep voice, filling the cabin as if it were from a loudspeaker.

The clouds gave way to a clear view of the sea, grey and shining below. It would have been a marvelous, reassuring sight if there were not the problem of our approach speed. We had not slowed down. Nor had we flattened out. The shuttle was still traveling at an angle that would hit would the water nose first.

'Seal-o,' Chen said, hopelessly. 'Close-o.'

'Hang on,' said the horrible voice at the entrance.

I had the rifle in my hands. I loosened my harness, turned and aimed at the enormous head and the tentacle that now stretched inside.

'We're going to hit the sea!' yelled Chen.

'Thanks for the ride to the Accord of Nations, guys?' said the creature. 'I'll be making the world more diverse, and diversity is our strength, right?' And it, or she, or whatever it was laughed deeply and mockingly as if this escape of ours had all been part of a plan.

So, with the shuttle about to crash, I pulled the trigger. As the rifle fired and the recoil threw me into a backward twist, the whole craft decelerated rapidly, slamming us forward in our harnesses.

Then, as if it had misjudged its own approach speed, the shuttle, hit the water, bow first, and plunged down with an almighty crash.

The view through the window turned milk white and then dark green as we went under. Chen and I were slammed forward a second time, the harness straps cutting into our chests. The hull shrieked as the body of the ship caught up with the bow. The shrieks were followed by tearing as if every rivet and seal was pulled and stretched and twisted.

Then, with the nose deep under the surface, the shuttle rolled like an old crocodile. We rolled one way and then the other and then, slowly, painfully, the massive shuttle's nose surfaced and the entire vessel settled upright on the sea.

'Is that it?' gasped Chen.

'I don't know,' I said.

'Is that thing gone?'

I looked around. The entrance way was clear. But that didn't mean the creature wasn't waiting just out of sight.

'For now,' was all I could say.

'Are we safe?' said Chen.

'We're alive,' I said.

No sooner had I spoken when the shuttle began to complain all over again through a series of moans and terrible tearing. The bow began to tilt upward. The window filled with the sky and the clouds, which could only mean one thing: the shuttle was sinking. The hull had been breached and now the giant, empty hold was taking on water.

'Now what?' yelled Chen.

Warning alarms began to sound all over the shuttle, and a voice spoke something in Latin, over and over.

Chen was shouting, but I couldn't hear him. I was thinking about how we could get out. The ports in the hold and the passageway were out of the question. The creature was down there. Water would be flowing in. Plus there was a huge drop to reach the deck.

So I looked at another way out—from the cockpit itself.

But all I could see was black metal.

'Aperta!' I shouted over the alarms. 'Aperta!' I shouted again. Then, to my amazement, a crack appeared in the hull, then a wider crack. It was opening up. There was a hatch up there after all.

Fresh, salty air rushed in.

Against all odds, against all logic and good sense, we had made it back to Earth from a hostile alien warship.

But new troubles were just beginning.

37

Chen and I watched the hatch inch open. Earthly light and fresh air flowed in. The air was cool and salty. It was familiar and reassuring. We breathed deep and relaxed a little. Soon, we would be out of the shuttle. The Navy helicopters would show up, thumping over the water. They would take us to the nearest AONS.

And once there, I could warn senior command about the danger posed by Octavia—if they would listen.

But no sooner had we breathed the wonderful air when the escape hatch stalled. It got as far as six inches open and then stopped dead.

'Aperta!' I yelled.

Nothing.

'Aperta!'

The hatch didn't move.

'Don't tell me we've come all this way only to be trapped at the end,' said Chen.

'It's not over yet,' I said.

I reached up, got my hand on the edge of the hatch and pulled. Then I pulled again.

The hatch didn't move.

'At least we're floating,' Chen said.

As if it were listening in, the shuttle released a long and plaintive moan that started at a low tone, then rose in pitch, higher and higher. It was joined by other moans from other sections of the shuttle until there were three or four competing moans, a chorus of complaints.

'Feel that?' said Chen.

The shuttle's bow began to rise out of the water, swinging up until it was as high as forty-five degrees.

I pictured what would happen next on a vessel of this size. The water would rise in the hold, causing the ship's bow to swing from forty-five degrees to vertical. Then, the whole vessel would sink under the surface and begin the long descent toward the seafloor, which in this part of the AON China Sea was two miles down. The ship would fall through the dark stern first, possibly spinning, gathering speed until it hit the sand, or rock, or mud, embedding itself. The rest of the vessel would either concertina behind it, or, if this hull was especially strong, not bend at all, which meant the ship would rear up and then, after its kinetic energy was spent, settle slowly into the mud of the seafloor, to rest in the cold, silent dark.

Unless of course, the black material floated on water.

But that didn't seem likely.

I came out of my daydream of sinking ships, back into the world of the sirens and warnings in Latin, shouted over and over. The hatch was still closed. The bow was still tilting upward. And we were still trapped.

I picked up the alien rifle.

'What are you doing?' said Chen. He was crouching

on the back of his seat.

'I'm going to shoot out the window,' I said. 'Move to the back as far as you can.'

As Chen moved, I raised the rifle towards the window and the cloudy sky in its view.

Then, I put the rifle down again.

'What are you waiting for?' said Chen.

'I'm putting my shirt behind my head to stop the effects of the recoil.'

'Why don't you just put the stock against the wall?'

'Because the recoil will sling the muzzle off target,' I said, 'and fling the rifle into one of our faces.'

'Just don't miss,' said Chen.

'Cover your ears,' I replied.

Once it was ready. I lifted up the weapon and aimed at the middle of the window and pulled the trigger. The recoil was just as violent as ever. The rifle threw my shoulder and head back against the shirt and the wall.

I looked at the window. Nothing. Not even a crack.

Alien glass.

I fired again, twice. Boom. Boom!

As if responding, the ship began to complain and sink even faster. Water appeared at the back of the entrance way, bubbling up as clear as gin.

'Nice knowing you,' said Chen.

'It's not over yet,' I said. 'I've got another idea.'

I looked at the control panels. They were still glowing. Maybe they would still respond to commands.

'What are you doing?' said Chen.

'Roma!' I called.

'What are you doing?'

'Roma!' I called again.

'Don't,' said Chen.

The image on the cockpit screen altered. Until now, it had displayed a map of the Earth. Now, the display changed to a starfield. Then it zoomed through the stars, zeroing in on one single star, then a solar system, then on one green colored planet. Symbols like hieroglyphs flashed and then remained static. Then the ship began to shudder, like it was flexing its muscles against the sea.

And to our disbelief, the shuttle slowly began to rise. The fact that it moved at all seemed impossible. The weight of water inside the hold was almost unimaginable in a vessel this size, and yet, up we went, slowly and tremblingly. Metallic groans came deep beneath the water in the hold.

'Now what?' said Chen.

'One step at a time,' I said.

'Stop saying that. What are we going to do?'

'If the water level drops enough, we can get to the exit port on the side—the same one we entered into when we boarded from AONS Accord Values.'

'It's a sixty-yard drop from here.'

'Not when the ship's vertical,' I said. 'It's a two hundred foot slide.'

'What about you know who?' he said.

'Let's just hope for the best,' I said.

We both looked back down to the port. We could hear water sloshing around in the passageway. I moved to the edge and looked out and down. No monster. No water. Nothing but the wet bulkhead which was now horizontal, like a deck.

I slid back into the cockpit, grabbed the rifle and

came back to the entrance.

'I'll go first,' I said.

I moved out onto the bulkheads. Chen came after me, careful not to put weight on his injured arm. We crawled on hands and knees along the bulkhead towards the port.

Meanwhile, the ship groaned and complained as it rose upward, hauling its cargo of water.

'Hurry,' I said, 'Or, we'll be too high to jump.'

'Jump?'

'To the sea.'

I reached the port. Chen came up behind me.

'Aperta!' I shouted. 'Aperta! Aperta! Aperta!'

Nothing.

'Aperta!'

Nothing.

I looked at Chen, and shook my head. 'Worth a shot,' I said, 'But it looks like either the water or the crash landing broke it.'

'Maybe it responds a different word,' he said.

No sooner had Chen spoken when the ship shrieked yet another series of groans, creaks, and bangs.

'What now?' I said. The ship soon provided the answer. It began to right itself from its vertical position, lowering the bow down, back from ninety degrees, to sixty, to forty-five, thirty, until Chen and I had stepped from the bulkhead and back onto the passageway deck. It kept tilting down until it was nearly horizontal again.

Which was both good and bad.

Good because we were now on a familiar footing. Bad because all the water in that enormous hold now had to flow elsewhere, which meant it would come right forward into the passageway.

Which it began doing immediately.

It came sloshing in from the hold, slamming into the bulkheads, as if a dam had burst. It flowed out, either side, like a forked tongue, flooding the passageway. Within seconds the water was up to our knees and rising towards our waists.

And then, right on cue, the lights dimmed, plunging us into wet semi-darkness. I tried not to imagine our friend, the prisoner, suddenly rearing up out of it.

Chen said. 'Any second now, this thing is going to try and take off to Rome.'

'One last try,' I said. 'Aperta! Aperta! Aperta!'

And then, quietly and slowly, the port slid upward, rising from the deck, letting in fresh air and revealing a high view over the grey and swelling sea.

Why did the port decide this was the moment to start working again? Perhaps it had to be level in order to work. Maybe its microphone had been underwater.

Whatever the reason, it now worked.

And we were going to be safe after all.

But then, right on cue, the next problem showed up.

38

In fact, two problems showed up.

The first was that the surge of water brought our prisoner, the creature, sliding out from the hold and into the passageway. The second was that the water began to pour through the open port, like a river suddenly unblocked, pulling both Chen and me with it.

So far, so good.

Except, that by this point, the port had risen two hundred feet above the sea. This was about the same height above the water as The Diversity Bridge in AON sub-territory San Francisco, which was too high for anyone who fell from it to survive.

And so, down we plunged—down through the cool air, with the grey sea rushing up to meet us.

In Navy training, the technique for surviving a high fall was covered briefly in the short section devoted to seamanship, specifically, the section on abandoning a ship. This was before the training moved on to the more important subject of gender-neutral bathroom etiquette.

PROTOCOL

To maximize your chances of survival, the instructors told us, you had to enter the water feet first with elbows tucked in tight. You had to keep one hand covering but not holding your nose. You had to keep the other hand holding the first hand's wrist so that it wouldn't be yanked aside when you crashed into the water. Meanwhile, you also had to keep your eyes on the horizon so that your body would stay upright. You never looked down, or you would hit the water face first. Finally, you took a big breath and tried to stay perpendicular. And you hoped the water wasn't shallow.

All well and good, but I was falling sideways. As I fell, I looked back up at the shuttle, water flowing beside me. And I could see Chen way up there too, following me down.

'Feet first!' I yelled. Then, I flailed in the air, trying to get myself into the feet-first position myself. My nose stung as I placed a hand over it. The wind whistled in my ears as I fell down and down. At least, I told myself, I had gotten this far, and that with a bit of luck, I would survive.

Then, fear whispered to me. It said that even if I survived the fall, Chen might hit directly on top of me. Oh well, I thought. There was nothing I could do, except to aim to go as deep as possible after I hit, and then try to veer off once under the water.

Some seconds later, I hit the sea. It was like an explosion, not a splash—an explosion followed by a rip —as if I had torn the sea itself. Then I was going down, way down, through the layers of light and shade, into darkness and cold.

Then I stopped.

I took my hand from my nose and moved my legs. They responded. Everything moved. Everything worked. I swam away and up toward the light. I broke the surface, lungs screaming, and was immediately slapped in the face by a wave. When the coughing was over, I looked around.

'Chen!' I yelled. 'Chen!'

I scoured the water in every direction, through all three hundred and sixty degrees. I could see nothing but waves, one after the other, rolling over me.

'Chen!'

Nothing.

'Chen!'

Nothing.

'Raise your arm if you can't speak!'

Nothing.

And then a new danger now presented itself.

The shuttle, having heaved itself into the air in its attempt to return to planet Rome, had now stalled. I looked up. There it was, high above the sea, a great black, elongated shape against the blue sky, water streaming from the open port and from breeches in the stern.

Slowly, and then quickly, it lurched to port, dipped its bow, and began falling, like an enormous football thrown by a giant.

Right above me.

I turned and swam as fast as I could—AONT-Australian-crawl style. Seconds later I saw the huge shadow grow around me, expanding outward and thickening. I kept swimming.

And swimming.

Then I heard the enormous, groaning crash, the huge

splash and then the shriek of the hull buckling after impact.

I stopped swimming and turned around to look where the shuttle had fallen.

The shuttle had hit bow first with an almighty displacement of water.

At the same time, the water already inside the shuttle had been thrown violently to the point of impact, causing the entire structure to burst, breaking off three quarters along its length towards the stern, clipping it, like a giant cigar.

Then the great vessel began to fall slowly and heavily to its side. I already knew where it was going to hit.

Right on top me.

Was there no getting away from this thing? It was as if it bore me a grudge and would do anything possible to kill me.

Or could it be that the grudge is borne by someone controlling it?

With my lungs aching, I dove under the water once more, breaststroking down for all I was worth, down and down again, pushing against the ocean, which fought to push me upwards.

Yet again, a dark shadow surrounded me. I heard the crash above the water. Saw the shadow deepen. Saw black debris shoot past me into the gloom. Then, the light disappeared as the enormity of the shuttle settled above.

Would I ever be free of it?

Not yet.

The shuttle lay directly above me, sinking all over again, so I had to keep swimming underwater to get out from under it before it came rushing down at me, catching me and dragging me with it. With my lungs really starting to complain, I pushed through the watery twilight world until I was in the light again.

Only then did I dare let my lungs bring me to the surface.

I bobbed among the choppy waves, sucking in breaths of air, one after the other. The shuttle's mass lay wrecked and twisted twenty yards away, bubbling in the water like a kraken.

It was a terrible sight, but I was too concerned with breathing to be worried. No breaths of air ever tasted as sweet. I savored that air, made it my total focus. Just the air and nothing else. In and out. In and out. I didn't dare look around me in case another threat was waiting: falling debris, a jagged section of the hull, fire, the creature, anything. I just wanted a moment to get my breath. Then, I would take stock.

If I were being honest, I also felt something else, something new that I had never felt before. Despite the danger and the fiasco of our escape from the alien ship, I felt a strange satisfaction. One I'd never felt before. It was the satisfaction of doing something right, of fighting a good fight. Call it what you want. It felt right. It was liberating. Call it seeing the world for the first time. Call it finally obeying the small voice of conscience within. Call it getting a glimpse of the true world and its ways for the very first time.

Not the world as the Accord wished me to see it.

Once I had got my breath back, I gathered my wits. This wasn't easy. I was tired and disoriented. Possibly in shock. First things first, I told myself. One step at a time. The most important thing was to try and find

Chen. He had fallen from the shuttle behind me. So he must have hit the water behind me. But with his injured arm, bleeding wounds and inexperience, he probably hit badly. I gave his chances of survival from the fall a fifty-fifty probability. Then, his survival from the shuttle crashing down, another fifty-fifty chance, which meant a less than fifty percent chance of surviving overall.

'Chen!' I shouted.

Nothing.

'Chen!'

Nothing.

The ocean sucked the power from my voice. Each shout seemed to go no further than the next wave.

'CHEN!'

Nothing.

He could have been anywhere—the other side of the shuttle wreck or even inside it.

Or underneath it.

I swam towards the wreck's largest piece. There was flotsam everywhere, dark black pieces of the hull, chunks of decking and bulkhead shards were scattered for hundreds of yards. Maybe Chen was clinging to one of them and unable to answer or even to raise an arm.

I checked one piece, then another, and another. Hopeless. It would take me hours to check them all. If only the choppers would arrive. From above, they could see everything.

I stopped and listened for any distant thumping blades.

Nothing.

For the time being, it was going to be just me out

here, somewhere in the AON China Sea. Me, the sea, and the wreck of the alien shuttle.

Then, as if on cue, as if waiting its turn, yet another problem showed up.

39

It wasn't an immediate danger, but I thought it might soon become one.

I stopped swimming and checked my arms, face, and legs. They were still clothed in the blue NWU, but the cloth was torn and I was bleeding. There were cuts on my legs and my back. My squashed nose was bleeding too.

Another lesson from the Naval training about survival came back to me: even small amounts of blood in the sea can bring predators. The predators could sense blood from large distances. And the warm water in this sea was home to many species of shark.

Sharks, I thought. What next?

The sharks were probably already on their way, I thought. They had told all their friends that there was a feast to be had near the smashed black thing. I expected any second to see shadows circling beneath me.

Where was the alien rifle? Had I brought it with me when I jumped? Would it float? It would make mincemeat of any shark. One shot would obliterate even the largest maneater. If only I had the rifle! Maybe it was floating among the debris?

What was that noise? The slap of a fin?

But it wasn't a fin. It was a voice. It came from somewhere beyond the waves.

'Chen!' I called. 'Chen!'

'No, Lieutenant,' said the voice.

I turned around.

The creature from the shuttle?

No, it was a boat, a small blue dinghy, riding low in the water. From its stern, the flag of the Accord flew in the breeze—the dove and the rainbow.

A man wearing an orange life jacket leaned over the side. Then I saw a Navy diver in the water beside me, as dark as a seal. The diver came up so close, we were face to face. Her diving mask was pushed back to the top of her head. Her brow was creased, her mouth was turned down at the corners.

'Lieutenant Alexander Burns,' said the diver.

'What?'

'Lieutenant Alexander Burns?'

'Yes.'

'I'm Lieutenant Fran Navarro from the Accord Of Nations Naval Ship Accord Values.'

'Have you seen Chen—the other guy?'

'Did you understand me, Lieutenant?'

'Sure,' I said. 'Sure. Did you see the other guy who jumped? It's Chen from the mission to the Roman mothership. He jumped into the water at the same time as me.'

I had gone forty-eight hours with little or no sleep. Maybe my words were slurred and my actions strange. I couldn't make myself understood.

'Hey!' shouted the diver. 'Eyes on me and nowhere else! You look here, at me. Do you understand? Hey, I won't ask you again.'

I turned to face this bobbing piece of fury. 'Yes,' I said. 'I understand. Completely. But do you understand me? I'll say it slowly for you. There is someone else in the water, over there where the shuttle sank. It's Andrew Chen from the Roman mission. Understand?'

'Too late, Lieutenant. You just violated the Navy Spirit Code by disrespecting an officer.'

'What?' I said. 'You're worried about a stupid code when someone might be drowning!'

'A stupid code, Lieutenant?' said the diver. 'Is that what you said?'

I turned away from Lieutenant Navarro, and began swimming back towards the sinking shuttle.

Three strokes in and I felt the tranquilizer dart hit my shoulder.

Navarro was soon back in my face.

She said, 'You can think about how stupid the Code is in the brig, Lieutenant. You're going to have plenty of time.'

I was back in the world of the Accord.

Very definitely back.

40

'You're a mess,' Lieutenant Burns. 'A real mess.'

This was spoken by Alexander Burns, the elder, leaning on the quarterdeck taffrail of HMS Vengeance. 'An utter sight,' he said in his bizarre accent. 'Enough to frighten the birds away. What happened to your face? And to your legs? You're not steady on your feet. You look sick. Truly. Mr. Collins! Mr. Collins, there! Pass the word for the Doctor.'

When I awoke again, I was lying down. I knew I was still aboard HMS Vengeance but I was below decks, not in a cabin, but in an open area with other patients. The deck above me was very low. And despite sea air drifting in from somewhere, the atmosphere was fetid. It smelled of damp rope, burned flesh, and sweat.

'Can you talk?' said the ship's doctor or the man I thought was the doctor. He stood over me, looking down. He wore steel-rimmed spectacles, and a yellow wig, which was something I'd never seen before. He frowned at me. I blinked at him. Could I talk? I wasn't sure yet. I was in a daze, too worried about what had happened over the last twenty-four hours, and also about what would happen next.

And what I could do about it.

I'd had an adventure, traveling to the Roman ship, fighting Goths, drawing the unearned obsession of a powerful alien beauty, causing the death of Le Seaux, causing the death of my mother, possibly of Chen too, and, through my recklessness I had given Octavia the pretext she wanted to launch an attack on Earth, presumably at the Establishment Day ceremony in two days' time.

It had been an adventure with terrible consequences.

Another face joined that of the doctor. The second face belonged to a younger man with brown hair and a beard. The doctor's assistant maybe. Both wore white shirts with handkerchiefs around their necks. They didn't look very navy-like. They didn't look very medical either.

'He's blinking,' said the younger face. 'That's something.'

'Leave him rest while we see to the others,' said the doctor. The faces withdrew.

What was I going to do? Part of me wanted to stay here on the Vengeance where no-one could find me. I could heal my wounds and join my ancestor's crew. I could learn real sailing skills and fighting tactics. It would be a new start, and a life at sea, the way I always wanted. But of course, this was all a daydream, a literal daydream, and my plan was a coward's plan.

I thought about what would be happening back in the AONE. My real self would be in the hospital brig on board AONS Accord Values, drugged with sedatives and who knew what other pills. When I woke up there would be a debriefing into all that had happened. There would be an inquiry too. There would be a court-martial. And, despite my warnings about Octavia and the Excidium, the Navy's leaders would ignore them.

Then I would be humiliated in front of the jeering mob at the morning anthem recital and sent to Naval prison somewhere out of the way, where I could never cause trouble again.

And in the meantime, the Accord Commissioners and their defense forces would sleepwalk into an invasion. No, not sleepwalk. They would welcome the invaders—welcome them in the names of tolerance and diversity. That's what the Accord philosophy was all about. In the Accord's way of thinking, there were no enemies except for homophobia, toxic masculinity, climate change denial, and the pre-Accord West's ideas of courage, self-reliance, science, markets, the family, and persistence.

So the Earth and its people would be enslaved without so much as a whimper of resistance.

There must be something I could do to stop it.

The two faces were back. A third face was there as well. It belonged to the famous Mr. Collins from the quarterdeck. I could see his blue coat. He held his hat under one arm.

'Well, Dr Bradall?' he said.

'He hasn't said anything since he opened his eyes,' grim-faced Dr Bradall replied.

'Nothing at all?'

'Nothing. However, I believe he is aware of his surroundings. As you see, he's following our conversation with his eyes. He's conscious. Can you hear me, Lieutenant Burns?'

'Yes,' I said. 'I can hear you.' My voice sounded slurred.

The Doctor looked at his assistant and Mr. Collins. Then, he looked back at me. 'Any pain, Lieutenant Burns? Pain?'

'No,' I said. 'I am very tired. Am I drugged?'

'What did you say?'

'Drugged,' I said. 'I was drugged.'

Dr. Bradall turned to Mr. Collins. 'Did you understand that?'

'I think he said he was drugged.'

'You were drugged, you say, Lieutenant?'

'Yes.'

'The Captain would like to see him,' said Mr. Collins.

'The Captain would like to speak to you, Lieutenant Burns, when you're up to it.'

Good, I thought, because I certainly wanted to speak to the Captain.

41

The day passed. The deck above me thrummed with the crew's bare feet as they changed each watch. The ship's bell tolled. Night came. The lamps were lit. And HMS Vengeance sailed on.

And suddenly, I was awake.

With my fellow patients snoring either side, I slid from my bunk and stood up. My legs were stiff and sore. I had a thumping headache, but I could breathe through my nose.

I walked to the nearest ladder, climbed through the hatch to the next deck. Then I climbed out onto the top deck itself and limped unsteadily under the great sails towards the stern and quarterdeck.

I was immediately intercepted by a young midshipman. He was dressed as Mr. Collins had been in a giant Navy coat and a cylindrical hat. He was startled by the sight of me, by my modern camouflage uniform, but his sense of duty forced him to confront me.

'Only officers may walk the quarterdeck,' he said.

'It's all right, Maitland,' said my ancestor's voice.

'Ask Lieutenant Burns to come up.'

Lieutenant Maitland stepped aside and I climbed onto the quarterdeck's hallowed boards.

'How are you feeling?' said Captain Alexander Burns.

'I've felt better,' I said.

The bell tolled twice down on the deck. Then there was a pause followed by two more tolls.

'Four bells,' my ancestor said. 'Four bells in the morning watch. That's six in the morning if you're wondering.'

'What did you do to Octavia?' I asked. I said it just like that. I didn't feel the need to play cat and mouse games. Not anymore. If my ancestor could see things in the future, then he could answer a direct question. By his reaction, I had caught him by surprise. He stood to his full height, all six feet four, which in that blue great coat was an imposing sight.

'That's not the tone to use when addressing a post-captain in His Majesty's Navy,' he said.

'My apologies,' I said. 'Things have changed since we last spoke.'

'So it seems.'

'And four bells in the morning watch is when our encounter ended last time. I might have only a few minutes. So, please, Captain, spare me a moment of your time.'

He turned to his right. 'Mr. Maitland.'

'Sir?' said Maitland.

'Step to the fo'c's'le to see if Skerrick has repaired the jib boom.'

'The jib boom is already repaired, sir.'

'Well, go and make sure that the repairs are holding.'

'Aye, sir.'

When Maitland had clattered away, the older Burns said, 'Now, then, Lieutenant.'

I said, 'I will make this as brief as I can. Back in the Accord Era, I am being held in a ship's brig for a list of charges over what happened when I met Octavia, the woman you referred to last time. She, Octavia, is preparing to invade Earth from her vessel, the Excidium and its fleet of ships, supported by hundreds of thousands of heavily armed Marines. Meanwhile, the Accord leaders believe she is a friendly ally. They have even invited Octavia and her senior officers to attend a ceremony on Earth tomorrow, which is when I think she'll begin to invade.'

'Anything else?'

'Yes, not that it ranks in terms of importance, but she is obsessed with me. Dangerously, irrationally obsessed to the point of endangering her own crew.'

'But?' he said, as if he already knew everything, and just wanted me to say it.

'She says her obsession is because of you. She says she met you hundreds of years before in this era, and that you broke her heart. She can't forgive you.'

He looked up into the night. He wasn't smiling. Maybe he was thinking how inappropriate it seemed to use a phrase such as broken heart on a warship.

'She doesn't have a heart,' he said. 'Not a woman's heart. Though she certainly appears to be a woman. There can be no doubt about that, as I'm sure you observed for yourself.'

'I would ask you what you did to make her so obsessed,' I said, 'but I don't think I have time. My question is, that knowing what you know about her, what should I do?'

'It seems you have done plenty already,' he said.

'I've triggered an invasion, if that's what you mean.'

'It was going to happen anyway,' he said. 'You are simply the excuse.'

'That's what I thought.'

'And this Accord will crush anyone who goes against its foolish ideology, the one that has made your military so weak, and convinced the world to distrust its own eyes and ears.'

'Yes,' I said. 'I am beginning to see that.'

'A great crime,' said Captain Burns.

'Yes, but I have to convince them to act or at least to see the truth before Octavia sweeps in unopposed.'

'Then, you already know what you must do.'

'But I'm just one guy,' I said. 'And I'm in prison.'

'Then do nothing,' he said. 'Easier that way. Events will happen with you or without you. You'll be no worse than anyone else in your Accord.'

Suddenly a voice shouted from the darkness above. 'Sail ho!'

'Where away?' called Maitland's voice from the deck.

'Port bow, hull down,' called the voice.

'That will be the Indomitable,' said my ancestor. He looked at me, excitement in his eyes. 'We have found her.'

'But it's still night,' I said. 'How can the lookout see?'

'It's not dark up there,' said my ancestor. 'He can see the dawn while we are still in the dark.'

There was a clatter on the stairs. Mr. Collins appeared, removed his hat and saluted.

'Sir, should we beat to quarters?' he said.

'Yes, Mr. Collins. Beat to quarters.'

'Aye, sir,' and he clattered down again. 'Beat to quarters!' he yelled. Instantly the ship came alive. Whistles sounded, a drum began to pound, hundreds of feet began thrumming up the ladders.

My ancestor turned to me.

'Stay for the battle,' he said. 'I'll enter you into the ship's register. You'll be rated as a midshipman.'

It was tempting. This world, the pre-Accord world seemed so much better than the Accord of Nations Era. There was so much I didn't know about it and so much I wanted to find out.

A golden glow appeared on the fringes of the horizon. I turned and looked to the port bow. There it was in the distance. The sails of a mighty ship of war blazing white in the sun.

I turned back to Captain Alexander Burns. He was looking at me. 'You'll find a way,' he said. You're a Burns.'

'What's the meaning of "Deiseil a-riamh?"' I said.

'It's the Burns family motto.'

'What's it mean?'

'It means "ever ready."'

'Ever ready for what?'

'Ever ready for anything important, for the hunt, for the rising tide, and for battle.'

'And what is the meaning of Excidium?'

'Now you're testing me on Latin words?'

'Do you speak it?'

'I learned it. Everyone does…in this era. The Romans and their achievements are studied as an example of how a nation should be governed. You have never heard about them?'

'It's forbidden to read pre-Accord history, especially

any history from Eurabia.'

'Now why would that be?'

'They say it's for our safety, but now I know why,' I said. 'It's because to know the past is to understand the future—and it would reveal all the Accord's lies.'

'A great pity to have lost so much,' he said.

'And the word excidium—what does it mean?'

He drew a long slow breath, exhaled and said, 'It means destruction.'

'Destruction?'

'Hey!' someone shouted.

A strong hand was tugging at my sleeve.

'Get up, Burns,' a voice said. The accent wasn't my ancestor's, nor the curious accents of the crew on his ship. It was a modern voice with an accent from the Accord Of Nations, territory USA.

'What?' I said. I was still in the grip of the dream. I was still there on the swaying quarterdeck of HMS Vengeance, wanting to know more about the pre-Accord era. Needing to find out all I could before I returned.

Then, suddenly, I wasn't there anymore.

'What's up?' I croaked.

'They want to see you.'

Two large shapes stood over me—not kindly Dr. Bradall and his assistant, but huge bulky types with Navy MA patches on their chests.

'Who does?'

'Now, Burns.'

'Give me a minute to wash up,' I said. 'It's the tolerant thing to do. And we're all about tolerance, right?'

'I said now, Burns. Get up or we'll kick you up.'

42

The two of them smelled of detergent, a bubblegum scent. They were practically bursting out of their shirtsleeves, like uniformed mastiffs. One name patch read Yiu; the other read Gupta.

'On your feet, Lieutenant.'

'What's happened?' I said. 'The invasion?'

'Shut it,' said the one called Gupta.

'Octavia?'

'Hey!' said the guard named Yiu. 'We said shut it.'

I got slowly to my feet, checked myself for injuries. There was a large white bandage across my nose. My ribs, arms, and legs all complained.

'Let's go,' said Gupta.

There were handcuffs hanging from Gupta's belt, but they remained there as the two MAs each took an arm and shoved me towards the door.

We walked down a passageway, climbed to the next deck and then to another set of stairs and up until we were level with the bridge itself. Then they shoved me into a cabin on the ship's starboard side and told me to wait.

The cabin had a large conference table and several chairs. There was a TV screen at one end. On the starboard side was a view to the deck where crew members fussed around the ranks of Slingshot aircraft or assembled for the morning anthem.

'Sit there and keep quiet,' said Yiu. The two guards left, locking the door behind them.

I was well and truly back in the world of the Accord and its Navy.

A few minutes passed. The door burst open. Yiu barged in, glared at me and then stood to one side. 'Atten…shun!' he or she barked.

I got to my feet. In came Admiral Zhou, Captain Paine, and Captain Odilli of Navy Spirit. They were followed by a guy wearing an Accord smock and two uniformed ensigns.

Apart from the guy in the smock, everyone appeared to identify as female.

I saluted as they sat down and arranged their papers. The two MAs, Gupta and Yiu, remained either side of the door, glowering. One of them, I noticed, held the Roman rifle beside his or her leg. A small tag hung from its trigger guard, and a plastic safety brace had been fitted to prevent its use.

I looked at the angry faces of Captain Paine and Admiral Zhou, and the even angrier face of Captain Odilli.

'Captain Paine, Admiral Zhou,' I said. They looked up at me. Both of them looked angry but I carried on. 'We have to talk about the Romans. They're…'

'Silence when you're in the presence of officers,' shouted Captain Odilli. Her voice was so loud, it rang on the room's metal walls.

Everyone took their seats. Then, the inevitable happened.

'Lieutenant Burns,' said Captain Paine, 'exactly what do you think you are doing?'

'Captain?' I said.

'Don't mess us around, Burns. We've heard all about it from our galactic allies.'

'Stealing a shuttle, stealing a weapon, firing at Roman Marines,' said Admiral Zhou.

'Participating in a foreign war,' said Captain Paine.

'Returning to Earth without orders,' said Admiral Zhou.

'Stealing a spacecraft from our allies and crashing it,' said Captain Paine.

'Endangering the lives of Captain Le Seaux and Andrew Chen,' said Captain Odilli.

'You mean Le Seaux and Chen are alive?' I said. 'Is my mother alive? Octavia sent a beam at her house.'

'Shut it, Burns,' said Captain Paine. 'We are still reading your many charges. We haven't mentioned the Navy Spirit Code violations regarding xenophobia, mansplaining, deliberate misuse of pronouns and misogyny. We'll get to those in a minute. First, we want to be fair. We want to give you a chance to explain yourself, which is far more than you deserve.'

'Well, Burns? Can you explain yourself?' said Admiral Zhou.

I cleared my throat. Took a breath. Told myself to calm down and speak slowly and deliberately, not like the madman I must I appear to be.

'Captain Paine, Admiral Zhou, sir, and samma,' I said, ignoring Odilli, 'the Romans are not what they seem.'

'No?' said Captain Paine. 'What are they?'

'They pretend to be friendly visitors, but they are in fact a hostile force, sirra. They aren't here to make friends. They are planning an invasion. You've seen the size of their ship. You saw how they acted regarding Blairia and Le Seaux and Chen. Those weren't the customs of their people. They were a display of force, and a test to see how we would respond. Their actual fighting force is large. Hundreds of thousands of Marines.'

'And what evidence do you have that they will invade us?' said Admiral Zhou, one eyebrow raised in derision. I ignored and pressed on.

'I heard it from Admiral Octavia herself. She told me they are here to invade. She said she was relying on our values of tolerance to invade unopposed. That is why we must get our defenses ready or it will be a complete walkover.'

'You heard it from Admiral Octavia herself?'

'Yes.'

'You're quite sure about that, Burns?' said Admiral Zhou.

'Yes, samma.'

She turned to one of the ensigns.

'Play the transmission.'

The adjutant pressed some handheld device and the TV screen came alive. After a few seconds, it showed Le Seaux. She was standing with Captain Drusilla and some of the officers. They were waving and smiling like old friends—as if nothing was wrong. 'We'll see you tomorrow in Hong Kong for the big day,' said Le Seaux, meaning today.

'We are really looking forward to it,' said Drusilla.

'Thank you for inviting us.'

'Best wishes to Lieutenant Burns. We hope he got back OK.'

They all smiled as the image on the screen faded to black.

Everyone in the room turned to face me. Paine. Zhou. Odilli. The smock guy. The two ensigns. Gupta and Yiu.

'Well?' said Captain Paine.

This was not going well.

'It's a trick.' I said. 'A trick to bring the full force of their weapons and army right into our midst unopposed, and right when the Accord Commissioners and senior military people will be in the one place for the Establishment Day ceremony.'

'Really?'

'Yes, sirra. Really.'

'You think Le Seaux's being forced to play along?' said Admiral Zhou. 'Is that what you're saying, Burns? Our allies are forcing Le Seaux to smile and wave for the camera, but there's really a gun being pointed at her, just out of the frame? Is that what you're saying?'

Outside, the Accord anthem began to play. The sailors on the deck sang the words. 'Equality of outcome; Accord values for all; Nations without borders; The patriarchy must fall.'

'That person in the video is not Le Seaux, I said. When Chen and I escaped, Le Seaux had been shot by a Roman Marine. The blast knocked her off her feet. We saw her fall.'

'Did you see her die?'

'I didn't need to. No-one, no human could survive a blast from one of those weapons.'

'Of course,' said Captain Paine. 'Because you fired one of those weapons several times, didn't you? Illegally and against Captain Le Seaux's orders. Ze told us, Burns.'

'Sirra, the Romans have the ability to change their size and appearances. Chen and I saw it on the ship on the way back. The pilot we captured changed into Le Seaux's form and even to Admiral Octavia's. It might have actually been Admiral Octavia.'

'The same Le Seaux who just appeared in the video?'

'Yes,' I said. 'I know how that sounds, but yes.'

'And then you fired your unauthorized shots from a stolen weapon.'

'We were attacked,' I said. 'It attacked us.'

'"It!"' said Captain Odilli raising her hands in exasperation. 'That person has a preferred pronoun, Burns.'

'All right, Kayla,' said Admiral Zhou. 'I think Lieutenant Burns understands the charges. And I think we have heard enough.' She turned to me. 'Lieutenant, you have been given every opportunity that the Accord and its Navy can afford a straight male. You have taken those opportunities and misused them in the worst possible ways, especially by abusing the hospitality of our new galactic friends, and in the process you have almost ruined the great achievement we are about to make for intra galactic diversity.'

'Hear, hear,' said Captain Odilli.

'You mean, you're not going to do anything?' I said.

Odilli's face quivered with rage.

'Intra-galactic tolerance. Intra-galactic equality. Intra-galactic diversity,' she bellowed, hurling the words at me as if they were weapons.

I stared back at her. 'Diversity, Captain, is not always a strength.'

As soon as I had spoken, I sensed a change in the atmosphere. The world seemed to skip a heartbeat. The room came to a total silence. The faces of Admiral Zhou, Captain Paine, Captain Odilli, Yiu, Gupta, and the Accord emissary in the unisex smock—all of them looked as if they had just been slapped, and slapped hard.

I looked from one outraged face to the next.

This was not going to end well.

43

'What did you say?' said Admiral Zhou.

'Diversity is not always a strength,' I said.

'Say it again, Burns. I don't think the world heard you.'

'Not when the people you're inviting don't share the same values it isn't. It's a weakness. Our weakness. These galactic visitors are our enemies. They want to invade us, to enslave us. Surely you can see that in this case diversity is not a strength. This kind of diversity is making us participate in our own destruction. Same with tolerance. You can't tolerate the intolerable. But you and the Accord are so used to throwing these phrases at people to silence them that you don't question them anymore. You heard Admiral Octavia's reaction. She said…'

Admiral Zhou was on her feet.

'We've heard enough. More than enough. I don't know what happened to you, Burns, to turn you into a misogynist, a xenophobe and a racist, but we are not going to tolerate it in this cabin, on this ship, or in the Accord. Diversity is a strength. That's an axiom, Burns.

MM HOLT

It's never *not* true.'

'Hear, hear,' said Captain Odilli.

'Well said, samma,' said Captain Paine.

The two ensigns and the smocked Accord representatives were nodding to each other.

'And you'll be saying it as the aliens burn our cities,' I said.

Admiral Zhou's righteous indignation gained new strength.

'One more word, Burns, and I'll have you gagged. Our galactic friends will be in AON sub territory Hong Kong today as our guests. They will join us as we mark the founding of the Accord and celebrate the values of tolerance, equality, and diversity. And while we are conducting these celebrations, Burns, we don't want you around, not even as a prisoner, not even as a memory. Not in any presence at all. You will be transported immediately to AONS Schumer on AONT USA and incarcerated there until your court-martial, which I can assure you will be thorough. Then your Navy career will be over, and your civilian existence will be over too. The world will no longer have to tolerate you.'

'Not even for reasons of diversity?' I said. 'Diversity of opinion. Diversity of thought?'

She looked at me with eyebrows raised, shaking her head left and right, disgusted. 'Is that it?'

'Just one thing more, Admiral'

'Admiral, I think we've heard enough,' said Odilli.

I spoke over the top of her.

'The Roman pilot aboard the shuttle, Admiral—her, she or it, might have survived the crash. If it did, Admiral, we should be on alert because…'

'We don't want to hear it, Burns,' said Captain Paine. 'Not one word of it.' She looked over at Gupta and Yiu by the door, who unfolded their arms and hulked towards to me. Gupta reached behind his back and brought out the handcuffs, and took the first few steps towards me.

And that's when I heard the first bang.

It wasn't an explosion. It was like a heavy metal object being thrown against another object.

Over the edge of the window, the bodies of several crew members flew like rag dolls. One actually hit the window with a sickening bang and left a smear of grease and blood. At the same moment, the entire ship pitched forward as if it had plunged over a wave and into a deep trough.

'What's going on?' said Captain Paine.

'I told you already,' I said.

'Told us what?'

'It's the creature that was on the shuttle with Chen and me.'

'You just want to keep adding to your charges, don't you Burns,' said Odilli.

I came to a decision. The only one I could make, really. I could go quietly, or I could speak the words that had been lurking in my mind my whole adult life. Then, I could do my best to get out.

'What can I expect,' I said, 'from a military and a whole government so deluded by its own ideology that it can no longer believe its own eyes and ears?'

'What?' Captain Odilli screamed. 'What did you say?' she yelled. 'What did you just say to me?'

Then she actually stood and slapped me. The thick palm landed across my face, squashing my nose for the second time in two days, but I wasn't going to let her see me as much as a flinch.

'I see who you are,' I said. 'I see all of you and I know what you want.' Odilli, Paine, Zhou, the smock guy from the Accord—all stood watching, their faces stunned, watching the maniac, Burns, speak the unspeakable heresies. Even the two guards, Gupta and Yiu froze. 'You want power and nothing more. You don't really believe all this nonsense. Not really. No-one can believe if they think about it.'

'Sergeant,' Odilli said. 'Now.'

Gupta and Yiu unfolded their arms. Smiles appeared on both their faces. I knew they were going to enjoy bouncing me around. I also knew this might be my last chance to do something about Octavia. Better to die on your feet, I thought, than to live in prison on your knees.

I turned to Captain Odilli.

'Get out of my face!' I said.

And then I broke the worst of the Navy Spirit Code violations. I stood up to my full height, raised my hands, put one palm against Odilli's astonished face, the other on her shoulder, and shoved her backward into the advancing bulk of Yiu and Gupta.

44

I'd crossed a line. No, not just crossed it. I'd jumped over the line and then turned around and spat on it.

Shoving Odilli was an unthinkable act. No-one ever touched a woman, even if the woman was biologically a man. To do so meant an instant sexual harassment charge. But that's what I did. I shoved Captain Odilli backward—not hard enough to cause harm, and careful where I put my hands, but hard enough to knock him/her/it off his/her/its feet.

The shove put Yiu and Gupta into confusion. They had to catch Odilli; but at the same time, they knew they couldn't touch her either. What to do? They chose to catch her, which created just the distraction I needed. I stepped around them, yanking out Gupta's handcuffs from his belt, and headed for the door.

Ten feet from it, Captain Paine was already standing up, moving to block me. I didn't dislike Captain Paine, but I wasn't going to be stopped by zee.

'Don't even think about it, Burns.'

'Too late, Captain,' I said and carefully grabbed her by the shoulders. They were surprisingly narrow. No doubt about it, she was still a female underneath all the talk. I expected a knee in the groin or a claw to the face, but instead, she went rigid, like a plank. Her mouth was stuck in the shape of a wide ellipse as I swung her around into the advancing form of Yiu, who had rested Captain Odilli back in her seat, and was now coming after me.

I could hardly believe what I was doing. Captain Paine struggled, but there was no way zee was getting out of my grip.

'Sorry, Captain,' I heard Yiu say as he put out his hands to prevent avoid another collision.

With Yiu's hands full of Captain Paine, I stepped the final ten feet to the door. Now the smocked emissary from the Accord Commission made his move to stop me. Like Paine, he stepped in front and stood in the way, but he was yet another guy without a clue how to fight. And he was barely as tall as my shoulders, and almost as thin as Captain Paine. I slapped aside his pathetic outstretched arms and flung him behind me. I heard his pathetic, outraged shout of 'Hey!' as he fell.

'The weapon!' called Admiral Zhou. 'Stop him getting the weapon!'

Too late. I grabbed the Roman rifle where it leaned against the bulkhead. It felt even stranger than I remembered, with its swirling metal carvings and weight.

At the same time, it felt reassuring to have it my hands again. What a weapon it was! What damage it could do! How foolish they were to bring it to this hearing. But that was the Navy all over. It had cowed the people so much they didn't know what proper security was anymore.

But not me. I was getting away. I pulled open the door and then pulled it shut before Gupta reached it from the inside. Then, I looked for a way to clamp the handcuffs on the handle to stop it from opening. No chance. The bulkhead beside it was smooth. There was nothing on which to clamp the cuffs—nothing but a sign that read, 'Remember the four Ps. Proper Preferred Pronouns make a Perfect voyage.'

So, I raised a boot and shoved on the door so that it crushed Gupta's grasping hands. 'Owww!' he yelled. 'Hey! Come on! Stop the violence.'

'You stop the violence,' I said.

I put the handcuffs in my pocket and rushed up the passageway, carrying the rifle.

I had to get to the main deck and to the rows of Slingshots. If I could just get to Hong Kong before they began…

Yes, but what would I do when I got there?

That was about as much as I had thought through my plan. Get a Slingshot. Get to Hong Kong. Find out where the Establishment Day ceremony would take place. Take it from there.

But what about the commotion on the main deck?

The ship had come alive. Crew surged along the passageway in both directions. A group of twelve Marines carrying PQ47 weapons ran toward the companionway leading down to the deck. I ran behind them holding the alien weapon by my side.

Somewhere, a siren blared over and over as if the ship were under attack.

'Stop that guy,' yelled either Gupta or Yiu, but none of the crew members paid any attention. I climbed the companionway with them and burst onto the deck.

None of them noticed me. When they pushed forward, I held back, slipped behind a Slingshot and crouched down.

As I did, the twenty-foot long form of one of the other Slingshots crashed onto the deck beside me and slid along in a shower of sparks.

Who or what could be behind it all?

But I already knew the answer.

45

Half on the deck, half in the water, was an enormous creature, shining gray and wet in the sun. It looked like one of the horrible animals from the deep ocean: a Goblin Shark or Vampire Squid, with an enormous maw and great, flapping side fins. Water streamed from its head.

It was a nightmare creature come alive.

The crew was in disarray. They were undisciplined, afraid, and unused to firing weapons. They ran like civilians. They were more a danger to themselves than to the creature. They were brave only when it was easy to be brave, facing the non-existent enemies the Accord told them were real.

Typical, I thought.

'This thing's gonna sink us!' someone yelled. 'It's gonna sink the Accord Values.'

In between smashing Slingshots, and flinging people into the air, the creature appeared to be searching for something or someone. It raised its head up to peer along the length of the ship, then down along the deck. It sniffed all the while, which was weird for a sea creature, but this was no ordinary monster from the deep. For one thing, it appeared to be morphing from a sea animal to something with limbs, and a snout.

Searching for me.

I had to get off the ship—for the sake of the crew, for the sake of myself. I guessed our location to be still in the AON China Sea somewhere between AONT China and AON Archipelago Philippines, which meant it couldn't more than an hour or so of flying to AON sub-territory Hong Kong itself. And if I could reach the coast, I could ditch the Slingshot and hide while I worked out my next move.

If only there were more time.

While the monster snuffled around on the bows, I crept out from the gun mounting and ducked towards the nearest undamaged Slingshot. The words Gender Fluidity were stenciled on its side. The name could have been worse. The Slingshot beside it was called Patriarchy Smasher.

I raised Gender Fluidity's canopy and peered inside. There was a helmet on the seat and a J-Pack behind it. The J-Pack was the Navy's jetpack. It was light, portable, and good for thirty minutes of flying. And it would be perfect for jumping between buildings in Hong Kong.

I laid the alien weapon in small stowage space beside the pilot's seat. Then, I put my boot onto the first step and prepared to climb inside.

Almost there.

Then a voice said, 'Going somewhere, Burns?'

I turned and saw the bulldog forms of Yiu and Gupta. Gupta had a pistol drawn, a semi-automatic A19. Like the PQ47 rifle, the A19 had been given a number, not a name. Names, such as Viper, or Piranha, or even makers' names were considered too patriarchal for weapons. So, they were never used. Gupta pointed the A19 at my chest. Yiu was beside him with another set of handcuffs ready. Gupta was breathing hard. His or her face was shiny with sweat. He or she looked mighty pissed off at having been humiliated in front of two captains, an Admiral, and the Accord guy. The A19 shook. 'Turn around and put your hands on the metal.'

I stood where I was. I told myself no matter what happens, I wasn't going back to a cell—not while I was alive.

'Weren't you listening?'

'Weren't you?' I shouted. 'We're about to be invaded and enslaved, cities burning, people killed, the Accord overthrown, and you're asking me if I know what's going on?'

'Shut it, maggot, and put your hands on the Slingshot,' said Yiu who had put the handcuffs back on his belt and brought out a taser. It was aimed it at my chest. Now I had two weapons to overcome.

'Come on, guys,' I said. 'What do you think is going on? What do you think that thing on the bows is all about? A fish deformed by climate change? An octopus that's finally had it with misogyny?'

'Turn around,' Gupta said.

'Can't you see we've all been deceived—you, me and everyone who lives under the Accord? They have lied to us about everything. You know it, deep down. You know that what they tell you is not what you see with your own eyes. Just look at the aliens.'

'They're not aliens,' said Yiu. 'They're our galactic friends.'

'Friends?' I said. 'That thing up there—the one that just swatted someone into the sea. Some friend! Next you'll be telling me that men can be women and women can be men.'

'Women *can* be men—if they identify as men. I was born female.'

'I don't believe it,' I said. 'Neither do you—not really. Come on, just walk away and let me go. No shame in it and it'll be better for you.'

'You don't know anything about what it's like to be me,' said Yiu.

'Just turn around,' called Gupta. 'You are going to a nice cell in AONS Schumer. You can tell them all about your gender theories there.'

'I'm not going anywhere, no matter what you girls do.'

'What did you say?' said Gupta.

'You heard me.'

'Have it your way,' said Yiu. He fired the taser, but not before I ducked way down, jumped forward and flung my right arm up, grabbed his wrist and kept pushing upward. The taser shot over my head, the bolt clanging against the Slingshot fuselage. Then with my left hand, I hit Yiu with three quick jabs, one on the side of his head, then twice on his or her nose, bending it sideways, as mine had been bent. Then for good measure, I leaned back and kick him in the groin. He or she fell back into Gupta who once again had to catch someone.

Then, I stepped around the falling Yiu and kicked Gupta in the side of the knee, just as I had tried with the soldier on the Roman ship. This time the kick worked. With the extra weight of Yiu in his arms,

Gupta's knee buckled straight away, and he clutched it like everyone does who has ever suffered a dislocation —with panicked astonishment. I stepped forward and punched him in the throat. That did the trick. Now both Gupta and Yiu were on the ground like a couple of dogs rolling on the lawn. I grabbed the taser and tossed it over the side into the sea.

Before they could get to their feet, I turned back to the Slingshot and climbed in. There was a helmet inside. I put it on, adjusted the chinstrap, and pulled down the perspex canopy, sealing myself in. Then, I fired up the engines. The Slingshot slowly lifted upward from the deck.

Freedom was just a thruster blast way.

But it was at this moment, that I noticed a development on the bow. The great creature had finally found what it was looking for. Its snout pointed my way. It reached one great paw forward over a rank of Slingshots. It was like a hideous giant predator, its eyes focused on me, unmoving. If it had a tail, it would have been swishing, like cat's before it pounces.

'Unauthorized Slingshot activation,' said a female voice in my ear. 'State your name.' It was the ship's control tower. It had somehow remained functional during all the chaos. 'State your name,' said the voice again. 'This is an unauthorized Slingshot activation. State your name.'

I ignored it.

'If you do not respond,' said the voice, 'we will presume hostile intent and will respond with force.'

'Force?' I said. 'That'd be a first.'

Meanwhile, the monster was advancing. It actually bellowed out something that made the canopy rattle, a deep, 'Ahhhhh-llleexx!'

With the Slingshot engines running, I opened the canopy again and climbed down on the deck, bringing the alien weapon with me. I took a stance to the side of the Slingshot, raised the weapon, looked down the sights at the creature's snout, and pulled the trigger.

As before the recoil threw me backward. I fired again and again until the creature halted.

Then, I climbed back into the cockpit.

I throttled up the vertical thrusters, slowly rising. The monster had recovered and was now bounding forward over the deck. With one great fling of its limb, it slapped the Slingshot's tail, sending it and me spinning over the side, plunging the eighty feet toward the green sea below.

The shadow of the creature descended with me.

'Lieutenant Burns,' said the voice in my ear. 'We are authorizing AON Navy pilots to pursue and disable you. Comply with the orders of Captain Paine or your craft will be shot down. Do you copy? Acknowledge.'

I throttled up the thrusters again and managed to level the Slingshot halfway down. Then, I put my hand on the red lever that fired the jets that would send me forward like a bullet. The green sea swelled ahead of me. The map in the cockpit showed the Slingshot's position next to the AONS Accord Values and AONT China and Hong Kong twenty minutes' flying time away.

Below me, the monster reached up from the water. On the ship's deck, the crew was recovering. I saw three sailors climb into the few undamaged Slingshots. The remainder took up positions with rifles on the deck.

Well, here you are, Burns, I told myself. Your career with the Accord Navy is over. The Accord wants you jailed and probably dead. The aliens are about to invade the planet and there is a monster in the sea reaching up to kill you—a monster that at other times is a beautiful woman.

I might last another day or no more than a minute. I might end up dead or imprisoned. But for the moment, I was free to act. I had control of a Navy aircraft. I had a weapon stowed behind me. And I had glimpsed the truth.

'Lieutenant Burns,' said the tower in my ear.

'This is Lieutenant Burns,' I said.

'Copy that, Lieutenant,' said the tower. 'Return your Slingshot to the deck and step down immediately, orders of Captain Bunyasarn, Captain Paine, and Admiral Zhou. Acknowledge your understanding.'

'Oh, I understand,' I said. 'It's taken me all my life, but I understand.'

It was then that I told myself that I had two enemies to fight: the aliens and the Accord.

'Do you comply?' said the voice from the tower.

'One step at a time,' I said.

Then I pulled the red lever and fired the jets.

Part 4: Excidium

PROTOCOL

'Where the rights of an individual conflict with those of the Accord, the rights of the Accord shall prevail.'

Accord Of Nations Constitution

46

I was soon a mile away from AONS Accord Values, flying low over the sea. For a whole minute, I had the wonderful sensation of flying alone, of freedom, of escape. Just me and my Slingshot. Clouds above. Sea below. No enemies. No Accord. No Accord values.

Freedom.

I savored every second of it, even though I knew it couldn't last. Within twenty minutes, I would be back in the thick of it, over the mountains and skyscrapers of Hong Kong. Then, I'd have to work out what to do next.

Just as I predicted, the moment passed, and new troubles began.

The Slingshot's radar displayed three objects approaching.

They were all Slingshots, all from AONS Accord Values, all in pursuit. Each was as maneuverable and fast as the Gender Fluidity, each flown by trained pilot. They could chase, climb, dive, swerve, and fire guided missiles.

I was a capable pilot too. I'd trained right up to the

level of aerobatics in Slingshots. I could roll, loop and fly upside down. I could do a Tail Slide, the maneuver where the aircraft falls backward and then recovers.

But would these moves matter against Navy pilots of Slingshots armed with guided missiles? The missiles were called A72s. Before the new regulation came in regarding offensive weapon names, they had been called Death Adders.

The only silver lining to this cloud was that the other pilots had no actual combat experience. They'd never fired a shot in anger.

I nudged the joystick. The Slingshot responded instantly. The merest caress sent it upward into the thick clouds, out of view. Within seconds, I was coursing along the cotton wool with the sun behind me in the east.

The three pursuers would know exactly where I was on their screens, of course, just as I knew where they were, but the clouds at least provided visual cover of sorts.

The speaker in the headset came on to remind me all was not well.

'Lieutenant Burns, this is AONS Accord Values. You are ordered to descend to one thousand feet and return immediately. If not, the aircraft pursuing you will deploy their missiles.'

'We've been over this,' I said.

'Captain Paine has ordered me to convey to you that you will be treated fairly if you return.'

'Define fair,' I said.

No reply. Seconds later, the Slingshot's instrument panel came alive with sounds and images. First time I'd had heard the missile warning system. Strangely, it didn't sound like an alarm or a siren. The Navy knew not to use those anymore. Sudden and shrill alarms startled pilots and stopped them concentrating.

Instead, there was a softer alarm, a female voice, calm and encouraging. It spoke gently into my ear, and said, 'MF3,' which meant three missiles fired. The image on the screen confirmed it. Three missile icons appeared. They were displayed ahead of the each of the pursuing Slingshots.

'IT15,' said the calm voice.

IT15. Fifteen seconds to impact, which meant fifteen seconds before I would be bits of metal. Not much time when you think about it. But it did allow at least a small time to react. My first three seconds were spent on panic. The next four seconds were spent in anger.

Not a good beginning.

The final few seconds were spent contemplating an image from an old movie I'd seen about dogfighting jets from the PAE. The trick to winning a dogfight in those old planes was to get behind your enemy— behind where he was most vulnerable.

'IT5,' said the woman's voice. Five seconds to impact. With the image of the dogfighting planes in my mind, I pulled back on the joystick. Not all the way, but three quarters, enough to climb the Slingshot into a loop.

Then, I hung on.

The Slingshot responded eagerly. It didn't so much as swoop upwards; it turned a vertical corner. The G-force was sharp and heavy. I hadn't buckled my harness, which caused no problem at first because I was shoved down firmer into my seat, but as the Slingshot climbed and looped, I slid out of the seat and up until, my head pressed against the canopy.

The missile alert spoke to me. 'IT7,' it said, which meant I'd avoided the strike, which was a relief, but apparently, the missiles had corrected and were back on the case.

I pushed the joystick forward and the nose leveled out. New missile icons appeared on the screen. Now the missiles were in front and below and two of them were coming directly at me.

'IT2,' said the voice.

I moved the joystick forward, plunging down, ducking under the missiles. I actually heard them fizz overhead, and I imagined them hitting the three pursuing jets, blowing them up.

But that was cartoon thinking.

As I descended, the clouds faded away and the sea rushed up. The white caps winked at me in the green. I pulled back on the joystick and leveled out about fifty feet.

Then I looked at what lay ahead. Heavy rain. A storm raging. But also, the green mass of the southern side of Hong Kong Island.

Almost there.

I urged the Slingshot forward. The screen showed the missiles correcting their paths once more. The Slingshot's onboard warning voice said nothing. Probably it was calculating. The pursuing Slingshots were still on my tail.

I stayed low and level, rocketing towards the Hong Kong coast. The sea beneath seemed dangerously close. One nudge of the joystick and I would cartwheel to my death along its surface.

If I could just get to Hong Kong Island.

The pursuing Slingshots must have seen what I was

MM HOLT

up to. More missile objects appeared on the screen. 'MF3,' said the missile alert voice. Three new missiles approaching. Then it added 'IT7.'

Great. I thought. Just great. Six missiles were coming for me.

Out in the real world, the coast of Hong Kong was coming closer. I could see the village of Stanley. Beyond it, the hill known as the Dragon's Back. Beyond that would be the skyscrapers and the famous harbor with its cluster of towers either side.

'IT4,' said the voice.

I fancied I could hear the missiles behind me, straining to touch my tail, straining to explode, to blow me to smithereens, as the phrase went.

Then, the green bulk of the Dragon's Back raced at me. I saw houses nestled in the trees, a road along the coast, cars driving along it, and hiking trails. A pretty scene that would soon turn deadly. The missiles gained on me from behind. The voice spoke. I didn't listen. I was wondering just how steep the Slingshot could actually climb.

'Last chance, Lieutenant Burns,' said the controller's voice from AON Accord Values. 'State your intention to return and the pilots will detonate the missiles.'

'It's too late for that,' I said.

When the first tree branch looked as if it would pierce the Slingshot's nose, I pulled on the joystick. The Slingshot climbed violently. The fuselage cracked. There was an awful clunk like a metal object had clogged the jets. I thought the engines might stall, but the Slingshot surged over the ridge of the Dragon's Back and out over the green forest of Hong Kong Island's high center.

PROTOCOL

Then I shot into the grey clouds, sliding back on my seat. This time, my head cracked on the canopy. But I kept on going up. If the missiles were going to hit, they could hit me way up high where I wouldn't explode near any civilians.

The screen showed the first missiles vanishing. 'IT2' said the voice said, in reference to the second set, which must have had time to correct and follow me over the ridge.

Two seconds to impact. Looks like the Accord didn't care about civilians after all.

Well, I'd given it a good shake.

Suddenly there was an awful bang, and the Slingshot pitched up and to port. The missile icons disappeared from the screen, and the two Slingshots pursuing me were banking away from the coast, out of the restricted airspace.

They'd detonated the missiles anyway.

I kept the Slingshot climbing, just in case. The altimeter displayed 15,000 feet—roughly three miles high. And with relief, I knew I was all alone.

I pushed the joystick forward, leveled off and then descended while I looked at the map.

I had overshot Hong Kong and its skyscrapers by twenty miles and was now flying over AONT Mainland China. I pulled a wide banking turn, back toward Hong Kong Island. That's where the Establishment Day celebrations would probably take place, down by the harbor's edge.

But now a new problem arose. A different voice in my helmet spoke. A gruff male voice. All business.

'Naval aircraft Gender Fluidity, this is the control tower at Hong Kong International Airport. You have just entered restricted civilian airspace above our runways.'

47

AONT sub-territory Hong Kong Airport was one of the busiest in the Accord. It was even busier than the airport at AONT sub-territory Los Angeles. The stack of aircraft above the airport was said to be thirty planes high at any time.

Today was no exception.

And I was right in the middle of it.

Looking up and to the left, I could see the stack itself, rising miles above me in the rain. Short haul CloudCastors, long-haul SkyClippers, enormous Skyships, sleek private jets, giant, bulb-nosed Colossus Class liners.

They could have come from anywhere—from AONT London (2 hours), AONT New York (2.5 hours) AONT Tokyo (0.5 hours), each bearing as many as two thousand passengers at a time.

The sky was full of behemoths. It was a very dangerous place for a fleeing Slingshot to suddenly find itself. But how to get out without causing mayhem?

Two ideas formed in my mind. The first was to make

a break for the wall of the spiral, to fly between the descending planes. The second was to go straight up, as high I could, up to where the spiral hadn't formed yet. Up there, I could peel off and away.

If the Slingshot could still climb that high.

The voice from AONS Accord Values spoke in my ear again.

'Fugitive Burns,' she said. 'Unauthorized access to civilian airspace is a violation of the Accord military operating code. We have alerted the civilian aviation authorities and given them access to our radar. They can see you, fugitive Burns. It's all over. I have patched in Civilian Radio for them to guide you down to a disused landing area where you will surrender to AONT Hong Kong police.'

Then the airport tower chimed in.

'Lieutenant Burns,' said a male voice. 'This is air traffic controller Kan. You are to follow my instructions. Understood?'

'Understood,' I said, 'but not accepted.'

'There are over thirty aircraft surrounding you. They're carrying over fifty-thousand civilian passengers. You are endangering all of them. So, unless you want to be responsible for a huge loss of life, including your own, listen to what I say. We'll get you down nice and safe. Remain at the altitude you are now, a thousand feet, no more, no less. Then, you are to...'

'Sorry, Controller Kan,' I said. 'You don't control me.'

'Lieutenant Burns,' he hit back. 'Military or even rogue military people do not take precedence over civilians. We're going to get you one way or the other.'

I made my choice. I had been holding the Slingshot's

joystick lightly inward to keep me circling inside the spiral of jets. Now, I centered it until I was heading north, toward the edge of the spiral.

'Stop, Lieutenant,' said Controller Kan. 'Return to your previous altitude and path.'

I ignored him and turned the knob on the joysticks top to increase airspeed. The Slingshot responded grudgingly with creaking and clattering.

'Change course immediately, Lieutenant,' Controller Kan said again. 'You are heading directly into the descent path of civilian aircraft.'

'No shit,' I said. 'Thanks for telling me the bleeding obvious.'

The civilian aircraft he was talking about loomed into view, above and to the right, as large as a warehouse. It also appeared on my cockpit screen, a dark shape, uncomfortably close.

'Pull out, Lieutenant,' said the air traffic guy. 'Stay within the stack, right now!' I wished I could find a way to switch him off.

I passed over the CloudLiner's great hulk. It seemed like just a few feet, which had me immediately worried about being hit by the slanted blade of its tail, the part bearing the Accord flag. But it passed beneath me, and I was soon out of the spiral way out over the green sea again, free and clear, if only for a few seconds.

I turned the aircraft east and headed towards the bristling skyscrapers of Hong Kong Island and to the squat, ancient robot shape of the HSBC building.

From simulator training, I knew it had a wide flat top. Maybe I could land there and get into my J-Pack before the police showed up.

'You have disobeyed civilian air controller

instructions, Lieutenant,' said the voice from the AONS Accord Values, who had suddenly come back on air. 'That is a serious Navy Spirit Code violation.'

Yep, I thought. Just keep adding them to the pile. You can read them out at my funeral when the Accord Of Nations becomes a province of the planet Rome.

That was the moment, the thumping in the Slingshot engines changed from a clatter to a series of very loud bangs.

48

Heavy rain hit the Slingshot canopy and streamed backward. Visual Flight Protocol was impossible, as the air traffic controller might have said. So I followed the image on the cockpit screen until I was above the HSBC building and descended onto the flat helipad.

The rubber landing pads slid slightly onto the slick surface, then settled with a squelch. The Slingshot fuselage creaked as it adjusted to the new distribution of weight.

Then all was silent except for the patter of rain on the canopy.

I opened up and climbed out of the cockpit, then down the three steps to the helipad, where water streamed around my boots. I reached into the cockpit, and retrieved the J-Pack and slung it over my back. I kept my helmet on. Then strapped the J-Pack tight at my waist and chest. Next, I reached in and pulled the alien rifle from the bracket beside the pilot's seat.

I was going to need it.

I stepped down from the helipad onto the main area of the HSBC building roof. Here too, the roof was slick with rainwater. The rain was so heavy, it was like a veil over the entire city. Thunder rolled along the Kowloon hills. The great metropolis was under siege from the weather.

I checked my watch. It was now 10:00a.m. The Establishment Day Ceremony would begin in an hour. The Roman visitors must be scheduled to show up soon. They might even have arrived already. Down below, by the harbor's edge, the Accord Flag stood proudly as always but was buffeted by the rain and wind. Around it, the empty grandstands and podiums waited.

Soon, the most powerful members of the Accord would assemble there to sing the Accord anthem, recite the Accord founders' pledge and to announce plans for the future. No doubt, they would also announce the great leap forward for tolerance and diversity created by the arrival the galactic visitors. Unity TV television coverage would be global.

I had to think of a way to sabotage the ceremony and expose Octavia's plans.

But first, I had to hide.

I put the J-Pack over my back and pulled the straps tight. I kept the rifle in my left hand so that I could control the J-Pack with my right. Every Navy personnel member was required to be familiar with J-Pack use. I'd even completed extra courses in J-Pack tactics. Even so, controlling one in the rain would be difficult.

While the pack idled on my back, I surveyed the scene. Where was the best place to hide? To my left and right, stood the skyscrapers of Central. Behind me, rose the hills of Hong Kong Island. In front of me, the Exhibition Centre on the harbor's edge. Beyond it, the grey surface Hong Kong harbor itself with ferries going back and forth through the rain. On the far side of the harbor, the skyscrapers of Kowloon.

Kowloon. That seemed as good a place as any—at least for the moment.

OK, J-Pack, time to go.

Suddenly, there was a commotion behind me. The door to one of the roof access stairwells opened. Guys in black SWAT uniforms streamed out and squatted either side of the entrance, their guns raised. Their leader barked through a loud hailer.

'Drop the weapon!' he yelled. 'Drop the weapon! Drop the weapon!' As if I couldn't hear already. Even the AONS Accord Values chimed in through my headset.

'Lieutenant, Burns, drop your weapon and surrender to the police.'

There was no way I was going to drop the weapon, let alone surrender to anybody. But what to do? The SWAT team had PQ47 rifles aimed at my chest.

'Drop the weapon,' the guy said once more.

Then nature came to my rescue.

Out of nowhere, lightning and thunder struck. The whole cityscape was illuminated as if someone in the sky had turned on a gazillion fluorescent lights. It was visually arresting and aurally stunning. When it was over, glass was raining down from shattered windows on the neighboring buildings, and car alarms were screaming from below.

And I had dropped off the side of the building.

I fired the J-Pack halfway down the building's side. The blast strained the shoulder straps, as they took my weight plus the extra force of the upthrust. I came to a halt in the air, then, shot out into the rain, above the shiny streets below.

Seconds later, I was out over the harbor, passing above one of the ferries chugging through the deluge. Then I reached the harbor's edge on the Kowloon side, low over the buildings, but not so low as to attract any attention. At least, I hoped I wouldn't. I touched down onto the curved roof of the Hong Kong Science Museum. From there I had a good view of whatever might be coming for me from across the harbor.

I brought the rifle up. Looked through its sights to scan the harbor, back towards the roof I'd just left. The Slingshot was surrounded by the civilian police in their SWAT gear. I could see them poking the Slingshot canopy. One had a radio to his ear. I guessed that meant I could soon expect a helicopter to come thumping my way.

As I was thinking this, there was another commotion. This time on the far side of the Science Museum roof. Another door to another stairwell opening up. Out came a pistol muzzle, followed by a guy crouching down, SWAT-style. Then three more men. Or women. Or the variations. They all wore loose-fitting uniforms so I couldn't tell what sex they might be. They took up positions behind an air intake unit and leveled their weapons at me.

Not again.

'Drop your weapon!' one of them yelled through a loudspeaker. 'Get on the ground!' It was quite a demand to make because, by this time, I was behind a concrete wall with my own weapon leveled right back at them. 'Come out. Drop the weapon!' the guy shouted again.

Sorry, pal.

I quickly scanned the cluster of skyscrapers behind me.

There was a tall building about five hundred yards away. A logo on its side said China Chem. If I could get to the other side of it and find a more secluded rooftop, I might be able to hide before they saw where I'd gone.

As I was thinking this, a small drone appeared over the edge of the building, hovering in the rain. It bore a camera and a light. Without hesitating, I swiveled the rifle, fixed the drone in the sights, and fired. The rifle bucked. The muzzle climbed. A pulse of energy shot out and hit the drone. And lit up the gloom.

'Weapon discharged against Navy orders,' said the voice in my ear. 'Weapon discharged in civilian territory.'

But once again, I was over the edge of the building.

I fired the J-Pack. It shot me forty-five degrees upward, away from the Science Museum. I sailed between the skyscrapers past office windows where people sat at their desks, screens in front of them. One guy was leaning back talking to a headset as I went by. Then I was past the building and heading towards a roof which I hoped would be out of sight.

I landed with a bit more elegance than my take off. A couple of steps and I was standing in the rain on a wet roof with a good view of Kowloon and plenty of air conditioner intakes for cover.

There was also a good view across the harbor towards Central.

I dropped behind one of the air-con intakes and, using the rifle, scanned the scene. Neighboring rooftops first. Looking for nosy security personnel.

Looking for police SWAT teams. Civilians with binoculars. Anyone.

I saw nothing but one or two security guards patrolling in the rain among the various pipes and other building top structures. Some had umbrellas; others wore ponchos, slick with water.

So far so good.

But that was when I saw *her* too, on a rooftop about fifteen hundred yards away, crouching down and scenting the air.

It was Octavia.

49

As if things couldn't get any worse.

Was Octavia the creature attacking the Accord Values or wasn't she? And if the creature was her, how had she reached Hong Kong so quickly?

The questions would have to wait because here she was yet again.

This time she wore a blue Navy uniform, the same kind as her crew wore back on the Excidium. But Octavia's own version of the uniform was different. The crew member's uniforms had been loose fitting; this uniform was tight, figure-hugging, and slick.

It emphasized her tiny waist, her unusually long legs, her narrow waist. Wearing it, she became a fantasy character, as tall and sexual as the superheroes in the comic books banned by the Accord Purity of Information Department. A glorious sight. And, without a doubt she was the only woman anywhere in the Accord to be so seductively dressed that day, or even that century.

But why dress in such an impractical way? Could it all be part of her twisted obsession?

I watched Octavia sniff the air, her nose twitching like a rabbit's. The heavy rain streamed down her ponytail, which remained upright as if it were made from materials other than human hair. She was a magnificent sight—so lithe and beautiful. So, desirable.

So deadly.

I looked down at her through the rifle's sights. Firing a monster was one thing. Firing at such a beautiful woman was another. Chen had managed it on the shuttle, but he fired in order to save me from strangulation.

This was different.

If I managed to kill Octavia—if that were even possible—would it mean the Romans would withdraw and take their ship away? Or would it simply mean that Captain Drusilla would assume command and complete the mission anyway? Or would I simply have no choice but to fire on her for my own survival?

I slid my finger into the loop of the rifle's trigger guard and began my routine. I settled the sights on the side of Octavia's profile and began breathing slowly, calming my mind, slowing my heart and stilling the rifle's muzzle.

But then Octavia ceased her sniffing, turned her head and looked directly down the scope and into my eye.

If ever I was going to pull the trigger, it should be now.

The small light on the rifle's side began to blink. Inside the rifle's magazine, the pulse gathered force, ready to shoot across the fifteen hundred yards between us.

As if she knew what I was thinking, Octavia smiled a

cold smile. Her teeth were inhumanly white, like a slice of fresh snow.

She slowly brought one slender finger to her throat and slid it horizontally across her slender neck.

It's time, Burns. Shoot her for goodness sake. Pull the trigger and shoot her! Shoot her now because there won't be a second chance.

Do it.

I took two more deep breaths, breathed out completely.

Suddenly, a door opened behind Octavia—the door to the stairwell. A man in a gray uniform appeared—probably a security guard making his rounds, or responding to what he'd seen on the security camera. He called out to Octavia and walked toward her.

But I had already squeezed the trigger.

I pulled the rifle away to the left, but it was too late. The light had stopped blinking. The rifle had fired its terrible blast.

The gunstock slammed into my shoulder. The recoil lifted me up from the wet concrete and flung me backward like a tossed plank. I hit steel piping behind me.

Then, I looked back to what damage the blast had caused.

Fifteen hundred yards away, smoke rose from the rooftop. The energy pulse had slammed into an air conditioner outlet to the left of Octavia. Concrete dust plumed in the rain above.

But Octavia, she was still there, a blue figure in the dust and the rain. The security guard was crouching by the stairwell exit. He had one hand shielding his eyes. Then, he got up and scrambled back through the stairwell door.

Octavia stood her ground.

Then, as if coming to a decision, she stepped slowly backward, step after step, like a high jumper preparing to address the bar. I couldn't believe what I was seeing. Was she was actually going to run to the building's edge and jump the fifteen hundred yards to reach me?

Immediately, I got to my feet, picked up the rifle and ran to the far side of the building roof. I scanned for another skyscraper, preferably one of a similar height, but any skyscraper would do as long as it was in J-Pack range. The buildings left and right were all too tall. They also had pointed roofs, which were no good at all. But straight I found what I was looking for: a building of the same height with a flat roof and plenty of pipes and air-con intakes that could provide cover.

That's where I would go.

I re-slung the rifle and adjusted the J-Pack straps. Then, I dropped into a staggered stance and pressed the button on the J-Pack harness.

And jumped.

For a second I was up in the rain, motionless, stationary, as if I were weightless, like a cartoon character in the few seconds before he realizes gravity will have its way and pull him to the streets below.

Then, I pressed the J-Pack button on the chest strap.

Nothing.

I pressed again.

Nothing.

I pressed three times.

Nothing, nothing, nothing.

Had the rain damaged the mechanism?

I pressed one more time.

Nothing.

Then the pack fired by itself, unexpectedly, randomly, violently. It flung me upwards and away from the building and the street, but in the wrong direction, toward the side of one of the shorter buildings nearby.

I put out my arms and legs, like a cat flung up in the air. I hit the side of the building just below the roof line, right into the dark blue glass window. Bang! The pack and rifle swung around on my back and clattered into the window after me. The bill of my helmet smacked into the glass. I saw a woman at a desk literally jump out of her seat.

Then I bounced off. Too fast and too far to get my fingers into the gaps between the glass panels. I was falling again with fifty, sixty or seventy floors to the street below.

Or just a few seconds of falling before impact.

The street rushed up at me I clicked the J-Pack button over and over, hoping it would fire. Nothing.

I looked down at the glistening street. There was a traffic jam. The cars roofs were slick with rain.

At least I would hit those and not any civilians—except the people in the car. I hoped there might only be one.

But suddenly I was stopped in mid-air. At first, I thought I'd snagged my uniform on a pole or a gantry sticking out from the building's side.

Then I realized it was something else. Something strong. Something with a very long reach.

I hung suspended between the raindrops falling either side of me. Then, I was lifted up and flung high over the building's edge. I landed in a heap and skidded along the wet concrete.

I looked up. Ten feet away from me in the hammering rain stood Octavia.

'Hello, Alex,' she said. 'You weren't trying to avoid me, were you?'

I stood up performing a quick inventory. A welt was forming on one side of my forehead. My shoulder felt like it had been wrenched from its socket. Ankles, feet both seemed OK. My knee throbbed—the wound from yesterday.

I straightened up and brought myself up to my full height. I shifted my shoulders to settle the J-pack and the rifle.

'The Accord knows what you're planning,' I said. 'They're mobilizing the armed forces.'

The falling rain made Octavia appear all the more magnificent. It streamed down the blue uniform, from her high collar right down to where her glistening legs disappeared into combat boots.

She stared at me through her cerulean eyes, full of anger, full of certainty, full of coquetry.

'The armed forces?' she said.

'All three branches,' I replied. '

'Well, that seems strange,' she said. 'Just yesterday, I accepted their invitation to attend your Establishment Day ceremony. It's starting soon Alex. Over there,' she said. 'By the harbor's edge—a fittingly dramatic location.'

'They're deceiving you. They have the forces ready.'

She took a step towards me. Each leg swung forward and inwards, her hips swaying.

'We both know they don't, Alex, but you made a good try. They're just as naive as ever. They're welcoming us, as you knew they would.'

She came closer.

'Stay back, Admiral,' I said.

'You went to see him, didn't you?'

'It was just a dream.'

'What did he tell you, Alex?'

'Nothing that I haven't already discovered for myself.'

She was now just a few yards away. She stopped, looked at me, smiling.

'Don't worry, Alex,' she said. 'I'm not going to hurt you.'

'I'm not worried.'

'Oh, but I know you are, Alex. You know what's about to happen.'

'Do I?'

As fast as I could, I reached up and unslung rifle, bringing it around and down. But I was too slow. Octavia crossed the remaining distance between us before I could even bring the muzzle level.

She knocked the weapon aside, grabbed me by the throat and raised me off the roof and up, into the rain. My flailing arms couldn't reach her, my kicks didn't hurt her.

She smiled and tightened her grip.

50

'If I put you down, Alex, will you behave?'

She kept up the pressure on my throat.

'Blink twice for yes and once for no.'

I kept thrashing, trying to escape her grip.

'I don't see you blinking Alex.'

I blinked twice.

'Was that a real blink or was it just because of the rain?'

I blinked twice again.

'Good,' said Octavia. She lowered me to the roof and released her grip on my throat.

I tried to keep standing up straight as I drew a deep breath.

'You are more aggressive than your ancestor. He never fired a weapon at me, never tried to kill me. But you did, Alex.'

I said nothing.

'I like that,' said Octavia.

'You are lucky I missed.'

'Am I? You think you can kill me?' She laughed. 'Once you get to know me, Alex, you'll be amazed at what I can do.'

'I've seen enough.'

'Are you sure? The best is yet to come.'

'What did you to Le Seaux?' I said.

'Your short-haired, thin-lipped friend?'

'Is she safe?'

'It's more the case that she's repaired. We healed her after that blast.'

'And she's co-operating with you without coercion?'

'There's no need to coerce anyone who is a true believer in your Accord. She will be talking about equality and tolerance right up until her throat is cut by one of my Marines. Anything to avoid being called a name. Transphobic—was it, or other-ist? They're some of the words she used. I don't think I've seen anyone so able to deny reality—unless she was just acting. Could she have been acting, Alex?'

'What about my mother?'

'You saw the beam, Alex.'

'And Chen?'

'Ask your superior officers in the Navy. They'll tell you.'

I shook my head. 'You might have noticed that most people of the Accord are no longer my friends.'

'Were they ever your friends?' said Octavia. 'To me, they appear to be greater enemies than I am—but you know that now, right?'

I said nothing.

'You might be able to say I revealed the truth to you, up there on Excidium.'

Lightning flashed on the on the other side of the harbor. Seconds later, thunder rumbled through the skyscrapers. The rain beat harder, actually bouncing upward from the rooftop.

'You don't need to explain it to me,' I said.

'Oh, was I woman-splaining?' she laughed.

'When's the invasion?'

'Invasion? Who said anything about an invasion?'

'You did.'

'But we don't need to invade, Alex. Your Accord Commissioners have invited us here to stay. They're allocating territory for us, somewhere in the east of AONT Russia. Imagine that!'

'But you want the rest of the planet.'

'In time.'

'Which time?'

'The right time.'

'When's the right time?'

'Alex, you are so impolite now that you aren't in the Navy.'

'Politeness is for people who aren't invaders.'

She smiled.

'You're the only one who thinks we're invaders, Alex. Doesn't that make you feel foolish?'

'Not when it's the truth. I've had a lifetime of lies. The truth is harder, but it's better.'

'What are you going to do with the truth, Alex? What did you think you were going to do after you ran from Excidium—which I allowed, by the way? And what did you intend with your mad dash across the sea and the great blasts of your rifle—or should I say *our* rifle? You don't actually have a plan at all, do you? That's why you stayed an extra day on *his s*hip, isn't it? But you don't have a plan. You'll just take things one step at a time. Is that how you say it?'

I didn't reply.

'You're just one guy, Alex. A very handsome guy, but you're just one man, one Earthman. It's not worth the trouble of trying to prevent the inevitable. And think about this, Alex.' She stepped closer. 'We won't be any worse than the government you have now. We might even be better. You've heard of the Pax Romana. It will be something like that.'

Her cerulean eyes were on mine. She put her arms around my neck, apparently unconcerned about the weapon slung over my back. I pulled one her arms away, but like lightning, her hand was back at my throat again, and she lifted me up into the rain once more.

'I don't want to kill you, Alex,' she said.

I couldn't reply.

She lowered me till we were level. She brought her lips to my ear.

'Just this once, Alex. That's all I want. Just this once.'

She brought her lips to mine. 'I let you cause me so much trouble for this.' Then she closed her eyes. 'Don't resist, Alex. It will be more pleasant than you think. Trust me.'

'Fugitive Burns,' said the voice in my helmet.

Before the voice could continue, Octavia raised a hand to the helmet, severing the strap and casting it off with one movement. The helmet dropped to the concrete beside us.

And then we were kissing in the rain like film stars. Everything was like an Accord romance movie: the city, the storm, the island in the distance with its crowded skyscrapers, the people on the street below, sheltering under umbrellas, and the two stars kissing in the rain. The only things different were that Octavia was dressed like a pre-Accord fantasy figure, and that we were apparently of different genders.

'See?' Octavia breathed. 'Nice.'

Soon her uniform was unbuttoned. I was amazed at the sensuousness of Octavia's figure. She was like a statue come to life. She was beyond perfection, honed and sculpted. In the Accord we were taught it was an example of patriarchy to desire bodies to be like Octavia's. We were told it was necessary to like larger people—of any gender.

But the touch of Octavia's body was enough to make me forget all sense of duty of anything.

'I know your secret,' she whispered.

'What's that?'

'You have never been with a woman, have you, Alex?'

She hooked one impossibly long leg over my hip and drew me closer, rifle, J-Pack and all.

The rain thundered down against my back and ran down my legs. I hardly noticed it. Octavia writhed and swooned. She raved in her language. She bit my shoulder. She growled again.

'Lieutenant Burns,' said the tiny voice from down at my feet. 'Lieutenant Burns.'

Octavia had reached some state of ecstasy. She threw her head back. She squeezed until I felt a rib crack. 'Alex,' she said through deep breaths.

Then she breathed heavily into my ear.

'I never want this to end,' she said.

I sensed a change in Octavia's form. It was just the slightest adjustment of her body. It was still slippery and firm, but now it was harder, not flesh, her skin no longer pneumatic. It felt different, almost brittle. Her forearm was sharper than I remembered; it had an edge. And her scent, so feminine, so seductive, now turned sour.

I opened my eyes and began to speak, but the pincer was on my neck.

'Shhhhh,' said Octavia. 'Don't worry, Alex. Hundreds of thousands of us are coming. But you won't have to worry about what happens. You'll be with me.'

The pincer grip tightened. I brought my arms to try and unlock it from my neck, but they were as immovable as the blocks on a vice.

'Shhhh,' said Octavia.

'Lieutenant Burns?' said tiny the voice, somewhere in the rain.

Octavia's grip tightened. I had escaped all kinds of holds in training. Even holds where your opponent has you in the worst possible disadvantage: headlock, arm lock, sitting on you, sleeper holds—you name it, but there was no getting out of this.

And the grip tightened by the second.

But then I had an idea—a last desperate idea.

The rifle had slipped off my shoulders and was now slung around my waist. The muzzle pointed to my right. I reached my hand behind my back and grabbed hold of the stock. Then I pulled it slowly around, trying not to alert Octavia. I closed my eyes as if I were slowly asphyxiating. My finger located the trigger guard.

'Won't be long now, Alex.'

I tried to force the muzzle around so that it pointed at Octavia but it was too far. The best I could do was angle the rifle at the concrete beneath us. Maybe the blast might hit Octavia. The best might be it would fling me out of her grip. Or break my neck. Or destroy my legs. Or kill me.

Too late to choose. I was passing out.

I pulled the trigger and hoped.

There was an almighty boom and the rifle flung my arm violently outward, wrenching my shoulder properly this time. Concrete and dust blasted into the air, mixing with the rain. Octavia and I were thrown to the side, breaking her lock on my neck.

As soon as I landed I reached for the rifle. I grabbed it with my left hand and swung it at her face.

For the briefest of seconds, we looked at each other. Alarms were going off down in the building. Bells, sirens, some kind of announcement over a loudspeaker. Octavia's expression changed from surprise to pure anger.

I pulled the trigger one more time.

The rifle boomed. But this time the boom was not followed by concrete shattering. It was the sound of a large object crashing into mud.

And it was followed by an ear-splitting howl—one that I'd heard before.

'Ahhhh-woooooo!'

The blast flung me over to the edge of the building. I caught a glimpse of Octavia as I fell. What I saw was not Octavia the beautiful woman with a hairstyle from *Fashion In The Twentieth Century.*

It was the other kind.

51

As I fell, my unbuttoned uniform flapped in my face. I plummeted alongside the raindrops down towards a busy street in Kowloon.

A person falling from a building accelerates down at thirty-two per feet per second per second. They reach a terminal velocity of one hundred and twenty-two miles per hour.

Not good odds for survival.

I knew enough from the short Navy training on jumping from sinking ships what would happen when my body hit the street. On impact, my legs would telescope up through my body, meeting my organs which would still be on their way down, followed by my head. If I landed on my side, there would be a different effect. My ribs would hit the street first, the organs would crash into those followed by the rest of my ribcage crashing into them. My head, making its own way down would slam directly onto the street, or the taxi roof, or the building awning, or an unfortunate person.

But I wasn't planning on letting any of that happen.

Five seconds to go.

I swung my legs so that I was falling feet first. With my left hand, I pulled at up my uniform until I found the broken J-Pack button. Two seconds to go. The street and the taxis roofs raced up at me. With about fifty yards to go, I pressed the J-Pack button.

Just as before, it took several clicks of the button to get it to fire. When it finally responded, I was thrown up and to the right. My right shoulder slammed into the side of a glass building just above street level, no doubt startling yet another office worker. Then I bounced off the window and down into the street, but not actually onto the hard concrete or the blacktop. I landed on the heads and shoulders a crowd of people scrambling to get out of the way.

I was in civilian territory.

The force of my landing had been enough to knock some of the people down. Several men and woman staggered backward and then toppled onto each other forming a heap on the sidewalk. All of them wore Accord Establishment Day smocks.

'Sorry,' I said. 'Sorry.'

I got unsteadily to my feet, nursing my shoulder. My arm felt limp. The shoulder socket felt loose.

'Sorry,' I said again to the jumble of people.

I reached out my unhurt arm to a stricken woman. She shriveled at the sight of me and yelled something in Chinese.

On the rest of the street, there was mayhem. People scattered, dodging through the jammed traffic. Car alarms shrieked. Drivers in moving cars honked their horns trying to get away.

Mayhem.

Around me, other people were responding to the cries of the woman—the one I had tried to help. I felt the sudden gaze of hundreds of eyes and saw the fronts of hundreds of rainbow-colored smocks turning my way. With my height, my blue NWU, and enormous rifle, I knew how I looked, which was exactly like the pre-Accord villain everyone imagined.

'Get the police!' someone shouted. Then, other people started shouting other phrases in Chinese. The chaos spread. There were more car alarms, more rain, more confusion, more shouting, more broken glass, and more injured people pointing at me.

And somewhere high above, Octavia must have looked down on the scene, apoplectic with anger, reforming herself from the beautiful fantasy woman into something unimaginable.

But there was no time to think about Octavia.

Several hands grabbed my waist, my arms, my J-Pack. Someone kicked me. Someone else put their hands around my neck from behind, pulling me down.

Time to get out—if I could.

I raised the alien rifle and aimed at a building on the other side of the street. Before I could pull the trigger, a man grabbed the muzzle and yanked on it. I took my left hand from the rifle and jabbed his throat. Then, I quickly raised the muzzle again and shot off a pulse. The windows shattered halfway up the building's side. People at their desks were exposed, holding their faces. It was like throwing back a shower curtain.

The blast had thrown me backward too, out of the clutches of the people trying to subdue me. I turned and ran, limping with the latest injury: a rolled ankle from the crash landing.

I rushed through the crowd, shoving people out of the way, hard on the men, as gentle as possible on the women. I was being sexist, or at least the Accord's definition of sexist. I didn't care. I had to get out of that scene and away from Octavia's view of me.

As I ran, a plan was forming—a very rough plan.

One step at a time.

If I could draw Octavia in her current form over to where the Establishment Day Celebrations would take place, I could reveal for a worldwide television audience the danger we were welcoming to our planet.

If they could see Octavia in her monstrous altered state, maybe there would be an outcry. Maybe the Commission would be questioned.

It wasn't a very hopeful plan. Octavia would probably resume her beautiful self for the ceremony, after killing me first. Or she would accuse me in front of the commissioners of extreme xenophobia and other-ism. The Accord would be sure to buy it. And even if they didn't, Octavia was invading anyway, so what did it matter?

On the other hand, if she was as crazy as I believed she was, the plan might just work. I gave it a thirty percent chance. Then, I immediately revised my guess to twenty percent, then ten.

As for me, well, I pretty much considered my future over. I'd either be killed by Octavia or by her Marines or be imprisoned by the Accord for the rest of my life. Probably they would make an example of me as a case of toxic masculinity and patriarchy that had gone bad, which I guessed would only fuel more calls for more restrictions and more power for the Accord.

But there was a small chance I'd escape.

Daydreaming, I told myself. Daydreaming.

None of these plans will work.

But as I thought this, I heard an almighty growl from the rooftops above. It was so loud and unearthly, the people stopped in the street. Stopped and looked up, trying to locate its source. Maybe they thought it was something to do with the Establishment Day celebrations.

Everyone would soon see for themselves.

With the J-Pack hanging from one strap, and clutching the rifle over my chest, I carried on, pushing through the people, towards the harbor front. Everyone seemed to have forgotten to grab at me. They were more curious about the noise coming from above.

The harbor's edge loomed at the end of the street. Now to get across it before the police showed up.

I looked at my watch.

Not long to go.

52

As I staggered on toward the harbor, people streamed past me, back towards the chaos. Men, women, and children of all the genders, most wearing rainbow smocks, hurried to see what was going on. It was so strange that they ran towards danger and not away from it. Was it simply because there hadn't been any real threats to people's safety for years?

I reached the corner of Nathan Road and Salisbury Road. It was a broad area along the harbor's edge. I looked up for signs of Octavia. No sounds. No commotion. She must still be searching for me.

I hurried to the entranceway of the Peninsula Hotel, which I recognized from my sessions in the combat simulator. The hotel was a replica of the original pre-Accord style hotel with all its decadent architecture. Residents of AON sub-territory Hong Kong could visit it on special occasions, such as Accord Establishment Day. They could see for themselves just how much progress the Accord had made since the evil PAE.

The most important thing for me was that it had a flat, wide terrace overlooking the harbor and the

Establishment Day celebrations on the other side. It was a good place from which to launch myself, as long as the J-Pack would cooperate.

The door person was wary the moment I appeared. He or she stepped forward as I limped up, and planted his or her feet in front of the doorway while looking suspiciously at my limp, my bandaged nose, and my torn Navy uniform.

'Excuse me. Are you a guest?'

'No, are you?' I said, and put my left hand on his or her rainbow smock and shoved.

'You can't go in there!' came the shout but I was already hobbling past. The rifle muzzle banged on the old glass door as I went inside. The guy didn't try to stop me. Instead, he reached for his handheld.

Inside the lobby was an airy cafe. People sat at tables with cups of tea and small towers of cakes and sandwiches.

I walked straight through them all, past every gasp, every man standing up, every open-mouthed waiter, every advancing security guard. I brought the rifle down to my hip. That kept them away.

I found my way to the lift. Thanks to the simulator, I already knew where it was. There were people waiting at the lift entrance. After the lift doors opened, none of them got into the lift with me. So I stood there alone, pushing the button to close the door.

Four security guards came running around the corner.

As they came up to the doors, I leveled the rifle muzzle at them. The four guys looked at it. They backed off. One of them said, 'The whole city is looking for you. You won't get far.'

'We'll see,' I said, as the doors clunked shut.

The lift rocketed upwards. The doors opened onto a restaurant. It was full of people in Establishment Day rainbow smocks.

More screaming. More open mouths. It was an expensive restaurant. The people would be more likely not to try anything. I decided to keep the rifle at waist height anyway. I didn't want to risk a tangle with anyone who wanted to be a hero for a day.

'Where's the door to the roof?' I yelled at a waiter. He didn't understand. I pointed at the ceiling. 'Roof! Roof!'

The guy pointed to a door at the back. I limped over to it through the tables.

The door was locked.

'Open it,' I shouted to the nearest waiter.

'We don't use that door anymore,' he said.

'Open it,' I said.

'I can't open it,' he said.

I took ten steps back, raised the rifle and fired at the door. The blast threw me back into a table. More screams. More cries of outrage. I looked back at where the door had been. There was now a yawning hole opening out into the rain.

'Now you can use it,' I said to the waiter.

I left him and the diners behind, and walked out through the hole in the wall and onto the roof.

There was scuffling back in the restaurant. The security guys must have arrived. I climbed the short ladder to the rooftop and stepped out onto the terrace. From there I had a high elevation view of the harbor. I walked to the terrace edge. Now, I could see the crowd gathering for the Establishment Day celebrations on the harbor's opposite side.

PROTOCOL

Down on the harbor itself, the ancient ferries crisscrossed the kilometer of water, as they'd done for centuries. They were about to have one more passenger.

I made some mental calculations about how much power was left in the J-Pack. Probably only enough to reach one of the ferries and no more.

I made some adjustments to the straps, settling them on my shoulders. Then I set myself in a staggered stance, orienting myself at a ferry that was now in the middle of the harbor. Then, I prepared to jump.

Right on cue, the security guys arrived. I cursed. Then, I turned around with the rifle in front of me.

'Just stay back, guys,' I said. 'No-one will be hurt.'

The guy with the pistol raised it. 'Stay where you are,' he said. 'The police are coming.'

'See this weapon I'm holding,' I said. 'It's a rifle from the Romans, the intergalactic visitors you've all heard about. Understand this: One blast from this thing will obliterate the four of you. The blast will go right through you. Then it will go right through the wall and blow out a hundred square yards of windows on the building across the street. You don't want that, do you?' They stared at me. 'So, go back down the stairs.'

They looked warily at each other but didn't move. I raised the rifle, aimed at an air conditioning intake. It was about the size of a car. The blast obliterated it. When the dust settled, the group backed down the stairs but no sooner had they gone when I heard the familiar sound of the police SWAT team coming up them.

I stood up from the recoil and walked quickly back to the terrace's edge.

'Freeze!' came the shouts from the SWAT team. 'Stay where you are or we'll shoot.'

For the third time that day, I jumped over a building's edge.

Once again, the raindrops floated beside me, and the street rushed up.

And as expected, the J-Pack failed to fire.

Once.

Twice.

And then, after a huge jolt, I was sailing high over the harbor's edge.

53

I hadn't expected any shots from the SWAT team. They wouldn't want to hit the buildings on the opposite side of the harbor. But someone must have fired some kind of weapon. I heard the shot behind me, then I felt a sting in the back of my thigh.

No time to worry about it for the moment. I was busy steering the J-Pack to the white top of one of the old ferries in the harbor's middle. That was the plan. Land gently on the wide, flat roof, draw the Octavia monster with me, then draw her into the Establishment Day ceremony itself—where everyone could see the monster in her real form.

If only the J-Pack would co-operate. It got me as far as skimming over the water forty yards up, but then it spluttered out when was I ten yards short of the ferry.

I hit the roof an angle, sliding on slick paint. Then, I lay there swaying with the ferry's motion on the waves. Swaying was good. Snipers can't hit swaying, especially from so far away.

First thing I did was to check that the alien rifle was OK. No damage except a wet barrel, which wasn't any damage at all. It had fired several times in the wet already.

Then I reached around and checked the back of my right leg. My uniform was torn above the back of my knee. I stuck my finger into the tear and found what I expected: a bullet entry wound. Not a large one. No exit wound. The bullet was lodged in my flesh. It hadn't shattered my femur, and it hadn't hit an artery. I was relieved. If could handle the pain, I could get by for the next twenty minutes.

I looked at the harbor side where the Establishment Day celebrations were about to begin. There were marquees, grandstands, a huge TV screen to display the ceremony to the crowds gathered below, and a large canopy in the center of the parade ground.

Using the rifle's sights, I zoomed closer. Already I could see an honor guard of Roman Marines standing to attention. Same slick uniforms. Same closed beavers on their helmets. Same imposing height. No weapons. Ceremonial only—or so they were playing it. No sign of Captain Drusilla and the other officers. They must have been sheltering in the rain somewhere, talking to Admiral Zhou and the others.

Placed around the parade ground were media tents and TV cameras. Each camera had its own small canopy to shelter it from the rain. The arrival of the visitors was being given maximum coverage. Everyone in the Accord would be watching, from AONT South America to AONT Iceland.

If my plan worked, they'd get a broadcast they'd never forget.

But first things first.

I had to find a building top nearby on which to play

out the final scene. There was a large, cubed shaped building beside the parade ground. Some TV cameras were already on its top. Perfect. On the building's side, a huge sign read, 'The Department Of Accord Markets.' The logo beneath it read, 'DAM'

If my J-Pack could get me there, DAM was where I was going, and with a bit of luck, I'd be drawing the monster with me.

I slid around to face the Kowloon side of the harbor. I scanned the harbor front through the sights. The roof of the Peninsula Hotel had quite a crowd on it now. The SWAT team was there. So were other police. At least five of them were speaking on their handhelds. Two had binoculars trained on me.

No doubt, an armed helicopter was on its way.

I ranged the sights over the rest of the buildings on the Kowloon side, looking for what I now called the Main Attraction. I didn't have to wait long. First, there was a commotion on Nathan Road, the main road beside the Peninsula Hotel. People fled from the road entrance, cars piled up at one end.

The source of the chaos?

Octavia?

Then, the beast itself appeared. Stomping along the street, as tall as an apartment building. As she reached the end of the road, Octavia's full monstrosity was revealed. This time she was humanoid in form with feet like slabs. And by the way she stomped on the cars, buses, and people, it was obvious she was also red hot with rage.

And she was coming for me.

She sniffed the air, as she had done earlier on the skyscraper top. Then, just as before, she sensed where I was and turned towards me. Through the swaying crosshairs of the telescopic sight, I watched as she narrowed her eyes and looked at me.

Then she was in motion—not jumping into the water, but climbing onto the roof of the low, flat Science Museum. Once up there, she clomped to the edge, feet sinking into the concrete. Then, she squatted down as if to jump.

That's when I decided I'd try another shot to make sure I kept her attention.

'Come on, Octavia,' I said. 'Come on.'

I reached for the trigger and braced myself as best as I could on the slippery swaying deck. I breathed out, counted my heartbeats, allowed for the sway of the ferry, and squeezed. The rifle boomed, the pulse raced away, and I was flung back along the slick paint towards the edge, stopping just feet from going over.

Back at the Science Museum, Octavia had disappeared. The shot had missed and hit a building behind. Glass exploded outwards. But where was Octavia? Had she jumped into the water? Had she gone back into the streets?

Then I saw her.

She was in the air. She must have jumped as soon as she heard the boom of the shot. Now she was up in the sky, coming closer, like a massive boulder.

No time to think anymore. I raised the rifle and swung it like a skeet shooter. I pulled the trigger. Boom! Missed. The pulse went right past her, up into the clouds. Octavia kept on coming.

Meanwhile, the recoil flung me back. This time, I went over the ferry roof's edge. I fell past the frightened faces of the passengers on the lower deck.

Then I was in the water.

As I splashed down, I heard an almighty crash like the sound of a bowling ball dropped into a metal sink. The ferry's metal groaned as Octavia crashed through the roof and into the top deck. Then she stood, like a giant ogre on a tiny surfboard, breathing hard, face furious, fists balled, staring down into the water at me, working out her next move.

But I didn't wait to find out what it would be.

Treading water, I brought the rifle up and leveled it at her chest, but the change of weight distribution sank me. I lowered the rifle, so that the barrel was just out of the water, the stock below. I made the best aim I could.

I pulled the trigger and hung on.

The rifle boomed, and I was pulled under by the recoil. When I surfaced, spluttering and gasping, Octavia was no longer there.

But where had she gone?

I didn't wait to find out.

I twisted in the water until I had a rough alignment to the cube-shaped building beside the parade ground and tightened the straps on the J-Pack.

First click.

Nothing happened. No surprise there.

Second click. Nothing happened.

Third click.

Not again.

Then, a cough under the water.

Fourth click.

It fired.

Dragging a veil of water with me, I was flung up in the air towards the parade ground, up and over the crowds of Establishment Day revelers, and the

assembled dignitaries of the Accord.
   The finale was about to begin.

54

I was halfway to DAM, the cube-shaped building, when the J-Pack began to splutter. It didn't exactly stop. Instead, the jets faded and surged, faded and surged, letting me drop, then flinging me up. It kept up this pattern all the way over the remaining stretch of the harbor and onto the harbor's edge.

The crowd of people on the shore cleared a space as I dropped down among them and began limping towards the cube-shaped building. They'd seen what had just happened on the ferry. Now they could get a close-up view of the crazed, tall guy in a military uniform, maimed and bloodied—and dangerous.

And so they scattered.

Umbrellas crashed into umbrellas, rainbow smocks crashed into rainbow smocks. People shoved each other out of the way. The men yelled at me in both Chinese and English. 'What the hell are you doing?' was said many times.

'Get back!' I yelled before anyone could stop me. 'Get back!' I brought the rifle around. 'Sorry, but please get back!'

At the parade ground's edge, police crashed through the crowd, weapons drawn, trying to clear a space. I pressed the J-Pack button. Four times, five times. It fired and launched me up high enough so that I was above the roof of DAM.

That's where I wanted to be.

I landed and fell, inevitably sliding on the wet concrete. One of the two television crews already had their camera on me. I caught a glimpse of the giant screen above. It changed from a view of the parade ground, of Drusilla and her officers standing with Accord Commissioners, to a shot of me and the weapon.

So far, so good.

But where was the Main Attraction?

From across the harbor, came the whump-whump-whump of a helicopter, probably carrying another SWAT team and snipers. To minimize my exposure, I ran limping to the far side the building and crouched beside a wall. I didn't want to be killed before I could even begin.

I tossed off the J-Pack. I wouldn't be needing it anymore. Then, I unslung the rifle and looked through the sights along the building tops. Snipers watched from a rooftop eight hundred yards away. Their weapons were mounted on tripods. Same with a second building beside it. The shooters would wait for the right moment.

But I also had a rifle, one that would obliterate them.

To shoot or not shoot?

In the end, the decision was made for me by Octavia.

There was a crash off to my right, a boom of glass panels breaking and metal straining. I looked over at the famous Bank of China building, the building shaped like a shard of glass, another example of the progressive architecture from the pre-Accord era.

Now it served another purpose.

Standing there, her lower half embedded into the side of the building was Octavia, or at least the life form that used to be Octavia. She was something else now, changed from the monster she had been a few minutes before into something even more bizarre. Never were the words 'alien life form' a more appropriate description.

She or it was about the height of a five-story building and about as wide. She was colored grayish purple. Her skin rippled as if there were boiling fluid beneath it, or something squirming underneath. And her feet were no longer slabs. They had claws.

She squatted and then leaped, sailing through the air toward me. Her clawed feet hit the roof of DAM with a massive crash, and sank deep into the concrete, throwing up dust and shards, scattering one of the camera crews. She paused a moment, letting the roof settle under her feet, then came slowly towards me, one horrible claw step after horrible claw step.

I was as ready as I could be. I looked at the remaining camera crew. They stayed grimly aiming at the scene. The giant screen above showed the action. I couldn't help but think that the announcer would say this was another example of the Accord respecting the fascinating culture of our visitors.

I just hoped the people weren't that stupid.

With Octavia clomping towards me, I raised the rifle and fired. A pulse slammed out. I pulled the trigger again, and again. Each time the pulse threw me yards backward. Meanwhile, they hit the creature in the chest, the neck the head, the arms—all to little effect. The blasts were as ineffective as slaps from a child. They didn't slow her down.

By now, the helicopter was hovering nearby. The whump of the blades was louder than the megaphone calling out my name. Whose voice was that? Captain Paine's? Le Seaux's? Chen's?

But I was only half listening. The rifle had finally stopped firing altogether. It was also too hot to hold. Octavia brushed the last blast away and then took one giant step towards me. Bang! She was right beside me, looking down, a colossus above an insect. I looked up at that horrible face.

'It's over, Alex,' said a voice. It wasn't Octavia's. It was a growling voice, deep and menacing.

So this is it, I thought. This is it. This is the way the world ends for Alexander Burns. At least I was going to die in battle. A kind of battle, anyway. That was something. And my cause was just, wasn't it? The Accord didn't deserve saving, but the people of the Accord deserved to be warned about the aliens. At least I had tried to do that.

And then I could have taken on the Accord itself.

Octavia had been watching. She actually shook her head in pity. Her pincer arm was just above me, lowering slowly. I tried one more time with the rifle and then let it drop. Not working. Too hot to hold. The pincer was on my chest. Then the pressure began, right on my Adam's apple. Heavier and heavier.

'Goodbye, Alex.'

The rain began falling again. Thunder rumbled. I thought I heard cheering from down on the square below. Were both the aliens and the Accord celebrating the defeat of the troublemaker, the rogue sailor, Lieutenant Burns? He'd tried and he'd failed to ruin the spirit of intergalactic goodwill, of tolerance.

He'd gone against the ideals of the Accord.

He deserved to die.

I squinted up at Octavia through the rain.

And then, as if my mind blinked, I was no longer there.

55

I was standing on the quarterdeck of HMS Vengeance —holding the taffrail to keep the weight off my ankle. The pain was still there. It had come with me into this dream, this other dimension.

Unfortunately, so had the bullet wound in my thigh. I winced as I stood on one leg, grimaced as I put weight on the other. It must have looked as if I were performing a jig.

My ancestor stood at the taffrail too. As always, he was calm, commanding, imposing in his great coat, but this time, something was different. Captain Burns's ramrod posture was stooped as if he was suffering from a back wound. His hair was loose and his immaculate breeches were stained a watery red.

'What's happened?' he said. 'You look worse than before.'

'I could say the same about you.'

'Was it Octavia?'

'Was it the Indomitable?'

'Not one hour ago.'

'And it was Octavia,' I said. 'Still is. I must have

passed out while she had me on the ground.'

He nodded slowly. 'Was she…?'

'Yes, big as a house, angrier than…'

'Than a shrew.'

'Yeah,' I said. 'She was furious, a monster.'

We stood in silence for a moment listening to the ship's sounds, the groaning of the timbers, the protests of the straining ropes, the shush of the sea moving along the wooden hull.

'She's going to invade,' I said, 'with more troops than the stars.'

I winced as my ankle yelped, grimaced as my bullet wound throbbed.

'You need help,' he said. 'Mr. Collins!' he called. 'Pass the word for the doctor.'

'I know what you mean now, grandfather.'

'You know? Know what?'

'Many things.'

'Such as?'

'Combat, battle. How exciting it is, and how terrible. How important it is to know the truth and to act on it. The lies the Accord has told us all.' Then I added. 'The importance of knowing the things that happened in the past.'

'What things?'

'All the things I wanted to learn about the PAE, but now there's no time.'

'There'll be time,' he said.

'I only wished I could have raised a family—to continue the Burns line.'

'It's not too late,' he said. 'It's never too late.'

'I think it might be,' I said. 'Octavia has me by the throat, and this time, I don't think this member of

Burns line will survive.'

'There's always a way,' he said. 'Never give in. Never.'

'I'm just glad to have lived,' I said, 'if only for a short time. All my life, I've lived a delusion about the world and about myself.' The pain swelled in my legs and my chest. 'Now, just when it's near the end, I've seen what's what.'

He looked at me, Burns to Burns.

'I'll say it again,' he said. 'Never give in! No matter how dark the hour. Never give in. Always tell yourself that.'

Then he said something else, but I couldn't hear because the wind began to roar and the great ship careened to starboard. Down on the deck, shouting began. Something was wrong with HMS Vengeance.

'What about you?' I said. 'Are you defeated?'

He straightened up, hobbled over to me. He put his hands on my shoulders and spoke something to me.

'I can't hear you, grandfather.'

He said it again.

'I can't hear you. I can't hear you.'

56

Octavia loomed over me, but now something had changed. She had released the pressure on my throat. She was looking upward into the rain, at the heavy clouds above us. Then she looked down at me and smiled—or what I thought was a smile.

'See?'

'See what?' I rasped.

'Look,' she boomed. I squinted against the rain and at the billowing mist of the clouds. There was nothing there—nothing but bulges and shadings, like bruises boiling inside.

'There,' said Octavia.

Then, I saw it.

At first, it was just another shade of darkness within the cloud—a black bruise, bubbling. But the bruise deepened and spread. It swelled all along the length of Hong Kong Harbor. Then, it spread outward over the Kowloon hills and over Hong Kong Island itself. The dull daylight faded to gloom. It was like a solar eclipse were taking place or a blanket had been spread over the city. The atmosphere thickened, and I saw flocks of birds racing away south to the sea.

'There,' boomed Octavia.

The first hull emerged from the cloud like a horrible black egg, first the curve of its bottom, then the dark mass of its belly. Then more hulls emerged as the great ship Excidium lumbered down from the clouds.

Five, ten, twenty, fifty or more shuttle hulls pushed slowly through the mist until half the enormous ship was visible, like the underbelly of a gigantic black whale.

The lowermost shuttle hull almost touched the skyscraper on the harbor's edge. Any lower and the ship would begin smashing the city itself, knocking down the skyscrapers down like skittles. Perhaps that was the intention, to crush and destroy without firing a single laser, to show the people they were nothing compared to it.

Then, the ship halted its descent and settled over the harbor, a hideous, gleaming cluster of shells from the far side of the galaxy. An awful display of power and technology.

All was quiet. Not sound emerged from any of the hulls, except for the silent opening of hundreds of ports. Through them the barrels of laser guns now appeared, ready to cause devastation. And, then with the clanking and groaning of metal, the first of the shuttles detached and began descending slowly but heavily downwards.

Octavia looked down at me, then, without warning stepped over me to walk to the edge of the building. She saluted her fellow Romans down at the square. I could imagine the cheer. Their mission was almost accomplished. They had deceived and then captured the Accord Commission; they had brought their entire invasion force into one of the Accord's main cities, all without a single shot being fired by the Accord's so-called defense forces.

And, through the television cameras and three million handhelds pointed up across the city, the invasion was broadcast around the Accord, from AONT Peru to AONT Greenland.

Octavia returned from the building's edge. Standing over me, she waved to the ship above. Then, her monstrous face leered at me. She leaned down and with one giant claw, scooped me upwards and brought me to her face. 'Give my regards to your ancestor on the other side,' she said. Then, she drew back her arm, as if she were going to throw me away, fling me far away into sea.

Her arm extended way back, like a baseball pitcher's arm. I felt the surge of her muscles ready to contract. I closed my eyes and waited.

But the day was not over yet.

57

A green flash shot from the sky, slicing through Octavia's wrist. Then a second flash shot from the clouds and hit Octavia in the back, blasting through and carrying on to the parade ground below.

What on Earth was happening?

Octavia shrieked in pain and clutched at her back. I hit the roof with a sickening crack. It was my pelvis this time, but luckily my head didn't snap onto the surface and knock me unconscious. Octavia's hand crashed beside me in thump of dead, glutinous weight. Above, Octavia herself twisted in agony.

But more blasts were to come.

Green pulses shot from the clouds to the left of the Roman ship. Some shafted down towards the parade ground. But the majority struck the various shuttles and other vessels, causing searing holes to open up in their sides, with one or two exploding.

Then the cause of all these shots revealed itself. A huge jagged spear pierced the clouds, followed by the rest of a wedge-shaped grey ship. It wasn't a quarter the size of the Roman ship, but it appeared to be a different class. It wasn't a troop carrier or transporter; it was more like a frigate. It was sleeker, more maneuverable, fitted with more weapons.

Then, I realized. It was another Goth ship.

Blasts of laser beams hit the Roman ship like green hail. Blue cannon fire was returned but it too late. The Goth ship was dominant. It sent rolling broadsides as it flew along. It also sent blasts down at the one Marine shuttle to have begun its drop to the Earth, hitting the troops as they emerged from the hatch, destroying them in an explosion of green laser and mud.

Octavia sank to her knees, clutching at her wounds. Then, like the colossus that she was, she crashed sideways onto the roof, smashing its tiles with a sickening whomp. I couldn't tell if she were still conscious or not, nor whether she realized all her plans were now being undone by this new threat. Her eyes closed.

Seconds later, so did mine.

Aftermath

PROTOCOL

THE NURSE LEANED in close while I lay flat on my back. She or he or zee pushed something pebble-like into each of my ears.

At first, I thought they were some kind of ear cleaners, but after I felt the wires dangling on my neck, I changed my mind. I knew what they were.

They were earphones.

As far as I could tell, I was in a hospital. I could see a white ceiling and white walls. And I could smell the bubble gum of antiseptic detergent—the same kind used on AONS Accord Values. Probably, it was a Navy prison hospital. Maybe one in AONT China. Or in AONT USA. But not on a ship, I could tell that much. There was no motion from the ocean, no ship's noises, no hum of engines.

How long had I been there? I guessed it had been about two weeks. I had been delirious right up until this morning. All I could recall were brows frowning over blue surgical masks, and disturbing dreams in which my limbs were pulled, pushed and cut.

'That should do it,' said the nurse prodding at the pebble in my right ear. 'He can't move his head, so they won't come out.'

I swiveled my eyes to see the nurse's face. She wore short hair, the same as most Accord women, but her hair wasn't as short as say, Captain Paine's. It was softer than the usual brutal style. The nurse actually smiled when I managed to catch her eye and blink at her.

Blinking was the limit of my movement. My head was secured by some kind of brace with spikes. I could feel other restraints too: something on my legs, and a hard length of something beneath my back.

'I'll set the volume low,' said the nurse, 'so he won't be alarmed.'

But now another voice spoke, a male voice.

'Set it high,' the voice said. 'We want to make sure he doesn't miss a word.' The speaker was out of my range of vision, but if all my other guesses were correct, this voice belonged to someone from Navy Spirit.

'We shouldn't overdo it,' said the nurse. 'He only woke up last night. It's too soon. The doctors say he might have brain damage, along with everything else.'

'No special treatment,' said the other voice, 'especially not for someone with a hundred and twelve Navy Spirit code violations.'

'Even so.'

'No, especially so.'

'He's in a hospital.'

'Yes, but a prison hospital.'

'He has suffered extreme trauma.'

'But he is a male patient who is an alleged traitor who rejects Accord values.'

'Even so.'

'Just press the buds in a little further to make sure he hears absolutely everything. If ever there were a guy who needed re-education, it's this piece of work right here.'

The nurse pushed at each of the earbuds one more time. As she did, I tried to speak. 'The attack? What happened? My mother?'

'What's he saying?' said the voice.

The nurse leaned in again. 'What's that, Lieutenant Burns? What are you trying to say?'

'The attack,' I said. 'Hong Kong, the aliens—what happened?'

The nurse stood up. 'I can't tell,' she said to the other person in the room. 'His jaw can't really open. And, he's probably still delirious after so many sedatives.'

'If he can't speak, then so much the better for his re-education,' said the male voice. 'Just leave him and start the lesson.'

'No,' I said to the nurse. 'Stop. I'm OK. What happened? Can't you tell me what happened? My mother? Is she…'

But it was too late. A female voice began shouting in my ear. 'Lesson One: The oppression of the people in The Pre Accord Era.' The volume was so loud that it was painful. I signaled the nurse to turn it down. I winced. I screwed up my face. I blinked over and over. I shook my head. I poked out my tongue. I tried to move my legs, my toes. I squirmed.

But the re-education lesson droned on.

'The Pre Accord Era was characterized by one word: oppression. The oppression was imposed by the evil powers of the Western imperialists. It took many forms: free markets, the subjugation of women, mistreatment of LGBTQ people, colonization of other lands, insistence on the certainty of science and mathematics, of the so-called scientific method, patriarchal privilege, the idea of progress at all costs, able-ism, sporting contests, hierarchies of achievement, hierarchies of power, corruption, meritocracies, an emphasis on the family unit…'

'Please,' I said.

The nurse mouthed something, frowning.

She looked to the side, looked back, still frowning. She put a cool hand on my forehead.

And on it went until I blacked out.

Several days later, I woke to a quiet room. The earphones had been removed. The re-education had ceased. The ringing of my new case of tinnitus filled the void, like a fire alarm ringing endlessly. A hand shook my shoulder. It was someone different. This person had a frowning face. Beside it was another face, also unfriendly, with brutal, short-cropped hair and a Navy Spirit insignia on the collar.

Another nurse, or perhaps a doctor.

'Lieutenant Burns,' said the nurse. 'Lieutenant Burns. Blink twice if you can understand me.' I blinked twice. 'Blink twice again for me again, please.' I blinked twice. 'Can you speak, Lieutenant?'

'Yes,' I said. 'I think so.'

'He can't really speak yet, Captain Dowson,' said the nurse.

'Well, then he can't have any visitors either,' said the Navy Spirit officer. She stood up, then clicked on some kind of device that squawked. 'Ensign Tambor, please inform the two civilians that they can't see the prisoner. Not today. Maybe not for weeks, if ever.'

'Wait,' said the nurse. 'He said something. I just heard him. What did you say, Lieutenant Burns?' She leaned in close.

'The idiot beside you has their hand on my leg.'

The nurse looked up and smiled.

'He asked you to remove your hand, Captain,' she said. The heavy hand was lifted. 'If he's awake enough to make jokes, he's probably OK to see visitors, for a short while. Who are these people, anyway?'

'One's army; one's a civilian.'

'How did they get permission?' said the nurse.

'A command from one of the commissioners. That's the only way we'd allow traitors like this to see anyone. We protested, but you can't argue, not against a commissioner.'

I wondered who this commissioner might be.

The Navy Spirit officer left the room while the nurse fiddled with the equipment by my bed. Maybe she also didn't like Navy Spirit people. There was always hope.

After a few minutes, several sets of footsteps came into the room. I recognized the footsteps from the original Navy Spirit officer and then four more people. Two sets of footsteps came close to the side of the bed.

The Navy Spirit officer said, 'I remind you one more time that this is a dangerous prisoner. He is charged with at least one hundred and twelve Navy Spirit code violations so far. You are not to talk to him about his charges nor are you to discuss with him the events leading to the charges. Is that understood?'

'He doesn't look too dangerous to me,' said a voice with an accent from AONT USA that didn't sound quite right. I recognized it immediately.

Chen.

'He doesn't look like he'll be saving the world either,' said a feminine voice with an accent from the sub-territory of France in AONT Eurabia.

Le Seaux.

The two faces loomed over me. Chen had a burn mark on his left cheek. The skin was blistered into a mottled lump. 'Last time I saw you,' he said, 'you were falling backward out of a spaceship.'

'And the last time I saw you,' said Le Seaux, 'you were going into one.'

'Stop!' said the Navy Spirit officer. 'I told you. No mention of the events leading up to his capture. Do it again and you'll be out the door and won't be allowed back. Have you got that?'

Le Seaux laid a hand lightly on my arm. I looked across at her. Her face was unmarked. In fact, she looked surprisingly fresh-faced, softer, her green eyes bright with health. It was amazing she was alive at all. But then I remembered. Octavia said they had healed her.

'The invasion?' I said. 'Hong Kong?'

'What?' said Le Seaux. 'Say it slowly this time.'

'The invasion? Hong Kong?'

'What was that?' said the Navy Spirit officer. 'What did he say?'

Le Seaux ignored him and spoke directly to me. 'Your family, Lieutenant? Is that what you said? They're devastated, of course, but surviving. They'll be here when you're better.'

My family? What could she mean?

'I didn't know you'd been in touch,' Chen said.

Le Seaux shrugged. She had some new kind of patch on her uniform, an award of some kind.

'Octavia?' I whispered. 'What happened to Octavia?'

Le Seaux leaned in close. I felt her breath on my neck. The Navy Spirit guard stepped forward as well. 'Too close, Captain. Way too close,' he said. 'Step back from the prisoner.' He grabbed Le Seaux by one arm, and pulled her away, but not before she managed to whisper something.

'I'm right here, Alex,' she said, but her voice was not the same accented English that I recognized as Le Seaux's. Instead, it was a mannered voice, the strange pre-Accord accent I'd heard weeks before.

'I'm right here. It won't be long now.'

—End—

Burns Returns in 'SHALE,' book three in The Burns Series.

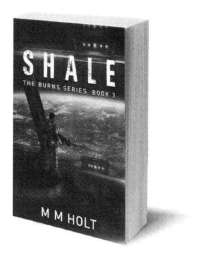

DIG DEEP. FIGHT BACK.

It's the year 250 in the the Accord of Nations Era. Things couldn't be worse for the people of the Accord. Octavia has landed her invasion force. The politically correct government has welcomed the invaders in the names of tolerance and harmony. And in their delusion, they have even offered Octavia a leadership role.

But achieving tolerance and harmony are the last of Octavia's intentions.

For Lieutenant Burns, the chance to fight back is almost gone. He languishes in a navy prison, half-mad from 'Re-Orientation.' In his future lies a show trial and decades in jail. That's if the earth lasts that long. That's if his sanity doesn't break.

But when all seems lost, help comes from the most unlikely source imaginable, and Lieutenant Burns suddenly finds himself aboard an alien ship crossing the galaxy to a dusty planet the size of the sun. There he finds a curious, glittering metal that could change everything.

If only he can find his way back.

If you were thrilled by the adventure of Book 1, 'Fifty Degrees South,' and were outraged by the future world of 'Protocol,' you must read 'SHALE,' the story of the Burns family's fightback against invasion and political correctness taken to extremes.

To buy your own copy, please visit Amazon and search for 'Shale,' by MM Holt.

To read the thrilling opening chapter, turn to the next page.

Best regards,

M.M. Holt

SHALE

PROLOGUE

I RAISED THE spear to the sunlight. It was over eight feet long, thin but stubbornly rigid, and it glittered like no metal I had ever seen before. It also seemed to emit a crackling hum, like an electrical cable.

It looked deadly too. The tip was sharp to touch, and the spear's shaft was light. In the right hands it could be wielded to cut, smack, and bludgeon, or just twirled around to create a diversion before the next stab.

But I had never fought with a spear before. I'd never even held one, not even in the combat simulator back at AONS Harmony in AON sub-territory California. Spears were not part of a modern arsenal of weapons, of course. Not just because they were primitive, but because they were symbols of male power; and male power was responsible for all the trouble in the world. Every Accord member knew it.

But this wasn't the Accord of Nations.

It wasn't even Earth.

And for a hundred thousand light years in every direction, I was the only human male alive.

I stood in a dusty clearing in the middle of a dense, tall, alien forest. The strange trees loomed on three sides, thick and green, and full of screeching birds I could neither see nor imagine. To my right, a tall, gray cliff dominated the clearing. At its base was a series of caves in which my hosts lived.

PROTOCOL

On my left was a sight that would strain the tolerance of the most dedicated Navy Spirit officer. A thousand bear-wolf monsters, known as Goths, howled and roared at me. They bared their teeth and unsheathed their claws, and they slashed at the air with great swipes. They were in a frenzy, a rage. They growled a single Goth word over and over. 'Gwanta!' they growled. 'Gwanta! Gwanta! Gwanta!'

Gwanta, the god of the Goths. Gwanta, the god of war and of vengeance.

The roars echoed off the cliff face. They bounced back across the clearing as if the cliff itself wanted vengeance, as did the forest and the sky. The whole Goth land called to Gwanta, beseeching him to avenge the terrible wrong done to the Goth nation by the strange alien creature from across the galaxy.

I raised a sleeve to my face and wiped away the sweat dripping into my eyes. I grabbed the collar of my soiled, blue Navy Working Uniform and peeled the shirt from my clammy back. Then, I reached up to my nose and pushed the small breathing device deeper into my nostrils, shoving it all the way until it hit cartilage. I didn't want it coming loose when the fight began, and I didn't want to smell the reek of the planet's foul air.

Then, I lowered my arm and gripped the spear in what I thought was the most natural way, left hand on the middle to guide the sharp tip, right hand on the lower third to provide the power. I twisted my boots around in the dust until I found a fighting stance. Then, forcing down the fear smoldering in my stomach, and closing my mind to images of claws and teeth tearing at my uniform, I raised the spear and leveled the quivering tip at my opponent.

Ten yards away, swaying on his hind limbs, the Goth warrior Granak glowered down at me. At the sight of the raised spear, he barked in disgust. Granak required no spears. Not at all. He had all the weapons he needed built in. His claws were as big and sharp as fruit knives. His canine teeth were as long as my hands. He was many times my weight, at least twice my height, a yard wider, and his hide was as thick and tough as old carpet.

He panted at me, his long, red tongue dripping saliva to the dust beside his hind paws, twelve feet down. His genitals swayed obscenely beneath him, and his sewage breath reached across the ten yards between us, like an advanced fighting force. That breath of Granak's was so foul, it could kill a man all by itself—if the man ever allowed him to get close enough.

The sight of him drained my courage. How could I ever hope to defeat a creature so enormous? How could I win with nothing but my boots, my wits, and a primitive weapon I didn't know how to use? Worse! How could I defeat such a creature when he was fighting for his king, his god, and the pride of his nation, while I was fighting only for myself?

The answer was that I couldn't—not without a miracle.

Standing there in the heat and dust, I asked myself the questions I'd struggled to answer all morning. How had I allowed this to happen? How did I end up in this nightmare? How was it that I came to be clutching a spear in the middle of an alien forest, fighting a monster on a planet one hundred thousand light-years from Earth?

And not just any planet, either. This was the planet Rome itself, the home of Octavia and her alien nation, the nation moving its enormous warships into formation around Earth while I stood with the spear, the dust, and the overwhelming odds of defeat.

But, of course, I knew how this situation had come about. No matter how much I shook my head, I knew all too well. I had chosen to be here. I had chosen to go with the Goths. Me, and no one else. It was a wrong choice, a stupid choice, the worst decision possible. Only a fool would have made it. A fool or someone out of his mind. But that's what I'd done. I'd chosen the Goths. Now I faced the terrible consequences.

'What are you looking at?' I shouted across the sand to Granak. His ears sprung up and twitched towards me like turret guns. He couldn't understand me, of course. Only Karz, the she-Goth interpreter understood a few words of Accord languages. But Granak got the gist. He knew a taunt when he heard one. He must have heard hundreds or thousands of taunts from enemies whom he soon ripped to pieces. Now, he faced another enemy, and another opportunity to rip and tear all over again.

As if hearing my thoughts, he smiled. The black seam lining his immense snout curled, revealing more of his teeth and brown gums than I wanted to see. Then, he snorted and sneezed with a great shake of his head before ducking his eyes under a wipe of his forelimb, and settling back into swaying tall in the sun with his ears twitching and his claws sliding in and out of their dark sheaths.

And so, we waited for some signal to start. The alien sun beat down, my eyes stung with sweat, the spear tip quivered and glittered. Meanwhile, the Goth mob howled, and my arms and legs, already tired from carrying the planet's heavy gravity, trembled with exhaustion and fear.

Come on, I thought. Let's get started. Let's get this over with, for better or worse.

But Granak was in no hurry. He looked casually at one shaggy shoulder, then dug his snout into his fur, checking for something, bites from alien bugs, or the bones of his last meal, or his last victim. Who could tell? His long shadow stretched towards me over the dust, revealing an enormous creature apparently eating itself.

Finally, Granak looked up from his fur. He lifted his snout to the chanting mob and bared his teeth at them and nodded a few times. Then, as if reaching a decision, he turned back to me, dropped from his great height, flopping down onto his four dinner-plate-sized paws, lowered his head, and charged.

I didn't need the Goth mob to tell me the fight had begun.

They had dropped their chant of Gwanta. Now they howled and bayed in a raucous free-for-all. Baying for blood. Baying for death. My blood and my death.

There could be no getting out of it now. Minutes ago, I might have wanted to run or protest or plead, to drop the spear and beseech the Goth king to pardon me, but those doors were now shut. There could be no going back.

Granak's shadow came bounding over the dusty ground towards me. His breath shushed from his open snout in rasping puffs. His black eyes gleamed. His dark fur shimmered. And his haunches drove him forward with astonishing power, like a charging buffalo, like a truck made of muscle, bone, and hate.

This is it, I thought. This is how it will end. I'll die with my head crushed like a piece of fruit, my ribs cracked and pulled apart, and my guts ripped out and dragged in the dust for the entertainment of a howling mob. That's how it will go. That's how it will end. And it will be all my own fault.

So I waited with the spear tip trembling five feet in front of my sweating face.

Soon, the edge of Granak's hysterical shadow reached me. I gripped the spear tighter, leaning forward, anchoring my boots deeper in the dust, bracing myself for the terrible impact.

All right. Here we go, I thought. Here we go. You won't survive, but at least you'll die fighting. You have failed yourself. You have failed your people, and you have disgraced your family, but you'll die with a weapon in your hands. At least you'll have that. A sailor's death in battle. At least you'll have that.

But what I couldn't know was that fate had something else in mind. I would soon make a discovery that would change everything, and that this ordeal of man against monster would lead to a weapon that could defeat Octavia and save the Earth and its people from invasion and annihilation.

If I survived the day.

If.

But with every bound of that horrible shadow, the 'if' grew bigger. On it came, till the *if* was like another enemy itself, in partnership with Granak, the monster.

And then, all too soon, the shadow rushed over me. The hot, foul breath hit my face, and the thick yellow claws came slicing through the poisonous air.

———— / ————

Don't stop now.

Join Lieutenant Burns in his continuing struggle against Octavia and the Accord of Nations.

Visit amazon and search for 'SHALE' by M.M. Holt.

And turn the page for more books by M.M. Holt

A few words from you
could make all the difference.

Thank you for reading 'PROTOCOL.' I hope you enjoyed it.

If you have a few spare moments, would you please do me a huge favor and post a brief review where you purchased it. Reviews are essential to drawing readers to the book, especially for a new series like this one.

Without them, the book would languish among the millions of other titles on Amazon.

Just a few words from you can make all the difference.

To leave a review, please bring up the page from which you downloaded the book, scroll down to the book image, then click the button that reads 'Write a customer review,' and type 'This book was astonishing!'

Just kidding. I know you'll write what you think best.

On the off chance you didn't really like the book, could you contact me with your thoughts. I would love to hear your criticism. Email me at mmholt548@gmail.com

My sincere thanks,

M.M. Holt.

PS: Keep reading to discover more titles by M.M. Holt. You'll be glad you did.

The book that started it all.
When Alex Burns's ancestor met Octavia the first time.

If you didn't start the Burns Series at the beginning, here's your chance to
catch up, with Book 1, where it all began.

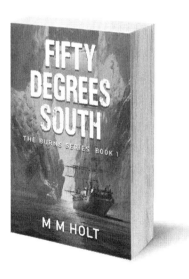

At the end of the earth, we fought an enemy from beyond the stars.

1803. The Napoleonic War. A Royal Navy warship is ordered to pursue an enemy frigate to the frozen waters far south in the Indian Ocean. There it must capture the enemy ship and retrieve a mysterious sea-chest, contents unknown. Failure not permitted.

For the determined young captain and his crew, this already dangerous mission turns into a battle with a mysterious vessel that appears not in the sea, but unbelievably, impossibly, in the sky above. The result is one of the most compelling and unusual encounters in science fiction.

Reviewers describe FIFTY DEGREES SOUTH as **'Brilliant," "A wonderful adventure,"** and **"Patrick O'Brian, CS Forester, Arthur C Clarke, and Naomi Navi, all in one."** It's also an unputdownable tale that will live in your imagination long after the final page is turned.

Join readers around the globe who were thrilled by FIFTY DEGREES SOUTH. Visit Amazon and check out the many five-star reader reviews. Then purchase a copy of your own or download the ebook version.

Whichever way you choose, you are in for an unforgettable adventure. You've never read a Sci-Fi novel like FIFTY DEGREES SOUTH. **Read on to check out the thrilling first chapter.**

FIFTY DEGREES SOUTH

Chapter 1

WHEN THE FIRST blue beam struck the sea just ahead of HMS Morgause, none of the seventy sailors in the first watch saw it. Instead, they were concentrating on the task known as wearing the ship, changing its heading from southwest to southeast.

At the helm, Jessop, the quartermaster, turned the wheel anti-clockwise, and the great ship's bow swung away from the wind towards port. The compass in the binnacle wobbled around to south-south-west, then south where it paused as Jessop waited for the next command. He was so engrossed in his task of feeling the ship's movement, he missed the sight of the blue beam entirely.

Forward of Jessop, on the main deck, the crew stood ready, the thick ropes in their hands, waiting for the commands to heave the yards of the main mast around to coordinate with Jessop's turn of the helm and with the other crewmen hauling on ropes at the foremast and the mizzen mast.

They too missed the blue beam as it hit the water, thick as a four barrels, and curiously light as it went down into the depths.

High on the mainmast, Trinity Evans was scouring the south for the enemy vessel, the Besançon, which the Morgause had been desperately pursuing for seven long weeks in heavy seas. But when he turned west with the movement of the Morgause's bow, he too missed the blue beam. He didn't see the three-second long blast from the sky, the cylinder-shaped shaft of light, wide and smooth, smacking the dark sea, going through it and straight down and distorting, like a twig in a glass of water. Nor did Trinity Evans hear the hiss of steam that followed.

On the quarterdeck, the view forward was blocked by the mainsail. The officer of the watch, Mr Kyte concentrated on Jessop's shouted compass readings. Mr Kyte didn't see the beam either, nor did he see the smoldering carcass of an enormous white squid surfacing ahead of the Morgause and sliding along its hull to be churned in the ship's wake.

But when the ship hard worn to her new southeast course and was pushing through the dark and swelling water at a good eight knots, the blue beam struck again.

And this time, it was noticed.

Trinity Evans ducked, held up an elbow, and thought it was lightning coming to strike him dead, but this was not like any lightning he'd seen before. For one thing, it was bright blue; for another, it was straight. It also wasn't flashing. It struck sixty yards ahead of the Morgause and blazed for a full five seconds. No lightning ever did that—not in Trinity Evans's experience. Not on your life. Not even after ten too many mugs of grog—the extra strong stuff.

He watched the beam, fascinated. The way it went right down into the water. Only when it finally ceased did he prepare to hail the deck. But still, he hesitated, wondering what he should say. This wasn't a regular sighting. It certainly wasn't the sighting of the Besançon, nor any other ship. This was something else entirely. It wasn't even in his list of hails, which was long. Still, he had better hail something before someone on the deck noticed it first. He slapped a hand to the side of his mouth and peered down at the darkened figures way below.

'On deck there!' he called. 'On deck!'

'Yes, Evans,' came the reply. 'Is it the Besançon?'

'No, sir. Strange light, sir! Strange light.'

'Where away?' came the reply but only after a few moments.

'Straight ahead!' he called.

As he said this, another beam hit the sea. Same place —directly ahead. Same thickness. Same intensity, it was the color of the blue in the plate glass windows back in his church in Penzance—which made Trinity Evans wonder. Was this a sign from God? Was the Second Coming at hand? Was this something mentioned in the book of Revelations? It certainly didn't look like a friendly light. Tomorrow, he thought. No more grog. No more ale.

'On deck there!' he called again.

'We saw it, Evans,' someone called back.

'Something new!' Trinity Evans countered.

'What?' came the reply.

'The strange light—it came from that big dark cloud.'

On the quarterdeck, Mr Kyte walked to the taffrail and looked up into the gloom at the gray cloud that had settled off the ship's port side, huge and glowering, almost like a ship itself, a ship of the air, with curious bulges. A ship of the air, he thought, then shook his head. His overactive imagination was at work again.

My Kyte made a note of the time. It was three bells in the morning watch, just as dawn was fighting off the night. Possible enemy activity sighted. A strange blue light.

'Did you see it, Poole?' he said to the youth beside him, one of the ship's young midshipman who were training to become officers, just as Mr Kyte himself had trained twenty years ago.

'Yes,' said Poole. 'I saw it, port bow, a quarter cable length away.'

'You mean, "Yes, sir,"' said Mr Kyte. 'You're in His Majesty's Navy, Poole, and we are at war.'

'Yes, sir,' said Poole. 'Beg pardon, sir. The light, sir— it made me forget myself.'

Mr Kyte scanned the darkness again. Nothing but the swelling sea in the soft dawn. Nothing but the shush of the water along the hull, and the creak of ropes as the ship rose and fell. He looked down at the main deck. The seventy men of the morning watch, dressed in their blue jackets and white duck trousers stared into the darkness. Others looked up at Mr Kyte —waiting for a command—and an explanation.

Then, without warning, another blue beam shot from the dark cloud. It was closer this time. He could see it clearly. It was a thick blue shaft of light, straight as a sun ray, coming from the dark cloud, going straight down into the sea, illuminating the underwater world beneath for a good sixty yards or so, and going down into the depths.

Trinity Davies was already hailing him from the

upper deck when a second beam struck the water. Same straight blue shaft of light. Same point of origin in the dark cloud above. Two beams. One to port. One to starboard. They were like a ceremonial gateway of light.

Mt Kyte turned around. Poole was behind him, crouching.

'Stand up straight, Poole,' he said.

'Yes, sir,' said Poole.

'The men must see that you are unafraid, that you are fearless.'

'Yes, sir,' said Poole. 'Beg pardon, sir.'

'Never again, Poole.'

'No, sir. Never again. Fearless.'

'Fearless of even the strangest things produced by war and the heavens.'

'Yes, sir.'

Mr Kyte turned back to the beams.

'Are we going to beat to quarters, sir?' said Poole.

Is was a good question. Beating to quarters meant the bosun's whistle would blow, drums would pound, commands would be shouted, and the crew would scramble for battle, the one hundred and thirty men asleep in the hammocks below would rush to join the men already on the main deck. The gun crews would rush to the cannons ranged along the sides of the Morgause, untying the ropes that held them fast on their wooden carts, readying them for the gunpowder and the cannonballs. The Marines would climb with their muskets into the tops. The powder boys would scramble to the magazine, deep inside the ship, and rush upward with buckets of powder for the gun crews. The wicks would be lit and set in tubs beside each cannon. The boarding crews would assemble for the armourer to hand out the cutlasses, rapiers and pistols. The gun ports on the main deck and below would swing open and the Morgause would be ready to unleash thunderous hell and utterly smash any ship within range.

Beating to quarters.

Mr Kyte made his decision.

'Yes, Poole,' he said. 'Give the order. Beat to quarters.'

Poole almost broke into a run before checking himself. He was eager for something to be done about the beams.

'Mr Pound!' he called to the bosun.

'Sir,' Mr Pound called up from the main deck.

'Per Mr Kyte, we shall beat to quarters.'

'What?' said Mr Pound.

'We shall beat to quarters!' called Mr Kyte.

'Aye,' said Mr Pound.

Instantly, the mood of the ship changed. Mr Pound's whistle piped its shrill two tones, and the ship came alive.

Mr Kyte watched the blue beams and wondered.

The year was 1803 in the Napoleonic war. The location was the Atlantic Ocean in the lonely waters far south the equator, off the west coast of Southern Africa on His Majesty's Ship, Morgause. Seas moderate to heavy. Wind from the northeast. Time at sea: sixty days. Mission: to capture the enemy frigate Besançon and retrieve a certain sea-chest, contents unknown, and return said sea-chest to the Admiralty in London.

Failure not permitted.

'Mr Poole,' said Mr Kyte without taking his eyes off

the beams.

'Yes, sir.'

'Pass the word for Captain Burns.'

—/—

To continue reading, search Amazon for 'Fifty Degrees South,' by M.M. Holt.

ACKNOWLEDGEMENTS

My sincere thanks to the many friends and family who encouraged me to persevere with this novel and the others in the series.

M.M. Holt.

About M.M. Holt

M.M. Holt is a mysterious figure who lives partly in the real world, but more often in his imagination.

He writes science fiction, horror and adventure novels, often involving a Navy lieutenant named Alex Burns who struggles to keep his sanity in a future world gone mad with political correctness. This same Alex Burns also fights alien invaders. Sometimes Burns's great seafaring ancestors also appear in the books. They are also named Alex Burns, and in their owns times they also battled invaders from beyond the stars. Battling aliens and dystopian regimes is like a family tradition.

M.M. Holt is a relentless traveler. He can usually be found writing in cafes by the sea, or in a bar on the edge of a crowded street, usually in far flung cities. If you see him, he'll be the handsome yet enigmatic stranger pounding the keyboard of his laptop, pausing only to sip black coffee and glance warily over his shoulder. He knows the Accord Of Nations is always one step behind.

CONTACT M.M. HOLT

mmholt.com

mmholt548@gmail.com

@MMHOLT3

Facebook
(Search for M.M. Holt, author)

Instagram: mmholt548

Printed in Great Britain
by Amazon

29805618R00223